HER MAINE

Attraction

A Pine Cove Novel
Book 1

REBECCA GANNON

More by Rebecca Gannon

Pine Cove
Her Maine Attraction
Her Maine Reaction
Her Maine Risk
Her Maine Distraction

Carfano Crime Family
Casino King
The Boss
Vengeance

Standalone Novels
Whiskey & Wine

To my mom, my number one supporter.

Chapter 1

I stare at the packed bags around my room and sigh. I didn't even know I owned this much stuff. But I guess when you shove your entire life into suitcases, boxes, and bags, it will always look like a lot.

I definitely didn't think my week would turn out like this, but yesterday was just one mishap after another. I spilled coffee on my white blouse while I was walking into work, I hit my leg on the corner of a filing cabinet that made a huge run in my tights, *and* I had to work through lunch – surviving off the mints in my desk. Then, to top it all off, my boss called me into his office at the end of the day and fired me.

I can't say that I was too upset about it, though, because I absolutely hated my job. Working in a small cubicle and answering questions about insurance policies all day was not something that made me jump for joy. What it did make me do, though, is want to drink a lot of wine.

I surprisingly felt free when he fired me. I was almost happy, really. Which is new for me.

I used to be an artist, and I'd like to think I still am, but the degree I have proving that has been sitting on my shelf collecting dust for the past seven years. Which also happens to be the same amount of years it's been since I painted anything, so I don't really have the right to call myself an artist anymore. It used to be my escape and my therapy, and I somehow lost touch with that side of myself. But I fully intend on finding it again.

The first step in making that happen is deciding that I need to leave the only place I've ever known. I need a new place, with new people, and new scenery. So, I did what every woman does when she needs to make big life choices. I poured myself a glass—or three—of wine, and took to the internet to find where I'd be moving to.

It took a few hours, and a whole bottle of wine, but I found the perfect place. It's a cute little cottage in a coastal town in Maine named Pine Cove. The pictures show it to be a quaint, small town, that looks like it was pulled straight from a Hallmark movie.

The owner, Dottie, only asked me a few questions before telling me I was exactly who she's been waiting for. She said she was holding off moving in with her daughter until she found the right person to rent her home to. I'm not really sure why she thinks that's me, but I'm not going to question it.

Dottie told me I could come as soon as Tuesday, and I jumped at the chance, not caring that I only had five days to pack up my life. I need to do something crazy for once.

"Are you sure you want to do this, sweetie?" my mom asks, coming to stand next to me as I stare at the twenty or so bags I have piled around my room.

"Yes, I need to do this. I promise I'll be okay."

"I know you will be, honey. I'm just going to miss you is all," she says, tears pooling in her eyes.

"Please don't cry, mom. You know I'm going to miss you more than anyone." I give her a big hug and kiss her on the cheek. "Let's order pizza. I'll need to get my fix before I settle for whatever they call pizza in Maine."

Laughing, she wipes away a few stray tears. "Well, when you put it like that, how could we not? Your sisters told me they're on their way over. We'll get to have one last Friday family night. A proper send off."

"Sounds perfect."

I smile as we walk downstairs, and just as the pizza arrives, my two older sisters come storming through the front door.

"I'm going to miss you, baby sis," Kelly says, hugging me tight. "But I'm really happy for you."

"Thanks, Kell. Love you."

"Love you too, Ally-bear."

"What about me? Come here!" Marissa grabs me away and sweeps me up into a warm hug. "I hate that you're moving so far away. But I guess this means I have someplace to get away to when Kev is bothering me."

"I'm glad to be your hideout whenever needed," I tell her, laughing lightly. "That goes for you too Kell. Whenever Mike gets on your nerves, just drive up and stay the weekend."

"I don't think I'll need to escape my husband, but thanks

for the offer." She smiles. "Mar and I will come and stay with you because we'll miss you, you idiot. We don't need excuses."

"Oh, okay." I smile, hugging her again.

"Now, let's go eat. I'm starving!"

Our Friday family nights are something the four of us have been doing for the past few years. After my sisters moved out and we were all working a lot, my mom wanted to make sure we had one night every month where we were guaranteed to all be together. We always order pizza from our favorite pizzeria down the street, and we spend the night drinking wine and watching chick flicks. Our monthly night wasn't supposed to be until next Friday, but my mom called an emergency one under these special circumstances.

I didn't want to think that this would be our last one, and tonight goes by way too quickly. The pizza and wine go down way too easy, the hours fly by, and when it's time to say our goodbyes, my sisters hug me tight.

"I'm just a phone call away, okay?"

"I got you Kells. Thank you."

"And same for me, too. Let me know if you need anything. I'll mail or hand deliver it. I don't care either way."

"I may take you up on that." I laugh. "I'll be craving pork roll, egg, and cheese sandwiches in no time. But, come on guys, I'm not saying I'll be gone forever. And it's only a six-hour drive."

"We'll see," she says, doubtful.

"Okay, well, we'll see you soon." Kelly frowns. "Be safe."

"I will," I promise, hugging both again before watching them drive off.

Taking a deep breath, I hold back the tears pricking my eyes. That's one set of goodbyes down, and one more to go. I know tomorrow night is going to be just as hard. I honestly didn't realize how overwhelming it'd be to say goodbye to everyone I love.

Opening the door to the restaurant, I'm hit with the delicious scent of freshly made tortilla chips and spicy food, and my stomach growls instantly.

José's Cantina is a small Mexican restaurant that always promises a smooth, delicious margarita, and five-star fish tacos. I've been obsessed with this place since I was old enough to drink, and will probably have dreams of it while in Maine.

I'm meeting my three best friends – Ashley, Melanie, and Elizabeth – here, and I know they're going to have something to say about my move. We've been inseparable since freshman year of high school. We were put in the same group during orientation for ice breakers, and when we all confessed our hatred for ice breakers, it was an instant friendship.

Elizabeth is the outspoken one of the group, Melanie is the voice of reason, I'm the listener, and Ashley is the wild card. And despite the four of us being so different, we all seem to fit together perfectly. Which is why we've remained best friends for over ten years.

I spot the three of them by the hostess stand and squeal with excitement. "Guys!! Ahhh!! I've missed you!" I go straight to hug each of them, but Ellie puts her hand up to stop me.

"Allyson Rose. What in the hell do you think you're doing moving to mother freaking Maine in three days?! And you tell us yesterday?!"

Shit, she's mad.

"Ellie, I'm sorry! This wasn't planned. I mean, *obviously*. Why would any sane person up and move five states away in a matter of days from the time they decided to move in the first place?"

"What?" she asks, confused by my rambling.

"I got it, don't worry," Ash says. "You're not sane, and we agree." Mel slaps Ash's arm and gives her a look. "Ow, what? We agreed we wouldn't be nice about this."

"Okay, listen. I just need to do this, alright? This will be good for me, I promise. And you can come and stay with me anytime, and for however long you'd like. That's a given." Looking each of them in eye, I make sure they see my sincerity.

"Fine. We'll be coming soon, though, to make sure there are no serial killers lurking in the woods or whatever."

"Wow, Ellie, always the positive one," I say sarcastically.

"This way, ladies," the hostess interrupts, leading us over to our table.

"I don't want to fight about this. I just want to eat delicious food, talk, laugh, and then afterwards, get super wasted at a bar while we dance the night away. Is that too much to ask for from my best friends?"

"No, it's not," Mel says, opening her menu. "It sounds like a hell of a hangover for me, but I'll get over it."

"Yes, you will." I smile, unwrapping my utensils and placing my napkin on my lap. When I look up, I see Ashley eyeing me with a devilish smirk.

"Ally, do you remember when you snuck out of your house in high school and climbed down that small-ass tree outside your window?"

"You're seriously bringing this up now?" I ask,

narrowing my eyes.

"Yes, I am. Because everything's game when one of your best friends acts like an ass and leaves you." I give her a dirty look, but she continues. "You used that shrub of a tree to climb down out of your window while I waited in my car. And like I knew would happen, it went horribly wrong. In the silence of the night, all that could be heard was *Snap! Snap! Snap!* and your muffled scream as you fell to the ground."

"Um, why have we never heard this before?" Ellie and Mel look at each other and then at me and Ash.

"Because it was a horrible sequence of events, and Ashley swore she wouldn't tell anyone, even you two, unless I did something bad to her and she needed leverage. Which, I may add, is NOT the situation here, Ashley."

"Anyway! As I was saying," she continues, "all I heard was your muffled scream, and when I looked around for you, I saw you army crawling across your lawn to get to my car!"

"I didn't want anyone to see me! I thought I woke everyone up falling out of that damned tree!"

"So, you thought crawling like a creeper instead of running like a normal human was your best bet?"

"At the time, yes I did. And I stand by that choice now, even while you're all looking at me like I'm an idiot. Whatever, Ash, just continue on." I wave her onward, wishing I already had a margarita in me, and knowing I'll need a few to get through this.

"Okay, so you army crawled to my car, got in, and then turned to me with visible scratches on your face and hands and said, 'I feel like I'm in an eighties teen movie sneaking out of my house about to meet the hot jock at a party where he'll realize I'm the most amazing girl he'll ever meet at our god-awful high school and then he'll drive me home in his hot car and we'll make out.' Yes, I remember bitch. Word for word!"

"OH. MY. GOD." I cover my face with my hands and shake my head.

"I then proceeded to drive us to meet that guy you met on Myspace so I could make sure he wasn't some axe murderer rapist who was going to lure you away."

Ellie throws her hands up in the air. "Whoa, whoa, whoa! What the hell? You told us you ended it with that guy because he started sending you nudes and you needed a magnifying glass to find his junk."

"Yes, I did tell you that. And it was true. Just not the part about sending nudes. It was more of an up close and personal encounter that had me finding that information out."

"You saw his peen?! You, Allyson, went on a blind date in high school? You, the high school virgin who swore all men were the devil incarnate, went on a blind date in high school and got naked?"

"Holy hell, Elizabeth! You need to keep your voice down! Ashley, I revoke your right to visit me in Maine now. You'll never see me again."

"Oh, don't be a baby, Ally-cat. Okay, where was I? Yes, so I drove you to the movies to meet what's-his-face. I then proceeded to casually walk in a little after you and bought a ticket to the same movie, and then sat a couple of rows behind you. Then maybe halfway through the movie, I heard you gasp, and I looked over just in time to see you slap him across the face. You looked back at me and signaled that it was time to make our escape. And what was it that happened in there, Allyson?" she asks innocently.

Ellie and Mel are looking at me like they don't know me

while Ashley waits for me to confess my sins. Sighing, I tell them, "I went in my purse to look for chap stick, and when I turned back, he put his hand on top of mine on the armrest. I thought, 'Oh, how sweet, he wants to hold hands.' So, I smiled at him and looked down at our hands. Except, what I also saw was his tiny penis out of his pants, and he was trying to move my hand to it!"

"Ally! I can't believe we didn't know about this! Why was it such a secret? It's hilarious!"

"Because it was a horrible night. And at that time, super traumatizing. You know how I was back then. I was super shy and hated talking to guys. I was actually *scared* to talk to them. And yet there I was with this creep I didn't know who thought he could just whip out his penis forty minutes after meeting me! I had only said like ten words to him before the movie even began, so I don't know why he thought I wanted to give him a handy."

That date was so bad. And looking back now, I guess it is super funny. A slow smile spreads across my face, and soon I can't contain my laughter – a shoulder shaking, stomach knotting, laugh.

"Okay, I haven't thought of that night in years. It's hilarious." Wiping the tears from my eyes, I smile at my best friends. "You girls have been there for me through so much. From awkward high school experiences, to the bad choices made in college. And then after college, we figured out life together. This is going to be a totally new experience for me, but I need to do it."

I can't help the tears that start gathering in my eyes or the catch in my voice. "Now listen up, because this is the sentimental part of my speech. No one will ever replace you three, and you better not find one for me. We're besties forever. Bitches forever. I expect all of you to support me in this and come visit me when I get settled. I mean, we have to show Maine what happens when a group of Jersey girls gets together." I smile at them with watery eyes.

"Of course we support you, Ally," Ellie says. "You know I was kidding before."

Ash and Mel both nod in agreement.

"I know. I love you guys."

"We love you, too."

After stuffing our faces with tacos and filling our bodies with margaritas, we move the party to a bar down the road where we drink and dance until last call.

My head is spinning, and I know I'm going to wake up tomorrow with a massive headache. But a night out with my girls is always worth the next day's blues.

As we all stumble outside to wait for our cabs, a round of hugs and goodbyes has me tearing up again. "I love you guys so much," I slur.

Ashley's cab is the first to arrive, and when she reaches the door, she turns back. "Now, Ally, listen to me. Make sure you find some hot piece of ass to show you around town. And by town, I mean his penis," she says, giggling through her hiccups.

"Wow, such beautiful words of wisdom," Ellie mumbles next to me.

Ashley gives her a dirty look, not finished with her speech yet. "I want you to fall in love. I want you to have hot sex."

"Sure, Ash. I'll just find a hot piece of ass straight away. First thing." I roll my eyes at the probability of that happening.

"Allyyy!!!! Yeesss bitch!!!" Ellie yells, and the people

around us turn to stare. "Get yourself a man who knows how to fix things. Like cars. And sinks!" She's always been attracted to men who work with their hands.

"Ally, you should listen to them. Maybe you'll have some fun," Mel chimes in.

"Oh my god, okay. The way you see my life is super sad. I didn't know it was so obvious I needed a man in my life."

Ashley throws me an air kiss. "It is. Sorry." She shrugs. "Alright, gotta go babes – home, then throw up, then bed!"

"'Kay, Ash, bye!" I yell after her as she closes the cab's door.

The rest of our cabs arrive while hers is pulling away, and we each stumble in our heels to their doors. "Text me when you're all home safe. Love you guys! See you soon!"

Smiling at Mel and Ellie, I get into my cab and close the door. I take a deep breath, trying really hard not to cry.

Chapter 2

"Please let me know when you get there, sweetie. Drive safe." Hugging my mom tight, she kisses my cheek. "Do you have snacks? Are you getting coffee?"

"Yes, and yes." I smile. "I love you, mom."

"I love you more."

"I'll see you soon."

"Of course." She smiles, her eyes watery.

Blinking away my own unshed tears, I get in my car, not wanting her to see how nervous I am. Taking a deep breath, I smile and wave back to her as I drive off – my body buzzing with the feeling of something new that's just around the corner.

A few hours, and many coffee stops later, I'm finally here. WELCOME TO MAINE – VACATIONLAND. The sign along the highway is a welcoming sight.

I roll my windows down and take a deep breath in, filling my lungs with fresh air and the sweet scent of pine trees. I'm still a little over an hour away from Pine Cove, but just being in Maine sends a jolt of excitement through me.

Everything I pass is beautiful. Even the highway is beautiful, with massive pine trees lining both sides, creating a wall of green all around me. The sky is a bright, light blue, with wispy white clouds painted across in strokes of perfection.

When it's time for me to take the exit off the highway that will bring me to my new home, goosebumps break out on my arms.

I made it.

Driving along a small side road for a few minutes, I come to a stop sign that directs me to go left for Freeport, and right for Pine Cove. Turning right, I drive for a few miles before I come upon Main Street, and I sit up a little straighter. It's so cute!

Both sides of the street are lined with small shops and businesses that all have colorful awnings and signs, and overflowing flower pots out front. Bikes lean against lamp posts, people walk hand in hand down the sidewalks carrying shopping bags, and everyone looks happy. It really does look like a scene straight out of a Hallmark movie.

Slowing, I roll my windows down and try to read all of the different signs. There are a few clothing boutiques, a restaurant, a café/bakery, a bookstore, an antiques shop, a hardware store, and a hair and nail salon. There are a few others as well, including lawyer, doctor, and dentist offices, but I can't catch any others as I drive past.

At the end of Main Street, I turn left, and drive on for another few minutes. Looking to the right, I see a wall of pine trees lining the side of the road, and I catch glimpses of water between the trunks of the trees. Curious, I pull over onto the shoulder.

When I get out of the car, I look around, hoping that there aren't any bears, moose, or wild animals hiding, ready to jump out at me. That'd be such a great welcoming for the girl whose only wildlife experience is knowing how to dodge a deer while driving.

When I've discerned that there's nothing life threatening around, I take a short walk through the tree line and my jaw drops.

The afternoon sun glints off the surface of a huge lake — the glare casting a hazy hue over the surrounding land. It's stunning.

Across the way, two large mansions sit along the banks, making a statement with their grandeur. But while they're nice, it's the home in between them that really catches my eye. A big, beautiful, modern log cabin sits nestled amongst the trees, looking like it's meant to be a part of the land. Each has a dock extending out into the water, but only the log cabin house has a boat attached – gently rocking in the breeze.

I would love to sit out there and read a book. Being near water has always calmed me.

I take in the view for another minute, and head back to my car. Driving on, the air coming through my open windows starts to smell deliciously salty, and I breathe it in, knowing the ocean is near.

When I come to a stop sign, I make the right onto my new street – Peach Place. Driving slowly, I notice that none of the houses are visible from the road. The only indication that there even are any somewhere back in the trees, are mailboxes at the end of each gravel drive.

Seeing number 25 painted on the next one, I turn off my radio and into the driveway. The gravel path leads me through tall, lush pine trees for about a quarter of a mile before it opens up into a clearing where an adorable little blue cottage sits.

It's like a Thomas Kinkade painting come to life, and I laugh at the quaintness of it all.

My eyes are immediately drawn to the flowers that seem to be coming from everywhere. The sills of the two front windows boast overflowing flower boxes, the three steps up to the porch are lined with flower pots on both sides, and there are hanging fern baskets in the arches of the porch's roof. Garden beds flank either side of the steps, and are filled with a vibrant variety of flowers in every color.

The porch holds a table and two wicker rocking chairs, and a swing hangs on the far right. I've always wanted a front porch like this. One where I can sit and enjoy a cup of coffee while reading and listening to the rain.

Parking, I turn my car off, and the front door swings open. A cute elderly woman with curly white hair, white sneakers, pink capris, and a pink and white floral blouse steps out onto the porch, waiving jovially at me. Dottie is adorable.

Climbing out of my car, I smile and wave back. "Hi, Dottie."

"Hello, dearie. How was the drive up?"

"It was good. Once I hit Maine, everything was just so

beautiful that time didn't seem to matter." Walking towards her, she goes in for a big hug that feels like a grandma welcoming home her granddaughter after a long journey.

"I'm so glad you're here, honey. I didn't want to rent my home to just anyone, and I had a feeling about you right away," she says, taking my arm. "Come, let me show you around. We'll have tea and pie out back after a little tour."

"Sounds perfect."

The scent of fresh pie hits my nose the second we step into the house. "Oh my, what is that heavenly smell?"

"That would be my award-winning blueberry pie, dear. I'm famous for it around here," she tells me, the ring of pride evident in her voice.

"Sounds, and smells, amazing. I love blueberry pie."

"Well, we're known for blueberries here, so get used to the flavor."

"You won't see me turn anything blueberry away," I tell her with a laugh.

I take a look around the living room, and I can see that Dottie's love of flowers flows from the outside, in. But where the outside is bright and vibrant, the inside is all muted pastels and shades of white.

A pastel pink, cream, and lavender floral crochet knit blanket is draped over the back of a beige couch. White lamps with rose patterns on the bases sit on either side of the couch atop whitewashed wooden accent tables. The matching coffee table in front holds a spread of Home and Garden magazines and a fresh vase of tulips. The area rug beneath is sand in color, with a rose pattern throughout that's similar to the lamps.

A large TV sits on top of an electric fire place that rests against the wall next to the front door, a wooden floor lamp sits in the corner next to a large comfy recliner with a fur throw pillow and a cream and pink flowered crochet blanket, and bookshelves line the wall next to it.

"I packed away most of my books, so you have plenty of space to put anything you have out on the shelves. Feel free to make personal touches anywhere if you'd like, too."

I smile warmly at her. "Thank you, Dottie. I did bring a few things with me."

"Okay, come along. I'll show you the bedrooms next."

Following her down a short hallway, I notice the floors are a beautiful medium shaded hardwood throughout that contrasts nicely with the light colors she chose to decorate with.

When Dottie opens the first bedroom door on the left, all I see is pink. Pink walls with paintings of pink flowers, pink sheets and a pink floral comforter on a queen-sized bed, and a pink floral area rug.

"This is so beautiful, Dottie."

"Let me show you the other one, and then you can choose which you prefer." She opens the door to the bedroom across the hall, and I step into a mirror of the other, this one being purple themed.

Leading me down the rest of the short hallway, Dottie points at the last door for me to open. The bathroom is on the smaller side, but it has everything I'll need. The walls are painted a dusty rose color, and the floors are a white tile that matches the tub and shower walls. There's a pink and red rose patterned shower curtain, and fluffy pink rugs lay in front of the tub, toilet, and sink.

"If you haven't noticed, I love pink." Dottie smiles.

"I did." I laugh. "But I do too, so it's perfect."

Walking into the kitchen at the back of the house, I can tell it's where Dottie has spent many hours cooking and baking. It has a well-loved, homey feeling to it.

On the left side, there's a small, round wooden table with four chairs and a vase of tulips in the center. On the right, is the stove, oven, and fridge. A farmhouse sink and dishwasher are against the back wall, and an "L" shaped countertop wraps around from the sink to the oven. Cabinets line above and below the counter, and a small window sits above the sink.

"Dottie, everything is so beautiful. I love it."

"Thank you, dear. Since my husband passed a few years ago, I have been doing little updates every so often. That's why it's so feminine." She laughs. "Now, let me show you the best part of living here. We'll just have to get the pie and tea first."

"What would you like me to do?"

"You can fill the tea kettle if you don't mind. I'll cut us each a slice of pie and meet you out back."

"No problem."

I wait for the kettle to whistle, and then I grab it with a pot holder and carefully carry it outside. I'm so focused on not spilling or dropping the kettle, that when I place it on the small garden table and look up, my jaw drops.

"Dottie, wow, I can't believe this." The yard is lined on either side with pine trees and wildflowers, and then grass stretches out for a hundred feet or so before it drops off into the ocean.

Fishing and sail boats dot the water in the distance, and islands rise up into view even farther out. Four white Adirondack chairs sit near the edge of the lawn, and they look like the perfect place to spend an afternoon or watch the sunrise.

I'm honestly speechless. No words can describe the picture perfectness of this view. When I tear my eyes away, I find Dottie smiling at me. "It's so beautiful."

"It's the best," she sighs.

I sit down in the wicker chair next to her. The back porch looks very similar to the front with large overflowing flower pots lining the stairs down to the yard and vibrant flower beds all around the base of the porch. There are no hanging ferns, though. Just a clear view of the Atlantic.

"It's magnificent. I don't know how you could leave."

"Well, it's not by choice, dearie. It's harder on my own then it used to be, and my daughter wants me to come live with her and my grandbabies about an hour north of here. They live on the water too, though, so it won't be a total loss. But you're right, it's hard leaving my home. However"–she pats my knee–"this is your home now, Allyson. Just because you're renting from me, I don't want you to feel like I'm going to come one day and take it back. Treat it like your own. Give it your personal touch. I love this cottage, this town, and the people here. And I want you to love it as well. I already told everyone I know–which is everyone in Pine Cove–that you were moving in. So don't be shy when you're out and about, and do expect folks to just come up and say hello. We're a friendly bunch."

"Looking forward to it." I smile, pouring us each a cup of tea.

"We're family here in Pine Cove. I'm glad you chose us."

"Me too."

As we eat our pie and drink our tea, Dottie tells me more about the town, its residents, and the local gossip. I can just picture a group of little old ladies, all like Dottie, gathering after church on Sundays to trade the week's newest scandals.

"I left the number of a man you can call if you need anything at all. I always call him when something needs fixing," she tells me, a gleam in her eyes. "Jake's a very nice man. If anything happens, just call him."

"Thanks so much. That's so thoughtful."

"No problem at all, dearie." She smiles, finishing her tea. "Okay, I better be off. I left my number on the fridge as well. Please don't hesitate to call me with any questions or concerns. I'm just a short drive away, and I wouldn't mind chatting with you again either."

"I will, thank you. And your pie is delicious. I know why it's award-winning."

"I can teach you to make it if you'd like. That's usually how I pay Jake when he comes around."

"I'd love that. Thank you."

"Good. And remember, don't hesitate to call if you have any questions, and then we can set up a date to make some pie."

"Sounds good."

Smiling, I walk with Dottie through the house and see her off. When the sound of her car crunching on the gravel starts to fade the farther she drives, I can't help but notice how quiet it is here.

A gentle breeze rustles the trees and a few birds sing to one another, but other than that, nothing.

It's peaceful.

I never found true silence back home. There was always the sound of cars or people nearby. Closing my eyes, I take a deep breath in, letting the purity of the air cleanse my body. I know this place will be good for me.

Glancing at my car, I decide I should probably start

bringing some of my stuff in, and so I go and grab my keys.

I spend an hour going back and forth from my car to inside, and I'm exhausted. I'm definitely not unpacking any of it yet. I don't have the energy. I'd rather sit outside and enjoy the view while there's still light left in the day.

Walking out the back door, I make my way down to the Adirondack chairs, the wind picking up the closer I get to the water.

The waves lap gently against the rocky cliff, and I gaze out at the endless sea of blue.

I can see many afternoons spent out here sipping cocktails and tanning. It won't be like the Jersey shore, but I think I'll adjust.

Chapter 3

After the sun goes down, the beautiful silence of the day has now turned into the creepy silence of the night. Every little sound I hear is making me jump, so I go around and make sure every window and door is locked, and close all of the curtains.

A little paranoid? Maybe. But I've never not lived right next to another house before. I know that if I screamed bloody murder, no one would hear me. And that is more than enough of a reason for me to be extra cautious.

After my safety check, my stomach starts to grumble, and I suddenly realize that I'm starving. I guess I never really ate a proper meal today.

Dottie told me she left me a penne, chicken, and broccoli casserole in the fridge, so I heat up a plate for myself. She really is the sweetest.

I watch a little TV, but the events of the day start to catch up with me, and I know if I don't get up now, I'll just end up passing out on the couch and getting a huge crick in my neck.

Digging around in my big suitcase, I pull out my toiletries and a pair of pajamas. After washing my face and brushing my teeth, the pink room is calling my name. The sheets are soft and the comforter is fluffy, and I'm out in a matter of seconds.

Waking with a start, I bolt upright in bed. What in the ever-loving hell was that?!

My heart is beating wildly in my chest and my blood is pounding in my ears, and I have to focus for a minute before I can hear anything again.

A loud crashing sound comes again from somewhere outside, and I pull the covers tighter around me. That's definitely what woke me up.

A second later, I hear a growl, and I scream, biting the comforter to muffle the sound.

What do I do?! What's out there?!

Oh my god, why did I move here?!

I hear another loud growl, and I shudder, my hands shaking as they grip the comforter. I'm going to die.

Throwing the covers off of me, I jump out of bed and run to the kitchen. I need to find that number Dottie left me. I don't know what's out there, but it sounds like it's trying to get in the house to kill me.

I have no idea if this Jake person can help me, but I don't know who else to call or what else to do. 9-1-1 seems like an overreaction, but I don't know!

Frantically searching the fridge, I find the piece of paper with his number under a moose magnet and pick up the kitchen phone. Dialing quickly, I pray he can come over fast.

It rings three times, and then a gravelly voice comes through. "Dottie? Are you okay?"

My answer comes out panicked and rushed. "Hi, no, this is Ally. I'm renting Dottie's house. It's my first night here and I just woke up to loud crashing sounds and growls outside and it seems like something is trying to get in the house, or, I don't know. I don't know what to do. I'm not from here. I don't know if it's an animal or some creepy woodland creature or what to do. She told me to call you if I needed anything, and I don't know what to do! Shit, oh my god, sorry, I just saw the time. It's the middle of the night and I woke you up! I'm sorry! Never mind, I'll just wait it out and see what happens."

I go to hang up with a shaky hand, feeling stupid, but then I hear his gruff voice again. "I'll be right over."

"But-" I'm cut off by him hanging up on me. Staring at the phone for a second, I place it back in the cradle and cover my face with my hands. I'm so dumb.

I go and wait on the couch for him, my knee bouncing nonstop. Ten minutes later, I hear a vehicle coming down the drive, but I stay seated. I am NOT opening the door until he knocks. The thing could still be out there just waiting for its opportunity.

Abrupt rapping at the front door comes a few minutes later, and I jump, letting out a little scream.

Freaking calm down, Ally! You called him! Just open the door, apologize for making him come over, and then say goodnight.

But the second I open the door, my plan flies out of my head. The sexiest man I've ever seen is standing in front of me, half in the shadows of the porch light. He's well over six feet tall, and he looks like a freaking Viking. Sweet baby Jesus, he looks like Thor.

His overgrown, dark blonde hair, hangs in his face, still a little messy from sleep, and the t-shirt he has on does nothing to hide the bulging muscles of his shoulders, chest, and arms. He's holding a rifle in his hand, and looks like a warrior ready for battle.

I'm too busy taking in all that he is, that I forget I'm standing here in nothing more than a little silk pajama set that shows way too much leg and braless boobs.

I quickly cross my arms over my chest to try and hide the goods, and when I look back up at him, I'm met with his intense eyes. I feel a jolt to my chest and chills run down my arms and legs as the cool night air clashes with the heat of his stare.

"Is something out there?" I ask, my voice just barely above a whisper. He doesn't answer me, though. He just continues to stare at me.

"You're Jake?" I try again, my voice a little stronger.

He gives me a curt nod, but still doesn't say anything.

"Is there anything out there? I'm really sorry for waking you up, I just didn't know what to do. It's my first night and I was scared I was going to be murdered or something. And Dottie said to call you if I needed anything."

"Just a bear," he finally says. "They can't get in the house. I'll fix the broken pots in the morning." His deep voice floats over me, and it feels like velvet caressing my insides.

"Okay." I'm starting to feel a little dizzy with him looking at me the way he is. "Do you want to come in for a minute? Dottie made her blueberry pie for me today, and she said that's how she usually pays you. I know it's after 2am, but a slice is the least I can do." I don't know what possessed me to invite him in, but I can't just let him leave.

"Sure. I can never pass up Dottie's pie. She usually makes me a whole one."

I throw a nervous smile over my shoulder as I walk towards the kitchen. "Well this one is mine, so I can only offer a slice."

The pie is already sitting on the table from this afternoon, so I go over to the cabinet to grab us plates. But before I can reach up, I feel his warm body come up behind me.

"Let me," he says over my shoulder, his low voice sending a shiver down my spine.

Reaching up, he grabs two plates from above me, and his chest brushes my back. I freeze, my skin instantly heating from just that simple touch.

Gripping the counter, I turn around when he moves away, and watch him pull two forks from the drawer near me before setting them on the table.

He dominates the kitchen with what has to be at least a 6'5" frame. And now that we're in the light, I can see all of him.

He's fucking gorgeous.

His wild blonde hair falls around his neck and frames a square jaw that's covered in a short scruffy beard. His eyes are framed by a strong brow bone, a straight nose, and high cheekbones. He's the most handsome man I've ever seen.

His back muscles flex under his shirt every time he moves, and his low-slung sweat pants are showcasing an ass that looks like two scoops of ice cream and thighs that look like they could crush a car like it's nothing.

He has this rugged mountain man look that makes me want to ask him if he can chop me some wood out back. Shirtless. Or maybe naked.

Get a grip, Ally!

I shake myself out of those thoughts and walk over to the kitchen table, taking a seat in front of the slice of pie he's already cut for me.

"Thank you," I murmur, my voice sounding a little nervous as I pick up my fork with a trembling hand.

I meet his eyes again, and I'm struck by their color. It's like I'm looking into the ocean. They're a swirl of blue and green that's becoming darker the longer I look into them. I feel like I'm drowning in the shallows of the tide.

My chest tightens. He's hypnotizing me. It feels like he's trying to see into the deepest parts of my mind.

Using everything in me to look away, I take a tentative bite of pie, trying to regain a semblance of my sanity. We sit in silence for a minute before it becomes too suffocating for me, and I blurt out the first thing that comes to mind.

"Do you help Dottie often?"

"When she needs me."

"I'm sorry I bothered you tonight. I probably overreacted. I was just picturing some creature crawling out of the trees to take me." I let out a nervous little laugh. "Where I'm from, we don't have bears that come knocking at the door."

"Where are you from?"

"New Jersey."

"I see," he says simply.

"Are you from here? Pine Cove?"

"Yes."

"Okay." I nod. He clearly doesn't like talking, so I remain quiet and finish off my pie. When I'm done, I stand up and bring my plate and fork over to the sink, needing to do something to break the awkward tension I'm feeling.

Who just sits, stares, and barely speaks?

The only reason I'm not freaking out right now is because of the fact that Dottie trusts him. But then again, I barely know Dottie. She could just seem nice, but is really out to collect bodies or something by posting fake rental ads online.

Oh my god. I'm alone in a house with a stranger who has a gun. My pulse starts to quicken, and my breathing becomes rapid as I grip the sink in front of me.

"Hey."

"Eeep!" I let out a very girlish squeal and I spin around to see that Jake's right there, not even two feet away.

What the hell? He doesn't make a sound when he moves!

I knew it. I'm dead.

I'm going to die at the hands of this sexy mountain man who's only said like fifteen words to me.

"I'm not going to kill you. You need to relax."

"Telling someone to relax isn't helpful," I fire back. Then what he said registers. "And why would you say you're not going to kill me? That's not a very normal thing to say when you're trying to calm someone down."

"Because you just mumbled something about a mountain man killing you."

"I said that out loud?"

"Yes. Now sit back down and I'll make you tea."

Tilting my head, I study his expressionless face. "You make tea?"

"Yes. Dottie taught me."

"Oh. Okay, then," I say, sitting back down, trying to settle my heart rate.

Jake takes out a cup and saucer and places it on the counter next to the stove as he fills the kettle. He moves around with a quiet, stealthy ease – completely in control.

I jump when the kettle whistles, and I watch as he pours the hot water into the cup. With his back to me, I can't exactly see what he adds to it, but when he places it in front of me, the sweet aroma fills my lungs.

With a tentative sip, I let the hot, sweet, and smooth liquid slide down my throat, warming me from the inside out. I'm genuinely surprised that he knows how to make this. I think he added something special to it, but I can't place it.

"It's good. Thank you. And I'm sorry. My thoughts just got away from me and I panicked. I guess I was still shaken from being woken up like that."

"It's fine."

I nod, closing my eyes as I sip my tea, loving how good it is. Who knew a man like Jake could make tea?

When I chance another look at him, I find him studying me.

"So, what do you do here in Pine Cove? Help distressed women when they're in need of saving?"

"No, that's just Dottie."

"Why? Are you related?"

"No. Her husband taught me everything I know about what I do, so I look after her now that he's gone."

"And what is it that you do?"

"I build boats."

My eyes drop to his chest, and I scan his whole upper

body. "I can see that."

"Do I look like I build boats?" My eyes flash up to his, and they hold me captive again.

"Yes, you, um, do." I feel my grip on my sanity waning, and I think he needs to leave before I say or do something stupid. "I think I'll be okay now. Thanks again for coming over here so late."

"I don't sleep much anyway," he states, trying to make me feel better.

Standing, I walk him to the front door, and he turns back right before stepping out onto the porch. "Goodnight, Ally."

Lord have mercy, my name just rolls off his tongue like he was always meant to say it.

"'Night," I whisper, watching him get into his truck.

Closing and locking the door, I lean against it, trying to wrap my head around what just happened.

I think I stand there for five minutes before I can gather myself enough to walk back to the kitchen to turn the light out, and then crawl back into bed.

But sleep eludes me. I just lay here, staring at the ceiling, replaying every second I just spent with Jake.

When I turn to look at the bedside clock, I see it's past four in the morning now.

Ugh! I can't stop thinking about him with those sexy ocean eyes and the body of a warrior I want to wrap myself around like a vine.

Damn it!

I close my eyes, but his beautiful face is all I see. And that, in no way, is making me want to sleep.

I hate that he's affecting me like this. I don't let men get under my skin. But the tight control I usually have over my emotions started to falter the second I locked eyes with him.

When the first rays of light start streaming through the crack in my curtains, I let out a frustrated sigh. I just spent hours thinking about a man who said maybe twenty words to me.

Sighing again, I throw the covers off of me and put on a pot of coffee. I can see the sun is about to come up, so I go and grab the crochet blanket from the back of the couch in the living room and pour myself a mug of coffee. I peek through the window on the back door to make sure there isn't a bear waiting to attack me, and when I see the coast is clear, I slip outside and sit in one of the wicker chairs, wrapping the blanket tight around me.

The sun begins to peek out from the horizon and paints the sky in hues of orange and yellow, mixing with the blues of the ocean and sky.

It's absolutely stunning. I can't believe I get to wake up here every day now. I don't know what could beat this.

Chapter 4

Taking a sip of coffee, I breathe in the warm steam.

When the sun is fully seated in the sky, I stand, yawning as I stretch out my stiff limbs. I head back inside for more coffee, and spot a loaf of bread on the counter, suddenly hungry. I guess only sleeping for a few hours before staying up all night thinking about a sexy mountain man will do that.

Sitting at the kitchen table, I spread butter and jam on my toast and think about what I should do today. It's my first official day as a Pine Cove resident. I think I'll do a little unpacking first, and then head into town to roam about. I want to take a closer look at all of those cute shops on Main Street.

Finishing my breakfast, I reluctantly go to my room and start sorting through the bags and suitcases. After putting away my massive amount of clothes and shoes, I'm exhausted, and my back hurts. I'll have to leave the other boxes for another day.

Dragging my feet to the bathroom, I take a nice hot shower to relax my aching muscles, but when I stand in front of the closet full of clothes I just hung up, I'm at a loss. I want any first impressions I make today to be good ones. I've already greeted one town resident with pajamas, messy hair, and no makeup. So, really it can only go up from there.

Deciding to go with a simple look, I put on black skinny jeans, a loose white t-shirt, a jean jacket, and black ankle booties. While May back home is already hot, the weather here is still a little unpredictable.

I keep my makeup subtle and natural with only a thin line of eyeliner against my lashes and mascara to make my blue eyes pop. I curl some gentle waves in my long blonde hair to give it a little volume, and then flip it over a couple of times for a tousled look.

Grabbing my purse and keys, I open the front door and immediately jump back, letting out a little scream.

"Jake, you scared me!" I exclaim, my hand flying to my chest. "What are you doing?"

Dragging his eyes from my feet to my eyes, his gaze leaves a trail of fire up my body. "I said I'd fix this in the morning," is all he says, and I look down to see that he's gluing the flower pots back together that the bear broke last night.

How long has he been here? I didn't even hear him.

Smiling slightly, I decide to try and take back control of my emotions. I can't keep letting him make me feel like I'm powerless. "Yes, you did. And you're a man of your word, aren't you?"

"Yes."

"Very few words, granted, but that's okay."

"And why's that?"

I flash him a smile. "Because I'll get you talking eventually, mountain man." I accidentally let my little nickname for him slip, and watch his eyes go a little darker when I do.

"Is that so?"

"Yup. And I'm a woman of my word." A ghost of a smile crosses his lips before he looks back down at the broken pieces in his hands. "Do you need anything? I was just heading out to go into town and walk around."

"No. I'm almost done here."

"You don't have to do that, Jake. I can clean it up."

"Dottie would want me to help you out."

"Well, thank you," I say, closing the door behind me.

Taking the first step down the stairs, Jake stands, blocking my way. Looking up, my eyes meet his, and my brain goes fuzzy.

"Are you going to let me by?"

He doesn't answer me. He just looks at me with those intense eyes, and then steps aside. But only enough to where I still have to brush by him to pass. When my arm touches his torso, I feel a fire spread across my skin like it did last night when he came up behind me in the kitchen.

I suck in a short breath and straighten my spine as I walk to my car, acting like I felt nothing. When I reach for the door handle, though, I hear him say, "Watch out for bears."

Turning back, I smile sweetly. "I could, but then I wouldn't be able to call you to come and rescue me again. And where's the fun in that?" Not waiting for a response, I get in my car and head off down the driveway. I chance a look back in my rearview mirror, and see him standing there by the stairs, staring after me.

When I get into town, I park my car at the end of Main Street. I go in and out of a few boutiques, and notice a few cute dresses and some nice jewelry that I will definitely be back to try on.

As I'm passing the hardware store, I glance in their window, and stop short. Off to the side, I see canvases leaning up against the wall and an assortment of brushes and paints hanging on the wall above them. For some unknown reason, I'm compelled to go in and take a closer look.

A friendly man behind the counter greets me straight away, and tells me to let him know if I need any help. Thanking him, I head straight for the art section, and smile when I see they carry the paints and brushes I used to use.

I run my fingers over the canvases, feeling a pang in my heart. I stopped painting a long time ago, but I think it's time I start again.

Grabbing a basket, I load it up with a variety of brushes, a new palette, and about twenty tubes of paint. I bring that up to the counter first, and then go back for an easel and four canvases in different sizes.

Hauling everything up to the counter, the man who greeted me earlier smiles down at me. "Hello there, young lady, I'm Jim," he says, sticking his hand out. He's an older man, maybe in his sixties, with short salt and pepper hair and kind blue eyes.

"Hi, Jim, I'm Ally," I tell him, shaking his hand. "I just moved into Dottie's place."

"Oh, yes, she said to look out for you. Good to meet you. I hope you'll like our little town."

I smile. "I do so far."

"I'm glad." He smiles back, ringing up my items.

"You have a great selection. My favorites actually."

"That was my wife's doing. She was an artist, and wanted to make sure this town had a place for people to buy good supplies without driving out of their way. She unable taught painting, drawing, and sculpture classes from our garage, but since she passed a few years ago, we haven't had many artists come through."

"I'm sorry to hear that. She sounds like an incredible woman. I always believed artists have the ability to feel deeper than anyone because you have to open yourself up when you create. Without that, art wouldn't mean anything to anyone."

"That's very true, young lady," Jim says, his eyes misty. "My Linda loved fiercely, and felt everything to her core. Thank you for coming in today, Ally. I hope you come back soon. And maybe I can see some of your work sometime. This place has a way of inspiring you."

"I haven't painted in a long time, but I'm starting to feel the pull again." After paying, I quickly realize that it's going to be difficult to carry all of this back down the street to my car. I guess I could make two trips? "Do you mind if I leave some of this here for a few minutes? I think I need to take two trips to my car."

"Of course."

"I can help you," a familiar voice says behind me.

"Jake, my boy, how are you?" Jim bellows to the man behind me. Shit, how long has he been in here?

"I'm good, Jim."

"Good to hear. So, you'll help young Ally here?"

"Yes, sir."

I turn to face him. "You don't have to. I was going to take two trips."

"Now you don't have to," he says before looking over my head at Jim. "Do you have my order?"

"Got it right here." Jake takes a brown paper bag from Jim, and then takes the bags from my hands, along with the two bigger canvases.

Nodding, he signals me to lead the way, and I don't bother arguing. I pick up the other two canvases and walk out the door, Jake falling in step beside me.

"You paint?" he asks after we walk in silence for a few seconds.

"Yes. No. Well, I used to," I answer, shifting the canvases to get a better grip.

"Used to?"

"I haven't painted in a few years." I shrug.

"Why did you stop?"

My eyes flash up to his. "Just life, I guess."

"I heard you in there. Everything you said about artists feeling deeper than others."

"And?"

"I just thought there had to be more of a reason then."

"You don't know me, Jake," I say, my voice sounding harsher than I meant it to.

"No, I don't. I'm trying to figure you out, though," he states, a frustrated look on his face.

When we get to my car, he puts everything in gently so nothing gets damaged.

"Why?"

"Because I want to."

"Okay, good luck with that, mountain man," I say through

a laugh. "I don't usually go around sharing my personal life with people."

"We'll see," he says, looking down at me with a strange look in his eyes. A few seconds pass as we stare at each other before he abruptly turns and walks back down the street.

What just happened?

I need coffee. Or a shot. But since it's only ten in the morning, I guess I'll have to settle for a cup of *very* strong coffee.

I take a short walk over to The Blueberry Café and Bakery, and a bell jingles above my head when I open the door. The aroma of coffee hits me immediately, and I breathe it in.

Ah, the scent of my soul.

Black and white tiles checker the floor, with ten or so tables and chairs on the right side of the café, and the left holding large display cases full of assorted cookies, pastries, and baked goods. Behind the counter, a really beautiful woman who looks to be around my age stands talking to a younger employee.

I smile at them when I reach the counter. "Hi, I'd like a coffee please."

"Sure, anything else?" the woman asks. She has medium length honey blonde hair, bright hazel eyes, and high cheekbones.

"Yes, actually," I start, scanning the cases, "I'll have a piece of blueberry crumb cake, please."

"Good choice. That's my favorite." Smiling, she pores my coffee and hands it to me. "There's milk, cream and sugar at the end there, and I'll bring the crumb cake over to you."

"Thank you so much. I'm actually new here. I just moved into Dottie's place, if you know her?"

She laughs lightly. "Yes, of course I know Dottie, everyone does."

"That's what she told me. I'm Ally, by the way."

"I'm Courtney, I own the place. And this is Dara," she says, pointing to the girl next to her. "She works here and goes to the university nearby."

Dara is a cute girl with curly brown hair and warm brown eyes that sparkle when she shakes my hand. "Hi, Ally, it's so great to meet you."

"You too." I add a little cream to my coffee and then take a sip, letting the liquid gold soothe my frayed nerves caused by the mysterious Jake.

This coffee is heaven. Pure heaven.

"Courtney, this is amazing."

"Thanks. I sampled a lot of varieties before choosing that one. I'm glad it's appreciated." Her smile is so genuine and full of pride.

"It most definitely is." I take another sip and sigh. "I know this is kind of forward of me, but are you hiring?"

"You love my coffee that much?" She laughs.

"Yes, I do love it that much," I say, taking another sip. "Which would make me an excellent person to sell it."

"Actually, I am looking to hire someone. My other girl just quit on me, so if you'd like the job, it's yours."

"Do you need me to fill anything out? References?"

"No, nothing formal like that. I know on instinct with people. You have the job if you'd like it."

"I would, thank you so much." I beam. "I didn't think I'd find anything so soon."

"Well, if you're looking to start right away, you can come back tomorrow at 9am and I can show you everything."

"That sounds great, thanks." Courtney walks with me to a table and places the blueberry crumb cake down in front of me. And after the first bite, I devour the rest in just three more. Holy hell, this is amazing. "I'm definitely going to love working here," I mumble around a full mouth, making both of them laugh.

Chapter 5

The next morning, I wake up around seven so I can be ready early for my first day of work at the café, and drink my coffee out on the back porch, breathing in the salty air.

I can definitely get used to this.

Relaxing, I take in the view for a few minutes, and then head back inside to get ready.

I stare blankly at my closet, though, wondering what I'm supposed to wear. I don't remember seeing a uniform of some sort on them yesterday, so I decide to play it safe with black jeans and a flowy white blouse. I style my hair in a low pony, curling it to give it bounce, and then I put on the same light makeup as yesterday. I have another round of first impressions today and I want to make sure I look good.

I've always been a curvy girl–big hips, thighs, and ass–and over the years, I've learned how to love who I am. Fashion played a big part in that. I taught myself how to dress for my body so I can feel confident. It's the armor I wear against the world.

Taking one last look in the mirror, I give myself a big smile, and then head out.

I get to The Blueberry Café at nine sharp, and see Courtney behind the counter setting trays of donuts in place. "Hi, Courtney."

"Hey, Ally. Come on around and I'll show you everything we sell. You can make a cup of coffee for yourself if you'd like. You can have as many as you'd like, too, since I have to keep it fresh."

"Sounds like the best deal to me." I smile, walking behind the counter and putting my purse away. I pour myself a hot cup of liquid gold and add a little cream before turning back to Courtney for the run down.

"Alright, so this side holds our pies." She points to the case in front of her. "Today we have blueberry, peach, and apple, and sometimes I'll throw in a specialty one if I'm up for it. But I'll always do custom pies upon request, too. The next case holds our cakes and cupcakes. Coffee cakes and squares are on the bottom there, and our other cakes are kept basic unless special ordered. There's chocolate cake with chocolate frosting, chocolate with vanilla, vanilla with chocolate, and vanilla with vanilla. Cupcakes are the same way, but we do have a weekly cupcake special, and this week's is red velvet with a cream cheese frosting."

Oh, my, I want to sample it all.

"The next case has the pastries and donuts," she

continues. "There are blueberry fritters, blueberry muffins, Danishes, scones, and cinnamon rolls. For donuts, we have glazed, Boston cream, jelly, powdered sugar, cinnamon sugar, crullers, and then strawberry, vanilla, or chocolate frosted with sprinkles. We also run a weekly specialty donut, and this week is Nutella filled with a Nutella and peanut butter frosting on top."

"Oh my god," I breathe, and she smiles.

"This last case holds our cookies. We have chocolate chip, salted caramel, white chocolate macadamia, oatmeal raisin, sugar, and peanut butter. And our fresh breads and croissants are over on the rack on the wall. You got that?"

"That's a lot of deliciousness in one place."

"Yes, it is." She laughs. "And very tempting to be around every day." Turning around, she points at the chalk boards on the wall. "Then we have all of our coffee and tea drinks. Do you have experience making the fancy stuff?"

"I just need to be shown once, and then I'll be good. I'm a quick learner."

"Perfect. We pretty much get the basic orders here for coffee, espresso, and cappuccino. But when the tourists roll in during the summer months, they bring the more complicated orders with them." She smiles, rolling her eyes. "Our tables aren't numbered or anything, just bring the order to the customer if they're not getting it to-go. And I think that's it! I'll be here with you for all of your shifts in the beginning, and then you'll be working with Dara, too."

"Sounds good."

Over the next few hours, I meet a bunch of Pine Cove residents, and they're all so welcoming and friendly. Each of them told me to let them know if I needed anything, and they'd be happy to help. It's so different from what I'm used to, and I can tell they genuinely mean it.

Talking with Courtney between customers, I learn she's only four years older than me and married to a fireman in town. I may have swooned at that. Surprisingly, she didn't grow up here. She only moved to Pine Cove a few years ago when she bought the café from an elderly couple who were retiring. She said she found her fresh start here, and never looked back.

"So, Ally, did you leave behind a man in New Jersey? Or maybe you're running from one?"

"No, there's no man back there. Never really was, actually."

"Hmm, interesting."

"I just needed a new start somewhere."

"So, you're not looking for a man then?"

I let out a short laugh. "Not really. I haven't dated since college."

"What?! Wasn't that like ten years ago?!" she exclaims.

"Seven," I correct, hating that I even admitted that.

"Girl, you need to get back out there, and I'm going to help. Jack has some hotties working with him at the firehouse. But don't tell him I said that." She laughs. "He already doesn't like me being around them because he knows I have a weakness for men in a uniform."

"Who doesn't?" I laugh.

A throat clears behind us, and Courtney and I both jump and turn to face them, not realizing a customer had come in.

Well, fuck. My chest tightens the moment our eyes meet.

"Ally." He nods, and I feel my face heat.

"Jake."

Seconds pass before Courtney breaks the tension. "Do you two know each other?" I can hear the curiosity in her voice.

Jake just looks at me, waiting to see what I'll say. "Um, not really. He just helped me on my first night with a rogue bear at my door."

"Yes, she needed rescuing," he says, a hint of a smile on his lips.

"Okay, not really. I just didn't know what to do." I don't want him thinking I'm some damsel in distress.

"You work here now?" he asks, letting me have that one. He knows damn well I needed rescuing based on my crazed phone call.

"Yes," I answer, tucking a piece of hair behind my ear that escaped my ponytail.

Following the movement with his eyes, Jake looks back at me, and then Courtney. "I'll have my usual."

"Sure," she says, looking between the two of us before she pours him a coffee. Grabbing a blueberry fritter from the case, she places it in a paper bag, and hands both to him. "Here you go."

"Thanks." He nods, his eyes on mine. "See you tomorrow."

"Okay," I answer automatically. But, wait, what? Tomorrow?

As soon as he leaves, Courtney grabs my arm and makes me look at her. "Holy shit, Ally! What the hell?! Jake Taylor is so into you! I can't believe you're going to be the one to get him. Women all over town will be so jealous."

"What? What do you mean? I don't have him. He just helped me because of Dottie."

"I saw that man staring at you like he wanted to strip you naked and lay you out. You need to tell me everything."

My cheeks heat. He wasn't looking at me like. Was he?

Starting at the beginning, I tell her everything that happened that night and in the morning. And by the end, her mouth is hanging open.

"Okay, listen close. Jake Taylor doesn't do that. Ever. He barely leaves his workshop. And when he does, he comes here, the hardware store, and the grocery store."

"Why?"

She shrugs. "I don't know. He works a lot at his house, and just doesn't bother to come into town. He's still sexy as hell though," she says, fanning her face. "I love when he comes in."

"You're married, keep it in your pants."

"Yeah, yeah, yeah. I know." She waves dismissively. "There are four Taylor boys, you know. All equally hot."

"There are four of them that look like that? I think that'd be too much to take in at once. Jake makes me nervous enough."

"Mhmm. I bet he does." She winks.

Looking away, I try and busy myself cleaning the counter.

"You know, you could always break something at the house to make him come over again to help you."

"Courtney, that's pathetic. I can't do that."

"Why not?" She shrugs. "Before I started dating Jack, I told him I smelled gas leaking from the stove so he'd come over and 'fix' it. Then I spent the next hour watching him bent over trying to figure it out. It was great."

"Seriously?" I laugh, thinking about the idea of watching Jake's fine ass bent over in my kitchen. I'd have free rein to stare all I wanted. "Okay, maybe. I'll think about it."

And think about it I did. When I get home from work, I look around for something to break that wouldn't be super obvious that I did it on purpose. This is so dumb, but her idea is stuck in my head. So, the next day at work, I decide to give in and ask Courtney for her help in devising a plan.

"He's going to see right through it!" I yell.

"Good! Then he'll know you want him. And I want a full report after. Like, a full report," she says, waggling her eye brows at me.

"Yeah, I definitely will," I say sarcastically. "When I can pick myself up off the floor from passing out when this all goes terribly wrong, I'll make sure to call you straight away."

"Good. Thank you," she says, ignoring my sarcasm. "And it's going to work. Trust me. I got Jack, and you'll get Jake."

"I never said I wanted to 'get' him." A man like Jake screams heartbreak.

"Oh, please, you want him. Just stop thinking so much and do it."

Chapter 6

I can do this. It's no big deal.

Walking over to the oven, I open it and try and find whatever the hell I'm looking for. I Googled how to do this, so I stick my head in and locate the heating component plugs. When I see them, I grip them hard and pull them out.

Okay, first part done.

I grab my phone next, and take a deep breath before dialing his number. After three rings, Jake picks up. "Hello?" Holy mother of Jesus he's out of breath. Is he working out? Building a boat? Oh no, was he having sex with someone? Wait, no, I hope he doesn't answer the phone during sex. "Hello?" he asks again.

"Hi," I manage to squeak out, despite all the images of his

sweaty body flashing through my mind. "It's Ally."

I hear him let out a low, throaty chuckle. "You need rescuing again, darlin'?"

Darlin'? He has a little drawl in his voice when he says it, and I sway on my feet, gripping the counter for support.

"Not exactly. It seems my oven is broken?"

"Are you asking me if it is?"

"No. I'm sure. It's broken." Smooth, Ally, real smooth. "Do you know how to fix ovens?"

"I do."

"Well, um, do you mind coming over? If you're free?"

"I'm just finishing up with something, and then I'll come." His sweaty body flashes in my head again, my mind thinking of all sorts of dirty things.

"Thanks," I choke out, hanging up right away.

I quickly send Courtney a text to update her, and then I run to the bathroom to make sure my hair and makeup are still good. I will *not* be greeting him with pajamas and bed head this time.

I'm a nervous wreck waiting for him to come over. He said he had to finish something, so that could mean a half hour? An hour? More?

Pacing the living room isn't helping, and I can't sit still, so I decide to start unpacking my boxes of chachkies, pictures, and books to distract myself.

A half an hour later, I'm singing along to the song playing on my phone, when knocking at the door scares me, and I drop the books I was holding. I didn't even hear Jake's truck coming down the driveway.

My palms get instantly sweaty just knowing he's here, and I wipe them on my jeans before opening the door. And he's there – all tall, dark, and ruggedly handsome. He looks like the Brawny paper towel man in his work boots, worn-in jeans, and a red and black plaid button down over a white t-shirt.

I will forever be turned on whenever I buy paper towels now.

"Hi," I breathe out, my voice soft.

His heated eyes meet mine, and then rake down my body and back up. Thank God I'm holding onto the door or I would be melting to the ground with how he's looking at me.

"Hi," he says, clearing his throat. "You rang?"

I smile, regaining myself. "Yes, mountain man, I did. And you dressed for the part, I see." I brazenly rake my eyes up and down his body, and when I meet his again, they've turned molten.

Stepping aside, he brushes past me, keeping his heated gaze on me as long as he can before walking towards the kitchen. Following behind him, I enjoy the view the entire way.

The second I step into the kitchen with him, the air around us starts to swirl with an electric current that has my heart racing.

"I don't know what happened to the oven. I went to make something, but it wouldn't get hot." What is getting hot, though, is me in this freaking kitchen with him. I need to distract myself. "Do you want anything? Water? Tea? Coffee? Whisky?"

That last one gets him to turn and look at me. "Water is fine."

Grabbing a bottle from the fridge, I hand it to him, and watch as he unscrews the cap and takes a big swig, his throat moving as he swallows. Everything he does is sexy.

He clears his throat, and I look away quickly. Damn it, he

caught me staring. Lowering my head, I go and sit on one of kitchen chairs and open a magazine, desperately trying to look nonchalant even though I'm freaking out on the inside.

Jake gets to work immediately. He kneels on the floor and sticks his head in the oven. Oh, sweet Jesus, what a view. I've never been one to be into guys' asses, but hot damn, his is nice. And now I get to look at it without him knowing.

A few seconds later, though, I hear what sounds like laughter coming from him, but I can't be sure.

"Did you say something?"

Jake backs out of the oven with a small smile. "Nope, all fixed."

"Really? That was fast." The disappointment evident in my voice.

"I just had to play with the wires. It should be good now." Shit. He's looking at me like he knows what I did. And the fact that my face feels hot isn't helping.

"Um, well, thanks for coming over to help me. Again."

"That's my job now I guess." He smirks.

My brow furrows. "It is?"

"I helped Dottie when she was here alone, and now you're here alone, so…"

I give him a small smile. "Alright, mountain man, I'll let you help me. If I need it."

"Let me?"

"Yes, let you. I can always call someone else."

"Who?" he asks, taking a step towards me.

Standing, I go and get a bottle of water from the fridge for myself, my mouth suddenly dry. "Okay, so I don't know anyone else here besides you and Courtney," I admit. "And she doesn't really strike me as the fix-it type." Closing the fridge door, I turn around, and he's right there in front of me, my eyes forced up to his.

"You broke it yourself, didn't you?" His voice is low and smooth, like a fine whisky.

"What?" I whisper, all cognitive thought leaving my head. "No."

"You just wanted me to come over." He says it as a statement, and my skin breaks out in goosebumps.

"Yes." My answer is automatic, and I don't even realize I answered truthfully until he takes a step towards me, almost touching now.

"Why?"

"Because"–I swallow–"I wanted you to–"

Jake doesn't let me finish my sentence. He grabs the back of my neck and crushes his mouth down on mine.

The bottle of water slips from my hand and I grip his arms to steady myself. I feel pure heat raging through me, and it's something I've never experienced before.

Letting out a soft moan, Jake uses that opportunity to slip his tongue past my lips, and I melt into him instantly.

I slide my hands up his chest and around his neck, pulling myself up towards him as he pulls me flush against his solid frame. There's a fire running through my veins as our tongues come together in a tangled dance.

Dizzy, I realize how long it's been since I've been kissed. And I've never been kissed like this.

Jake slides his hands down to my ass and grips hard, lifting me up and onto the counter. I wrap my legs around his hips instantly and pull him as close to me as I can.

He kisses his way across my jaw, his teeth grazing my neck – licking, sucking, biting. Moaning, I slide my fingers through his hair, gripping the ends hard. His throaty growl vibrates through me, and he sucks my earlobe into his hot mouth, coaxing a low moan from my lips.

His hands continue to explore my body – moving up my back, down my sides, and snaking up under my shirt. The second he touches my bare skin, I feel it light with fire. My stomach muscles contract as his fingers move up my torso, taking my shirt with them. Throwing it somewhere behind him, his lips are on mine again instantly, and he yanks down the cups of my bra, filling his hands with my aching breasts.

Pulling away from my lips, Jake leans down and closes his mouth around my left nipple, sucking it deep into his mouth.

Throwing my head back, a ragged cry is torn from my body. I grip the back of his head as he moves to my right one, and I push myself into him, wanting to fuse his mouth to my body.

Jake smooths his hands down to my hips, making a sweep down my legs that are around his waist, and back.

When his hands move to the button on my jeans, though, I freeze, and push him away.

I want him. Badly. But this is too much, too fast.

Breathing hard, I adjust my bra so I'm covered again, and I stare at his throat, not able to look him in the eyes. "I'm sorry. It's just…" I start, but pause.

Placing two fingers under my chin, he lifts my head up so I'll look at him, but I close my eyes. "Look at me, beautiful." Taking a deep breath, I open my eyes again, and look into his that are swirling like a tropical storm. "I'm sorry. I got carried away."

I can only nod in response. If I speak, I know I'll start crying. My emotions are all out of balance right now, but I focus on Jake's reassuring eyes, and breathe in and out slowly.

Stepping back, he picks my shirt up off the floor and hands it back to me. Holding it tight against my chest, I watch his every move as he fills the kettle with water and places it on the stove. He's making tea?

When I know I can stand steadily, I hop down from the counter and go into the bathroom. Looking in the mirror, I take in my flushed cheeks and swollen lips.

Touching my lips gently, I close my eyes – still feeling his hands and mouth all over me. My breathing becomes shallow, and I have to sit on the edge of the tub.

I want him.

I want him with every fiber of my being.

But all I can think about is how every man I've ever let close to me has fucked me over – always breaking me just a little more than the last. I can't do it again. I'm already made up of so many broken pieces that there's not much left of me to break. One more is sure to be the unraveling of the thin thread I use to keep myself together.

A light knock on the door startles me, and I have no idea how long I've been sitting here.

Opening it, I find Jake standing there, his frame taking up the entire doorway. Even if I thought about running, I couldn't.

When I have the courage to look up at him, his eyes slice right through me, and I know he can see the dark battle I'm fighting inside.

"You okay?" he asks softly.

Not trusting my voice, I give him a small nod. Holding my gaze for a second longer, he moves aside, letting me walk back into the kitchen. I take a seat at the table, finding a steaming cup of tea waiting for me.

He made me tea.

Taking a sip, I let the warm, sweet liquid slide down my throat, and my muscles relax instantly. From the corner of my eye, I can see Jake watching me from across the kitchen, leaning against the counter he was just kissing me on.

"I'm sorry," I tell him, staring at the wood grains of the table in front of me.

"Why are you apologizing?"

I sip my tea and shrug my shoulders. I know I shouldn't be sorry, but it just feels like I should still apologize.

"I don't want your apology. You stopped me when you didn't want to go any further."

"I know. It's just that…" Closing my eyes, I try and focus my thoughts.

"Did someone hurt you?"

"Yes. And no." I take another sip of tea and I see that Jake's gone still. "It's not in the way I'm assuming you're thinking, though," I tell him, trying to assure him.

"I doubt you know what I'm thinking."

"Okay. What are you thinking?" I chance a look over at him, and his face has gone hard as stone. "Jake?"

Growling, he rakes his hands through his hair and turns his back to me, gripping the edge of the counter – his back muscles flexing.

Standing, I go to him, placing my hand on the center of his back – his muscles seizing at my touch. I gently rub my hand in a circle, sliding it up to his left shoulder and down his arm, stopping at his wrist.

"Jake, look at me," I whisper, and his eyes flash to mine. I hold his gaze, letting him see me.

When he finally loosens his grip on the counter, I slide my hand into his and lace our fingers together while I bring my other hand up to rest on his cheek.

Jake closes his eyes at my touch, and when he opens them again, I see the storm starting to pass. He covers my hand with his own, and rubs his thumb back and forth across my knuckles – reassuring and comforting me.

Leaning up on my toes, I press my lips to his in a gentle and soft embrace, squeezing his hand in mine.

Breaking apart, Jake leans his forehead against mine, and I settle back down on my feet, squeezing his hand again.

"Come on," I say, pulling him towards the back door.

The sun is starting to set, and the sky is transforming into hues of orange, yellow, and red. I'd love to paint this. My heart wrenches at that thought, and I'm overwhelmed with the need to put onto canvas what I'm seeing and feeling right now.

I haven't thought that in so long.

My emotions are on high alert, and whenever I used to feel like this, I'd paint. But this time, the emotions swirling through me feel different, which makes this need to paint feel different. I just can't pinpoint why.

"Have you painted yet?" Jake asks. I'm sure he can read every emotion that crosses my face, but I keep my eyes on the retreating sun.

"Not yet. But I want to. I want to paint this moment."

"Then do it."

"It's been a long time."

"That's exactly why you should do it."

He's right. Standing, I go inside and grab the supplies I'll need and the smallest canvas I bought. When I settle back into my chair, I set everything up, and try to block out Jake next to me. I focus on my breathing and mixing my colors, preparing myself for that first brushstroke. It's in that single motion where so many possibilities lie.

The restraints around my heart squeeze and then loosen as I breathe out with my first stroke, and it feels like reuniting with an old friend.

Time seems to move in slow motion while I lose myself in the moment. The sun continues to descend, but I feel like I have all the time in the world to capture it.

I put everything I'm feeling into this, and with every brushstroke, it feels like I'm coming home.

When the last of the light has left the sky, I put my brush down, and look at the first painting I've created in what feels like a lifetime.

The red sun bleeds out orange and yellow, meeting the darkening blue of the sky while the ocean welcomes it down under the horizon. At the water's edge, the silhouette of a man and woman holding hands makes my chest tighten. He's looking at her while she looks out at the sea. I didn't even second guess doing it. I gave myself over to my emotions and this is what came of it. This is what I'm feeling.

Tears start rolling down my cheeks, and the next thing I know, Jake is right there, kneeling in front of me and wiping them away.

"You did amazing, Ally." I close my eyes and let his soft, sweet voice pour over me like warm honey. "Open your eyes, darlin', look at me." My eyes flutter open, and a few more tears escape, but Jake is there to catch them as they fall. "So blue, so beautiful," he says, searching my eyes.

"I don't let people see me like this," I whisper, looking down at my paint splattered hands.

Jake slides two fingers under my chin, tilting my face back up to look at him. "Tell me what you're feeling."

I don't know how to describe it. "Seen. You make me feel seen."

Leaning in, Jake brushes his lips against mine, and I can't help the feelings bubbling up inside of me. I wrap my arms around his neck, threading my fingers through his hair and pulling him closer. Sliding my tongue across the seam of his lips, Jake opens for me, and I dive in – sweeping, tasting, and exploring.

Slowing the kiss, I pull away, my eyes closed and my lips still just a breath away from his. "Jake," I whisper, afraid to hear his response to my next words, but needing to hear the answer. "Tell me what you're feeling."

"I feel like I can see in the dark for the first time. I opened my eyes to see an angel lighting my way."

Rubbing his stubbled cheek with the palm of my hand, I softly trace his lips with the tips of my fingers. "Why are you in the dark?" I whisper.

"I just am. And you deserve the light, not darkness."

"I'm already in the dark," I tell him, tracing his jaw lightly.

He doesn't say anything more. He just rolls back onto his heels, breaking contact with me, and I watch him with wide eyes as he walks back into the house. Standing quickly, I follow him, catching up to him just before he reaches the front door.

"Why are you leaving?"

"I have to go. I have work to finish," he says, not even looking at me.

"Seriously?"

"Yeah, I have to go."

What? Stunned, I pull the front door open for him and

step to the side. "Thanks for coming over to help me. I'll just see you whenever." Bitterness drips from every word I say, and when Jake walks past me without a single look, I slam the door closed behind him.

Letting out a frustrated growl, I throw myself down on the couch and reach for my phone in my back pocket.

I text the group chat I have with Ash, Mel, and Ellie to see if everyone is free to talk, and then I conference them all in.

"Ally-cat! How are you?!" Ellie yells first. "You were supposed to call us days ago!"

"Yeah what the fuck, Al?!" Ash chimes in.

"Guys, oh my god, let her talk!"

"Thanks, Mel. I miss you guys, and I just really wanted to talk to you."

Mel is quick to pick up on my tone. "What's wrong? Do you hate it there?"

"No," I sigh. "I love it actually. I just…I'm having a man issue." A round of screams from them has me holding the phone away from my ear for a second. "And he's, well, I don't know. Complicated and confusing."

"What man isn't? Did you do the nasty yet?"

"Okay, Trash-ley, just dive right in there," Ellie says, using our favorite nickname for Ashley.

"No, we haven't. But I want him more than I've ever wanted anyone. We barely know each other, but I'm a jumbled mess whenever he's near me."

"AHH you went and found yourself a hot piece of ass right away like I told you to!"

"You're going to have to tell us everything if you want our advice," Melanie says.

Starting from the beginning, I tell them all about Jake. And when I finish, all I hear is silence. "Hello? You guys there?"

"Yeah we're here," Mel says.

"Just processing," Ellie adds.

"And thinking about moving up there with you so I can find a man like Thor."

"Well, he does have three brothers who Courtney says are just as hot."

"Who's Courtney? Have you replaced us already?"

"No, bitch, I got a job. Courtney is the owner of the café/bakery in town where I work now. And yes, we're friends. She actually came up with the plan to break the oven so Jake would come over and fix it."

"Well, it worked, so I guess she gets some points for that. But we'll have to vet her when we come up there to make sure she's good enough to be in our group."

"In our group?"

"Yes. Any friends you make will have to be brought into the fold so we're all on the same page with Thor and how you're going to get him to be yours."

"I love you guys. I miss you."

"Miss you too, Ally-cat. Now, I think we can all agree that you need to just go about your life for a few days and wait for him to come to you. You called him over today, and then he left like an ass. Let him make the next move."

"Alright. I think I can do that. It all just got intense so fast. I wasn't expecting that."

"That happens when you meet someone who you have a genuine connection with, Ally. There's no holding back because you can't. You feel this pull towards them, and it's near impossible to ignore or resist. You want to be near them, with them, know them."

"How do you know that, Mel?" Ellie asks.

"Don't worry about it."

"It's from your books, isn't it?"

"It still applies!" she yells back, always so sensitive when she's teased for reading so many romance novels.

"Look, Ally-cat," Elizabeth's soft voice cuts in. "Just let it happen. Let yourself feel something for once. I know you don't trust men easily, if at all, but don't let your past keep you from experiencing what could be something great."

My eyes burn with unshed tears. "I'll try."

"Good."

"Okay, I have to go. I'm hungry."

"Alright, we'll talk soon though, okay? Keep us updated."

"I will. Love you." Hanging up, I throw my head back against the couch and sigh. This is all going so fast for me and my head is pounding. I go from seven long years of isolation to an over intake of every emotion known to man.

Picking my phone back up, I dial another number.

"Hi, sweetie," my mom says as soon as she answers.

"Hi, mom. How are you?"

"It's a little lonely here without you, but I'm trying to keep busy."

"I'm sorry."

"Don't be sorry, sweetie. It was inevitable that you'd move out. I'm adjusting is all. The last of my chickees have flown the coop."

"I miss you."

"I miss you, too. What's wrong?"

"Why do you think something's wrong?"

"I can hear it in your voice. I'm your mother."

"It's nothing. I sort of met a man, and he's, I don't know. I think he's too much for me."

"What do you mean?"

"What I'm feeling scares me."

"Don't let that stop you from diving in without knowing how deep the water goes. Without risk, you can't have reward. I know your father and I weren't an example to follow, but love exists, sweetie. Good, genuine men, exist."

"Mom," I choke out.

"Please, try for me."

"Okay," I whisper.

"Thank you, sweetie. I love you."

"Love you too."

"Now go eat something, I know you're probably hungry and it'll make you feel better."

"Yes, mom." I don't know how she already knew. "Talk to you soon, okay?"

"'Night, honey."

"'Night." Hanging up, I wipe my hands down my face.

The pizza here better not suck. That would be the topper to a shit night. Washing my face, I throw my hair up into a messy bun and head out. Only pizza, wine, and a lot of TV will start to fix my jumbled emotions.

Driving into town, I'm lucky to find a spot right in front of Anthony's on Main Street – the only place that sells pizza in Pine Cove. When I open the door, I'm greeted with the delicious smell of Italian food. Mmm, I love that smell.

Not even ashamed that I want a large pie, I order one that's half peperoni and half plain. I'm definitely not in the mood to talk to anyone in the restaurant, so I keep my head down and walk back outside, needing to find a store that sells liquor. Pulling out my phone, I Google it, and see that the grocery store around the corner does, so I head off in that direction.

The fresh night air feels amazing on my face, and cools it down. Looking up, I see the sky bursting with stars. I didn't even know there were that many up there. The skies back home are so light polluted that I could only ever see a few. But here…I can see everything.

In the grocery store, I pick up four bottles of wine and a bottle of Maker's Mark. I'm going to need something strong to help me go to sleep later.

Dropping my bags off at my car, I go back inside Anthony's to pick up my order. I make my way to the counter with my head down, still trying to avoid anyone who wants to say hi. But before I even make it a few steps, I hear my name being called from a table to my left.

Damn it.

I turn and see Courtney with a man I'm assuming is her husband, Jack, having dinner together. And wow, go Courtney. He's really living up to that fireman's dream all of us woman have.

"Hey, Courtney."

"How are you? How did our plan go?" She smiles, but I really don't want to talk about this in front of her husband. "Oh, don't worry about Jack, I already told him everything." She waves her hand in the air like it's no big deal.

"You did?" I ask nervously.

"Yeah, we're married." She shrugs, like that explains everything.

I look at Jack, but I can't read his expression. I really

don't want to talk about this here.

"Tonight went okay, I guess," I tell her, shifting on my feet and looking away. "I have to pick up my order now, so I'll just tell you about it at work tomorrow." Turning away quickly, I hurry up to the counter before she can ask me anything else.

Chapter 7

Waking up the next morning with a dry mouth and a pounding headache are signs of a night well spent in sorrow. At least I wasn't kept up all night with thoughts of Jake, and I was able to just pass out cold.

Stumbling into the bathroom, I catch a glimpse of myself in the mirror and I almost scare myself. I look like hell. My eyes are red and puffy with dark circles underneath, and my skin looks paler than usual. I'm definitely going to need a little extra makeup today to make myself look like a human.

Wow, hangovers in my late twenties are a lot different than my early twenties when I would spring awake at seven in the morning and be good to go.

After I take a long hot shower, I feel so much better, but

then look at the clock and realize how much I'm running behind. Shit, I forgot to set an alarm last night and now I'm going to be late for work. It's Courtney's fault though, because of her dumb plan. So she'll have to forgive me.

When I walk into the café, Courtney comes rushing up to meet me before the door even has a chance to close behind me. "Ally, what happened? I know you didn't want to talk last night with Jack there, but you looked upset."

"Well, your dumb plan worked. It got intense and hot really fast, and then he left." Walking past her, I go behind the counter to put my purse away.

"Tell me everything."

"For starters, he saw right through the oven ploy."

She smiles. "Good, that means he's not dumb."

"Courtney," I sigh, rolling my eyes.

"And then what happened?"

"We sort of made out. Hard." I feel my cheeks heat.

"Hot damn, yes! So, wait, why are you upset? What happened?"

"I'm not upset, I'm frustrated. I showed him something personal, and I thought it was all going great, but then he just stood up and walked out. I was left standing there feeling vulnerable, and I hate that."

"He just walked out? Why?"

"I don't know. He said he had work to finish, but I know he was lying."

"Maybe he doesn't know how to handle getting close to someone?"

"I don't know. But I came here to move forward in my life, not let my past hold me back anymore. And all Jake does is remind me of my past."

"Do you want to talk about it?"

"Not really. Maybe over cocktails one night." I shrug. "But not now."

"I'm here, though. I hope you can consider me more than just your boss."

"I already do, don't worry." I smile. "We schemed together. We're friends."

"Good." She smiles. "And just give it time with him. You guys just met."

"I know. And you owe me coffee and breakfast because your plan gave me a raging hangover and I woke up too late to have time to make something before coming in."

Laughing, she says, "Of course, take whatever you want."

And take I do. I eat a strawberry frosted donut with sprinkles, my favorite since I was a kid, but I still need more sugary goodness to wake me up. Grabbing a blueberry fritter next, I wash it all down with the biggest cup of coffee we have, and finally start to feel like a human again.

Luckily, the day passes without having to see Jake, or talk about him anymore with Courtney. My mind has already been overanalyzing everything on a loop when him and I are probably never going to actually work anyway.

And just when I thought I was home free, and ready for another night of food wine alone at the house, Courtney yells over to me from across the café as I wipe the tables down. "Hey, we're going out tonight!"

"We are?"

"Yes. We're going to go have dinner and drinks at The Rusty Anchor. You need to go out."

I give her a look. "Is that so?"

"Call it staff bonding." She shrugs.

"What's The Rusty Anchor?"

"Our small town's only bar. But they serve good food, too, so grab your stuff. It's just a short walk down and around the block."

"Alright, fine," I sigh. "But don't get me drunk."

"I can't make any promises." She winks.

The Rusty Anchor is not what I expected. The floors are a dark wood that matches that of the ceiling and the horseshoe shaped bar at the far end of the room. Two pool tables separate the bar area from the twenty or so tables that are scattered on the side closest to the door. The walls are painted a deep navy blue and are lined with neon signs, posters, and all sorts of nautical memorabilia. I pictured a hole in the wall dive bar, but it's surprisingly decent, and just what a coastal town bar should be.

"This place is surprisingly pretty cool."

Courtney laughs at my response. "What did you expect?"

"I don't know. The bars in New Jersey are mostly shitty, so this is cool to me." We walk past the tables, opting to sit at the bar instead.

"The first round is on me since I made you come here."

"That's a given." I laugh. "But don't think getting me drunk will make me talk about shit."

"We'll see," she says, like she already has a plan to get me to spill all of my secrets to her.

I turn towards the bartender to order a drink, and I find myself locking eyes with a very sexy man. "I'll have a gin and tonic with extra limes, please." I smile sweetly at him.

"And I'll have a Jack and coke, Alex, thanks."

He nods and gets to making our drinks. Alex is walking sin. He has tattoos, dark hair, a short beard, emerald green eyes, and I'll even bet he rides a motorcycle.

Turning to Courtney, I whisper, "He's–"

"Yeah, I know." She smiles. "Every girl has a thing for Alex. He's our resident bad boy."

I let my eyes wander back to him. "Mhmm, I can see that."

"Don't go there, though, he only breaks hearts."

"A girl can look." I give her a sly smile, and when our drinks are done, I flash Alex another sweet smile. "Thank you."

"No problem, gorgeous." He winks.

Feeling flirty, I flip my hair behind my shoulder and stick my hand out. "I'm Ally, by the way. I'm new here."

He takes my hand in his much larger one, but I don't feel the heat like when Jake touches me. "Alex. Where are you from?"

"I'm a Jersey girl."

He flashes me a smile that I'm sure have made woman swoon and drop their panties from here to Cali, and back. "The best kind of girls."

"I've always thought so."

"I can show you around our small town if you need someone."

"Yeah she's good, but thanks," Courtney chimes in, and Alex holds his hands up in front of him.

"Offer still stands, Ally." He smiles, walking over to the other side of the bar.

"Courtney!" I yell at her.

"He's an ass. I just saved you some time figuring it out for yourself."

"Uh, I think I would have enjoyed figuring that out for myself. Especially on the back of his motorcycle." I swirl my straw around my drink and look back over at Alex.

"How do you know he has a motorcycle?"

"Look at him. He does, doesn't he?"

She laughs lightly. "Yeah, he does. But what about Jake?"

I roll my eyes. "Please, you and I both know Jake is the obvious winner, no competition. But I can still appreciate a hot man. Can't you? Marriage doesn't make you blind."

"No, it doesn't. But I love Jack."

"Of course you do! I'm just saying that a woman can always appreciate an aesthetically pleasing man without having to do something about it." I gesture towards Alex. "He's pleasing to look at, thus, I'm looking. That's it." Smiling, I take a big sip of my cocktail.

"You're terrible," she says, shaking her head.

"You should see me when I'm out with my friends from back home. I'm the wing woman, so I talk up all the hotties before passing them off to whoever wants them. It's great, actually."

"Seriously?"

"Yeah." I shrug. "None of the guys ever interest me, so I figure what the hell, you know? I'm thinking of asking the three of them–Ashley, Melanie, and Elizabeth–to come up for MDW. You can meet them then. And they want to make sure you're good enough to fold into our group."

"What?" Courtney chokes, spitting some of her drink out.

"Don't worry about it," I say, waving my hand in the air. "You'll be great. I called them last night and filled them in on everything, and so now they like you because of your oven scheme and want to be a part of any future tricks."

"Well, okay then." She laughs. "I like them already. What are they like? And what the hell is MDW?"

"Memorial Day Weekend." I laugh. "Come on, Courtney, keep up. And we'll need more drinks if I'm going to tell you about them. Hey, Alex?" I yell, waving him over. "Can we have another round, please?"

"Anything for you, beautiful." He smiles, laying on the charm.

With fresh drinks in hand, I dive in and tell Courtney all about Ash, Mel, and Ellie. I tell her about some of our shenanigans together, my life back in Jersey, and what ultimately led me to moving up here.

Alex continues to serve us drinks whenever our glasses are empty, and I think I'm starting to feel the effects.

"Hey, Ally, I'm so glad you moved here," Courtney slurs slightly. "I only moved here a few years ago when I bought the café. And then I found Jack, and I love him, and I love Pine Cove."

I giggle at her rant. "Me, too. And I know all of that already."

"We need another round, Alex!" she yells, and he looks over at us, shaking his head.

"You ladies haven't had enough yet?"

"Nope," I answer. "We'd like another, kind sir."

"Yeah, you're drunk. You better not be driving home later."

"Why?" I ask, leaning forward on the bar. "If I need a ride, will you take me home on your bike?"

"If you want me to," he says in a low, sexy voice, leaning toward me too.

Smiling, I take I sip of my drink and shake my head, leaning back off the bar. His eyes don't hold me captive like Jake's.

Looking around, I see the place has filled up while Courtney and I have been talking, and I didn't even notice.

"Okay, Ally. We've had a lot to drink. Now it's time to spill."

"What?"

"You said this morning that you'd tell me everything over cocktails, and we're drunk enough now. I think." She hiccups, then giggles.

"This was your plan? Liquor me up and make me talk? How very romantic of you."

"Oh, shut up," she says, swatting my arm.

"Fine, I'll give you the short version of my life." It's sad to say that her plan worked, because I start to tell things only a very few know about me. "I used to paint, and it was my life. Then I graduated from college and real life set in, so I gave it up. My dad is an asshole and I don't speak to him anymore, but my mom is the best person I know and we're more best friends than mother/daughter. I have two sisters that are great. They're both happily married and I'm jealous that they've found love and I haven't. I've been on a seven-year man hiatus that was just broken by Jake and his fantastic kissing skills. And now I'm trying to find my way back to being an artist again."

"Wow, okay. I don't even know where to start with all of that. You paint?" she asks.

"Yes."

"I'd love to see some of your work."

"Yeah, no," I tell her. "I only just started again."

"And what about your dad? Why don't you talk to him anymore?"

"It's a long story." I shrug, not wanting to get into it. "But I'll just say that I have a hard time trusting men because of him.

My mom said he was good once, until he wasn't."

"Is that why you're worried about Jake?"

"What do you mean? Who said I'm worried?"

"I can just tell. Was your hiatus because you don't want men to turn out like your dad?"

"Something like that." I take a long gulp of my drink.

"Didn't you say your sisters found love, and they're married and happy?"

"Yeah, and?"

"Love is always a risk. But when you meet the right person, you know that everything will be okay, even decades down the line, as long as you have them by your side."

"And you've found that with Jack?"

"Yes, I have." A dreamy look comes over her face, and my heart pangs with jealousy.

"I'd love to find that," I admit somberly.

"Maybe you have and you just don't know it yet."

I give her a skeptical look and sip my drink some more, needing the buzz the alcohol is giving me. "Jake is the sexiest, manliest, most beautiful man I've ever met. But he's also closed off and guarded and doesn't really talk." *And my body gets hot just thinking about him*, I add silently.

Courtney smiles wide and yells, "I knew it! You've got it bad for him."

I slap my hand over her mouth. "Shhh, stop yelling! And yes"–I look around to see if anyone is listening–"maybe."

I feel her laughing behind my hand and then she licks my palm, and I pull it away quickly. "Ew! Why did you lick me?"

"Don't put your hand over my mouth." She shrugs.

"Wait! We didn't eat!" I yell out, suddenly starving.

"Shit! Alex, can we get food still?" Courtney yells over to

him.

"Sorry, kitchen's closed, ladies."

"Courtney, I'm starving! Is there anywhere open still? What time is it?"

"It's 11 o'clock, I think," she says, squinting at her watch. "I don't know. I can't read my watch right now, my eyes are blurry."

"11?! We've been here for freaking hours! I need food!"

"Let me call Jack! He can bring us food!" she exclaims, dialing her husband's number. "Hey, baby," she slurs. "I'm hungry…Yeah, I'm drunk…I'm with Ally…Yeah, she's drunk too…We're starving babe, can you feed us? Alex said the kitchen is closed, that hot ass hole." She giggles.

I tune out the rest of her one-sided conversation, and let my hazy mind drift off to thoughts of Jake. Images of him kissing me while his hands roam all over my body flash in my mind, and my heart starts racing and my palms get sweaty.

"Ally! Hey!" Courtney yells next to me, and I snap out of it, turning towards her. "I've been talking to you. Did you hear me?"

"No, sorry. What?"

"Jack is coming to bring us food. I said burgers and fries were obviously needed. Is that good?"

"Mmm fries," I say, thinking of the delicious greasy food until my brain registers the song that's playing. "Oh my god, Courtney! This is my jam! We have to dance!" I grab her hand and stumble off my stool, taking her with me, nearly making us fall.

"No, no, no. I don't dance," she protests.

"Of course you do, come on!" I start to move my body to the Luke Bryan song that's playing – rolling my hips, raising my arms, and spinning around. I let my body move to the beat.

By the end of the song, we manage to get most of the girls in the bar to dance along with us, and we all keep going for the next few songs, laughing and singing along. We don't even notice Jack is here until he's right behind us, wrapping his arms around Courtney's waist.

"Hey, baby!" she yells over the music, throwing her arms around his neck. "I'm having so much fun! Did you bring us food? I'm starving!"

He pulls her in close and kisses her. "Of course, babe. It's my job as your husband to feed you."

"Well aren't you two sweet? Barf. Did you happen to bring your wife's new best friend some food, too?" I smile at him, and he holds up two bags of fast food.

"Of course I did. I'm not stupid."

"Ahh thank you!" I jump up and kiss his cheek. "What a peach!" I take one of the bags from his hand and sit back up at the bar, ready to devour my food.

When Alex sees me, he comes right over. "Are you eating outside food in here right now?"

"Yeah, because you wouldn't feed us," I mumble around a mouth full of fries. Shaking his head, he starts to walk away, but I yell after him, "Wait! Bring me another drink! Oh, sorry, I mean please bring me another drink. Thank you!" I think I've had like eight gin and tonics by now, and am well on my way to a nice drunken state.

When Alex puts another cocktail down in front of me, he doesn't let go when I grab it. "You are not driving home."

"Obviously," I say, rolling my eyes.

"I can drive you, if you want." Why is he looking at me like that?

"She has a ride, Alex," a deep, angry voice says from behind me, and I swivel around to see Jake with a sexy murderous look on his face.

"Hey, mountain man. What're you doing here?" I run my hand up his arm, and rest it on his perfectly chiseled chest. He's wearing a long sleeved blue Henley tee that's soft beneath my fingers. His hair is all messy like he's been running his hands through it, and his jaw is set tight as his eyes shoot daggers at Alex. "How'd you know I was here, Jake?" I ask, curling my fingers into his t-shirt, needing him to look at me. I crave his eyes on me.

Loosening his jaw at my touch, he finally meets my eyes, and I'm hooked. "Jack called and said you were drunk and needed a ride home."

"Alex said he'd take me for a ride on his motorcycle," I tell him, purposefully trying to provoke him.

"You are not going on the back of his fucking bike," he growls, his eyes starting to swirl.

"Why would you care if I did?" I uncurl my hand and run it farther up his chest, draping my arm around his neck as he leans forward, placing his hands on the bar on either side of me.

"You're not going anywhere with him, or any other man here." Damn, he's sexy when he lays down the law like that.

"Mountain man, you have no claim here since you walked out on me last night."

"I didn't walk out on you, darlin'."

"You did. But I could be persuaded into thinking otherwise," I tell him, stroking the nape of his neck and tugging on the ends of his hair. "You could kiss me right here, right now, and I'd forget that you rejected me last night."

He takes a step closer, and I spread my legs, letting him get as close as possible. "I didn't reject you, darlin', I never would. I just needed some space. A little time to think."

"Do you need more time? More space? Because I can't stop thinking about you," I whisper, placing my other hand on his leg in front of me.

"Baby, you're going to have to stop touching me if you want me to keep my control in this bar."

"I don't want you to. I want you to kiss me. I thought I already said that." Tilting my head to the side, I bite my bottom lip and smile.

"You're drunk, darlin'. I can't take advantage of that."

"You better. I'm drunk because of you anyway," I confess, pulling on his hair again. "Please? Otherwise you can go, and I'll just catch a ride home with Alex."

As I start to pull my hands away from him, he leans in further, holding me captive with the intensity of his stare. He must see what he needs there, because the next thing I know, his mouth is on mine. Pressing me back into the edge of the bar, I pull him close, not caring that we're in a bar full of people.

My body ignites, and I feel him sweep his tongue across my lips, asking for entrance. And I'm about to let him in when Courtney clears her throat next to me.

"Hey lovebirds, you should probably remember you're in public and know that everyone is staring at you."

Pulling away, I tuck my head into the crook of Jake's neck, my face heating with embarrassment.

"Am I forgiven?" he whispers in my ear.

Smiling, I kiss his neck and pull back to look into his sparkling eyes. "Yes, you most definitely are."

"Uh, Ally?" Courtney asks, looking at me with a knowing smile.

"Yes?" Oh my, the room is starting to spin a little. The alcohol mixed with the power of Jake Taylor has my head floating in the clouds.

Her smile disappears and her brows furrow. "Are you okay? You don't look so good."

"Well, that's not very nice," I say, slurring a little.

"I think you should take her home now," Jack tells Jake.

"Yeah, mountain man, I think you should take me home now." I giggle. Grabbing my purse, I hop down from the stool and stumble into Jake, who's right there to grab ahold of me before I fall over. "Thanks," I say, patting his chest. "Bye, Courtney, see you Monday? I think? And Jack, thanks for the food, you're a lifesaver. Truly." Jake puts his arm around me to support most of my weight, and I look up at his handsome face, ignoring all of the eyes on us as we walk out of the bar.

On the ride home, I curl up against the window of Jake's truck and close my eyes, hoping the world will stop spinning a little. And the next thing I know, I'm waking up in his arms as he carries me up the porch stairs.

"Let me have your keys," he whispers in my ear.

"Hmm? My purse," I manage to mumble, snuggling closer into his chest. He sets me down gently on the chair outside, and I try and object, but the words aren't forming as he leaves me to go and open the door. "Jake?"

"Right here, darlin'," he says, back in front of me, lifting me into his arms again.

Walking inside, he carries me into my room and sets me down on my bed. I reach out and grab his arm before he can leave, and peel my tired eyes open, trying to find his in the shadows.

"Stay. Please," I whisper.

"Ally…" he trails off, his voice strained.

"Jake, please."

I hear is him sigh, and then he carefully pulls away from my grip and walks out of the room, closing the door behind him. Shrouded in darkness, with only a sliver of light coming through the crack at the bottom of the door, I hug my pillow to my chest and try to not think about the rejection. Again.

Drifting off, I suddenly feel my boots coming off my feet and a blanket covering me before the bed dips next to me. "Jake?"

"Right here," he whispers, his whisky smooth voice flowing over me while his arm drapes over my middle. "I couldn't leave you again, darlin'."

Smiling into the darkness, I wiggle back, snuggling tight against him, and drift off into a deep sleep.

Chapter 8

Feeling groggy, I reluctantly open my eyes to see the first light of the day starting to stream through my curtains. I'm a little foggy on what happened last night, and my mouth feels like I swallowed cotton. I need water.

Swinging my legs over the edge of the bed, I gather all the energy I have, and stand. Shuffling out of my room, I make a stop at the bathroom, and then go and get a bottle of water from the fridge, taking a few swigs right away. As I let the cool liquid sooth my bone-dry mouth, I'm suddenly struck with what happened last night. The bar, getting drunk, Jake coming to get me, kissing him, and him carrying me to bed.

I could have sworn he slept next to me, but he wasn't there a minute ago when I woke up. Great. He probably snuck out after I passed out.

Grabbing the aspirin bottle from the counter, I pop a few in my mouth, sure of the headache that's about to come. Two hangovers in a row. Wow, I'm pathetic.

Starting a pot of coffee, I lean against the counter and cover my face with my hands. My God, I made a fool of myself last night. Why do I continuously do that with Jake? *Kiss me so I'll forgive you?* Good one, Ally. Force a man to kiss you, and then make him stay with you after he carries you to bed because you're lonely. I'm pathetic.

Grabbing a sweatshirt from my room, I pour myself a mug of coffee, and then shuffle outside to watch the sunrise.

"Morning, beautiful," a deep voice greets me, and I let out a little scream, nearly spilling hot coffee all over me.

"Jake! You need to stop scaring me like this!" I tell him, my breathing coming fast. "I thought you left," I say when my heart rate settles. "You weren't there when I woke up."

"I don't sleep much. I came out here to watch the sunrise. Come sit."

Taking the empty chair, I sip my coffee, and let it give my tired brain some clarity. "There's coffee inside if you want some."

"Thanks, I do." Getting up, he goes inside, and my head is still trying to catch up with what's happening. Last night I drank copious amounts of gin with Courtney, we talked, we danced, and then Jack brought us food. I was flirting with the bartender—what's his name—and then suddenly Jake was there, kissing me senseless.

My God, I love kissing him. It's like flying into a twister – wild and head spinning.

"Do you remember last night?" Jake asks, startling me out

of my thoughts. He hands me a blanket and I drape it around my cold legs.

"Yeah, sorry if I was terrible. That bartender just kept feeding us drinks, and we were having too much fun to say no."

"Fucking, Alex," he growls.

"Huh?"

"He was getting you drunk so you'd sleep with him."

"Who?"

"Alex, the bartender," he says sharply.

"Oh, that was his name. And, no, I don't think so," I scoff.

"Ally, all the men in that place wanted to take you home. If Jack hadn't called me to come and get you, I don't know what would've happened."

I look at him in disbelief. "Jake, all the men did not want to take me home," I tell him, shaking my head. "And it wouldn't have mattered if they did. It's not like I was going to sleep with any of them."

Jake just grunts in response, taking a gulp of his coffee. I really want to shout in his face that I wouldn't sleep with any of them because they aren't him, but I don't.

"Thank you, though," I say, looking out at the water. "You came to my rescue again. It seems moving here means I need saving a lot."

"I don't mind. Just call, and I'll be there."

Looking back at him, I see his eyes are soft and sincere, so I give him a slight nod.

As the sun peeks up from the horizon, the sky starts to turn the telltale hues of yellow and orange, with the blue becoming brighter and brighter.

"It's so beautiful. I can't believe I get to see this every morning." The quiet of the early morning surrounds us as we watch the world come to life.

"Do you have plans today?" Jake asks, breaking the silence.

"No, I don't."

Now that the sun has risen, I can see his handsome face more clearly. "I'd like to show you something, if you want."

"Yes, I'd like that." I smile softly. "Should I go and get ready now?"

"In a few minutes. No rush," he says, looking out at the sea, sipping his coffee.

We each enjoy the sunrise, and it's not until its fully risen and my coffee is cold, that I decide to go inside and get ready. I throw on jeans and a light sweater, hoping this will be okay for whatever he has in mind.

Sitting next to Jake as he drives, I contemplate for the fiftieth time where he could be taking me. We're driving down the road with the lake, and I try and catch a glimpse of it through the trees. "There's a lake there." I point. "Just through those trees. I stopped on my first day and it was so beautiful. The houses on the other side looked so nice, and the sun was hitting the water just right – casting a glow over everything."

"Sounds nice," he says.

"So, where are we going?"

"Somewhere personal to me."

"Really? You want to show me something top secret?"

"Something like that," he says, smiling softly. I haven't seen him smile fully yet, but I'll coax one out of him soon.

A few minutes later, Jake pulls off the road and onto a gravel driveway that's lined with huge trees. Now I'm even more curious. And just when I think the gravel drive will never end, we come up on a massive modern log cabin house.

Jake clears his throat. "My house," he says nervously.

My wide eyes sweep around to his. "This is your house? Jake, it's beautiful."

It's two stories, with large windows spanning between the two levels, and a huge wrap around porch. I didn't even know log cabins could be so big, and nice, and not just shacks in the middle of the woods.

Jake gets out of the truck and comes around to open my door. Hopping down, I land a little funny and stumble forward, bracing myself on his chest as his arms come around me in an instant.

"I don't bring people here," he confesses. "But you let me see you paint. That was you letting me see a piece of you, and I want to give you something in return."

"That's…that's, thank you," I whisper, feeling honored. But I'm not sure if he's doing it because he wants to, or because he feels he owes me something. Either way, he's letting me in.

Moving my hand from his chest to his cheek, I smooth it back and forth across his beard, loving the feeling against my skin. Pushing up on my toes, I give him a soft, sweet kiss. "Now, show me around. I want to see your secret lair."

Smiling softly again, he takes my hand and leads me toward the front door. There aren't flowers everywhere like Dottie's, but there are big, beautiful trees all around. I bet the pine trees look gorgeous covered in snow in the winter, and the oak and maple trees will look amazing when they change colors in the fall.

Walking up the steps of his porch, Jake opens the front

door, and I immediately gasp. "Jake, oh my god!" I pull him into his own house, going straight to the back wall. It's made completely of floor to ceiling windows so the sun can shine brightly through into the living room, and offers an uninterrupted view of a sparkling blue lake. "I've never seen anything so beautiful."

"I have."

Huh? I look up and see him watching me. Oh, he meant me. A blush creeps up my cheeks, and I playfully slap his chest and smile. Squeezing his hand in mine, I look around the rest of the living room. It's an open floor plan with high vaulted ceilings, a huge brick fireplace, and big leather couches. The mantle holds pictures of Jake and his family at various ages, and I take notice that Jake is definitely the best-looking brother, despite all of them being attractive.

A wooden coffee table sits in between the two couches, and holds a few magazines and a half-filled glass of water he must have forgotten about.

Plaid throw pillows and blankets lay haphazardly on the couches, and it feels so warm and homey in here. I can see myself curling up with a book on the big leather chair by the fireplace and enjoying a glass of wine.

When we walk into the kitchen, I almost faint. It's practically my dream kitchen with dark wooden cabinets, shiny new appliances, lots of counter space, a deep farm sink, and an island with bar stools. There's a breakfast nook off to the side, jutting out past the far wall, where a large bay window offers another unimpeded view of the backyard and lake.

"Jake, this is all so gorgeous," I tell him, squeezing his hand. "I love it."

He ducks his head, but doesn't say anything. Is he shy

about showing me his home? Well, isn't that cute. I found a small soft spot in the big, strong Jake.

"Want to see the back?" he asks, and I nod, letting him lead me through the back door.

We step out onto a large deck with a table, chairs, umbrella, and a huge grill in the corner. We walk down the stairs to the ground level, and to the right there's a patio area with a couch, three chairs, and a couple small tables sitting around a fire pit. It looks like the perfect place to spend summer nights relaxing and roasting marshmallows.

Continuing on, we walk down a stone path that leads to a dock where two Adirondack chairs sit at the end, and a tied-up row boat rocks gently in the water. As I take in the panoramic view of the lake, something occurs to me.

"Wait, Jake. Is this the lake? The one I said I stopped at on my first day?" I look up at him and he nods. "Wow," I breathe out. "It's even more beautiful from this side."

"The sunrise isn't like at Dottie's, but it's still nice."

"I'm sure it is." I look down at the boat in the water next to me, and see that it's made from a deep, rich colored wood with carvings all around the top of it – vines intertwining together so beautifully.

"Did you make this?" I ask, and he nods, running a hand through his hair. "It's amazing, Jake. I love the carvings all around the top. That must have taken a long time."

"It did. But that's why I do it."

"To keep your hands busy?"

"Something like that."

"Do you have any others I can see? Are you working on any now?" I'd love to see what else he can create, but he hesitates, not answering right away. "Hey, I showed you mine, now you show me yours."

"Alright, darlin', I'll show you mine. Come on." He smirks, leading me back up the dock and around the side of the house. We come up on a large garage, and Jake lets go of my hand to pull up the bay door, exposing his workshop.

Two boats are up on tables, mid-construction, and a bunch of work benches and machines are spread throughout with tools lining the walls.

"I think I would cut something off if I just stepped inside," I say, eyeing the saws.

"I wouldn't let that happen," he assures me, taking my hand again, and walking me inside. But I let go of his hand the second I see what the boats are.

I step up to the first one that has roses running along the side, and I run my fingers over them, feeling the carvings. They're raised, 3-D cut outs, not just a pattern carved into the surface. He must just start with a large piece of wood and then carve into it, leaving behind these beautiful, intricate flowers.

Moving over to the next boat, I'm immediately mesmerized. This one is even more impressive. The bow of the boat has a dragon's head with its mouth open, and it looks like it's trying to fly out of the boat and breath fire. The details are something I would have never thought possible to achieve in wood. Its eyes seem like they're looking right at me, eyeing me like I'm its next meal.

Running my fingers along the side, I make my way to the back where the dragon's tail curls off and around the end, attaching to the side of the boat.

I'm in awe.

"Jake," I whisper. "This is incredible. I've never seen anything like it. It's so lifelike and intricate." I run my fingers over the dragon's scales, feeling every curve. "So beautiful."

Turning to him, I see his eyes are guarded and unsure. He's watching me, and watching my response to his work.

"Jake, I'm serious," I say, making sure he can see the sincerity in my eyes as a shy smile curves at his lips. "Are you making these for someone?" I ask.

He nods. "Some of my pieces are commissioned to be specific designs. But these, like most, are things that just come to me. Whatever I'm feeling."

"Each one is a piece of you."

"Yes," he says, sounding uncomfortable.

"Has anyone ever been in here before?" I ask, and his eyes blaze into mine.

"No."

"Why me, then?"

He's looking at me with such intensity that I almost want to look away, but I can't. "Because I want you to see. I want you to know."

He wants me to see him.

"Thank you," I say, running my fingers along the dragon's scales again.

I like being the only one he's let in here. It's like he's saying I'm the only one allowed to know this part of him. I would kiss him right now, but I'm afraid I'd get carried away and then bump into something and cut a limb off.

"Are you hungry?"

"Starving, actually," I say, and his eyes go dark. Clearly, his mind has gone to dirty things, and even though I'd love that, I really am starving.

"Come on, I'll make us something." Taking my hand again, we walk out of the garage and he pulls the door back down.

"You cook?" I ask, my shock evident.

"Surprised?"

"A little." I shrug, smiling. "I can't wait to see my mountain man in the kitchen cooking for me."

"*Your* mountain man?" he questions, pulling up short, and looking down at me.

My eyes go wide. Oh shit, I did say that.

"I didn't mean it like that. I just meant seeing a man like you cooking would be a sight to see." Well, that's not any better. Just shut up, Ally.

"I like the idea of being yours," he whispers, like he was afraid to say it.

"You do?"

"Yes." He nods. "Just like I like the idea of you being mine."

"Oh," I say, not really knowing how to form words right now.

Jake takes a step forward so our bodies are touching. I can't think straight when he's this close to me and looking at me with those deep, seductive eyes.

He tucks a lock of hair behind my ear and holds the side of my face, leaning down. The instant his lips touch mine, I press up on my toes and give in to the kiss, an electric jolt thrumming through me.

Our tongues come together in a tangled dance that makes my body hot, and my blood rush. It's primal, hungry, needy, and I know I won't be stopping him this time around.

Jake puts his arm around my lower back, pulling me flush against him, spreading his fingers out, radiating his heat into me. His body is a solid wall of muscle and I can feel him against me – hard as steel, and growing with every sweep of our tongues.

Moaning into him, his hand slides down the column of my neck, and when he brushes the side of my breast, I push harder against him, sighing into the kiss.

His hands grip my ass and he pulls me against him, making me moan when I feel him right where I need him. Lifting me up, I wrap my legs around his waist automatically as he walks us across the lawn and up the deck stairs, only stopping to adjust his grip to open the door, never breaking our kiss.

As soon as we enter his house, Jake slams me into the nearest wall and kisses my jaw, neck, shoulder, and chest while his hands smooth over every inch of me that he can reach.

His hands slip under my sweater and he pulls it off of me, throwing it to the side. Lifting me higher on the wall, Jake kisses, sucks, and bites his way up my stomach.

I arch my back and he unclips my bra, taking my nipple deep into his mouth straight away – a breathy sigh escaping my lips. I feel the pull all the way to my core.

"Jake…Please. I need…" Panting, I can't finish my thoughts. He looks up at me with dark eyes, and I know he already knows exactly what I need.

Moving away from the wall, he starts to walk again, and I kiss his neck – biting my way up to his ear. "I need you, mountain man," I whisper, taking his earlobe between my teeth.

Growling, he runs up a set of stairs and kicks open a door. Throwing me off of him, I let out a scream before landing on a big bed, bouncing once. Jake stands there, looking down at me with pure hunger in his eyes as he takes in all of my exposed flesh he just marked with his mouth.

Whipping off his shirt, I'm greeted with the naked expanse of his sculpted abs, chiseled chest, and thickly roped arms. I can't wait to run my hands all over him.

Sitting up on my elbows so I can enjoy the show, Jake undoes his boots and kicks them, and his socks, off. Next is his belt and jeans, and he pulls them down, taking his boxers with them.

Oh. My. God.

I'm left staring at a naked Jake, and my core clenches and throbs with anticipation.

He really is a warrior.

I've never seen such a perfect man before.

He's huge–long and thick–and I want every glorious inch of him. Seeing me staring, Jake puts his hand on himself. One, two, three strokes, and I rub my thighs together trying to relieve the tension.

Putting one knee on the bed, he takes my shoes off and makes his way up to me, eyes on mine. The blue in his seem to be swirling like a hurricane, and I'm drowning in the waters.

Settling over me with his arms on either side of my head, he leans down and kisses my lips before trailing kisses down my body. He swirls his tongue around each nipple, biting gently, before continuing down my stomach, swirling his tongue around my bellybutton. I squirm under him, my breathy sighs and moans filling the room.

Looking up at me, Jake undoes the button of my jeans and slides the zipper down slowly. Pulling them down, he kisses the skin he's revealed, so close to the apex of my thighs. Tugging harder, I lift my hips, and Jake peels my jeans down my legs, leaving me in only my pink lace panties.

Dragging his fingers up the sides of my legs, they fall open at his touch, begging him to touch me. He kisses his way up my thighs, but stops every time he gets close to where I need him most.

"Jake," I moan. "Please." But he ignores my plea and continues to kiss my inner thighs, licking and biting my sensitive flesh. I grip the sheets next to me and close my eyes, trying to hold back from grabbing him and shoving him between my legs.

Feeling the scrape of his teeth against my hip, I force myself to look down, and see him with my pink lace in his mouth as he drags it down my legs. Keeping his eyes on mine as he crawls down my body, he frees me of them, throwing them on the floor.

Fully naked, Jake puts one knee between my legs and hovers over me, sliding his hand from my ankle to my hip – a trail of fire singeing my flesh. Kissing me hard, he presses me deep into the mattress, his hand sliding across my hip and between my legs.

I sigh into his mouth. Finally.

Parting me, Jake drags one of his thick fingers up my slit and circles my clit, coaxing a low moan from me as I tear my lips away from his, unable to focus on anything but that single finger. Another pass down, and he circles my entrance lightly, not going any farther – just a tease.

"Please," I groan.

"Shh, just feel, darlin'. Let me give you this."

He slides his finger up again, circling my clit, then down, circling my entrance. Over and over until I'm writhing beneath him.

"Please, Jake, I need you." My voice is foreign to my ears as I beg him for more, but he continues to torture me with just the tip of his finger.

"I know you need me, baby, but I want my cock to be what enters you first, not my fingers." Closing my eyes at his words, I grip the sheets harder, delirious with desire until he pulls away, and I whimper at the loss.

"Look at me," he demands, and I open my eyes, seeking his. I hear the ripping of a foil package, and watch him roll a condom down his massive length. "Open for me."

My legs widen at his command, and he settles between them. Grabbing my knees, he pulls them up and out, spreading me further. I feel him so close, right there at my entrance, and I close my eyes. "No. Open," he growls, and I do as he says. "Keep those sexy eyes on me, darlin'."

He pushes into me, and I have to use all the strength I have to keep my eyes on his and not let them roll back into my head.

Slowly, Jake slides every glorious inch he has into me, and when he's settled all the way in, he groans, low and long. "You're strangling me, baby. So tight. So hot."

Moaning, he slams his mouth down on mine, swallowing every sound I make. I throw my arms around his neck and I rake my fingers through his hair, pulling on the ends. I bite his lip when he starts to pull away from me, and he growls, feeling the vibrations all the way down to where we're joined.

I need him to move. Now.

Pulling his hips back a few inches, he pauses, then slams back into me. Screaming, I grip his hair tight, my back arching off the bed.

He does it again, and the room begins to spin. Keeping my legs pinned up to my sides, Jake doesn't give me any room to move as he pulls out farther and farther with each stroke until he's practically all the way out of me before he slams back into me.

The sounds being ripped from my throat are unlike any I've ever made as I scratch at his back, trying to get as close to him as I can.

I've never felt anything so consuming – this connection, this raging fire I feel inside of me. I never want him to stop, but I feel the buildup inside of me, and I know he can feel it too.

"Not yet," he growls. But his gravely, commanding voice has the opposite effect, and it sends me over the edge. White dots blind my vision as I explode around him, my body strangling him inside of me. My screams flood my ears as an all-consuming tidal wave washes over me.

Pulling out, Jake flips me over onto my stomach while I'm still pulsating, and he lifts my ass up, slapping my right cheek hard – once, twice, three times. "I told you not to come yet."

Gripping my hips hard, he slams back into me from behind, my screams being muffled by the pillows as he reaches someplace deeper inside of me than before. I can do nothing but brace my hands against the headboard as he pounds into me over and over. Jake is in complete control.

One of his hands slides up my back and grabs my hair, pulling hard. "Jaaakkkee," I groan out his name low and long as I feel myself getting close again, trying hard to hold off.

"Not until I say," he commands.

"Please!" I scream as he continues to torture me.

Releasing my hair, I fall back into the pillows, and he reaches around to press down on my clit – hard. "Now!" he yells, and I let go instantly, my muffled screams filling the room.

The world around me disappears as my body shatters into a million pieces. I think I lose consciousness for a second before I hear Jake release a guttural groan,

Collapsing on top of me, he rolls us over so that I'm draped on top of him, and I have no words, no thoughts.

Chapter 9

Waking up, I roll over and spread my hand out on the bed, searching for Jake, but only come up with cool sheets. I have no idea how much time has passed, and the curtains in the room are closed tight, obscuring the time of day.

Sitting up, the sheets fall from my body, and I look down, seeing the marks Jake left all over my chest. I touch them lightly and smile, loving that my body holds evidence from what we did. It's proof that it wasn't just a dream.

Standing, I pull the top sheet from his bed and wrap it around me as I take a look around his room. It's such a masculine space with a deep colored wood for the floors, bedframe, tables, dresser, and bookshelves. The walls are a rich dark green like the pine trees surrounding the house, and the sheets on his bed are navy with a green, navy, and white plaid comforter.

I smile, this is definitely the room of a mountain man.

My cheeks flush just thinking about Jake, and I walk over to the windows to peek through the curtains. The midday sun streams in on me and I squint, seeing that his room looks out over the glistening lake.

Closing the curtains again, I go in search of the bathroom, finding it when I open the door that's directly in front of the bed.

It's bigger than I would have expected. White tiles cover the floor and go halfway up the walls, with the rest painted in a deep, masculine burgundy. A long, double sink vanity with white and grey marbled countertops and grey wooden drawers lines the left wall, while a huge black clawfoot tub sits on the right with a glass shower right beside it. The toilet is in the far right corner with a fluffy burgundy rug laying in front of it, as well as in front of the vanity, shower, and tub.

Walking farther inside, I open a closet that's in the back left corner to find it houses the towels and other bathroom extras. The window next to it looks out to the forest on the side of his house, and I love that there aren't any neighbors right next door. If he wanted to, Jake could just leave all of his curtains and blinds open and walk around naked. No one's around to look in on him.

I decide to take a quick shower while I'm in here, and throw my hair up in a messy bun before stepping under the hot stream of water. I squeeze some of the woodsy shower gel I find into my hand, and sigh as I rub it in. So, this is why Jake smells like the outdoors. It's intoxicating.

Rinsing off, I step out and wrap myself in one of the fluffy towels from the closet.

I know my jeans are up here, but my shirt and bra are still downstairs, so I walk over to Jake's dresser and open a few drawers until I find the one with his t-shirts. I choose a dark grey one with Pine Cove High School written across it, and slip it over my head. It's big, but comfy.

Putting my jeans back on, I shove my panties into the front pocket, and grab my boots. I stick my head out into the hallway before stepping out, and see that his room is at the end of the hall. I pass a few closed doors before reaching the top of the stairs, and as I walk down slowly, I start to smell something delicious, and my stomach growls on cue. But when I enter the kitchen, expecting to find Jake cooking, it's empty. There's no food and no Jake, just a note sitting on the island that says I should check the oven warmer.

Opening it, I gasp, finding eggs, bacon, pancakes, and hash browns. When did he do this? Looking around, I notice the clock above the stove, and it reads one o'clock. Oh my god, I slept for four hours!

Taking the food out, I go sit at the breakfast nook and enjoy the view. Jake really has a beautiful home. I can't believe I looked out at the lake that first day and saw his house across the way, thinking about how nice it would be to sit out on the dock and read a book. I never would have thought less than a week later I'd be sitting in it, or better yet, having mind blowing sex with its owner.

Flashes of this morning flood my mind and I smile, taking a bite of bacon. Jake really is something else. He makes me feel so beautiful and desired. And he's so commanding. Just thinking about that stern voice he used on me is making my skin tingle.

When I finish eating, I wash the dishes and go in search of my mountain man. On my way out, though, I spot my bra and sweater laying neatly on the back of one of his couches so I quickly whip his t-shirt off and replace it with my clothes. I can't have the girls on full display while I wander around outside.

Stepping out onto the deck, I tilt my face up to the sun. It's warmer today, and feels like spring for the first time since being here. I walk down the stairs and go left, following the sound of music floating through the breeze.

The garage door to Jake's workshop is open, but I hang back by the entrance so I can watch him work without disturbing him. He's sitting in front of the dragon's head, a carving tool in his hand, and a look of complete concentration on his face. Lost in his work, I can tell this is what brings him peace. His hair is a little messy, and his jaw is set – determined. He's focused, but relaxed at the same time.

Stepping away quietly so he doesn't know I'm here, I walk down to the dock where the Adirondack chairs are calling my name. Taking a seat, I look out at the pine trees across the lake where I stood that first day, wishing I could sit out here. And here I am.

I lose track of time and drift off, the sun and water lulling me to sleep. But then I'm startled awake by a hand on my face, gently brushing my hair away.

"It's just me," Jake says, his voice low and soothing.

"Sorry, you scared me." Looking up at him, his eyes are bright – shining a brilliant shade of blue in the afternoon sun.

"Did you sleep well?"

"Yes." I smile wistfully. "And I ate, thank you."

"I promised you food this morning, but we got a little

sidetracked." He smirks.

A blush creeps up my face at the reminder of what we did, and Jake caresses my cheek, feeling the heat there.

"I saw you working earlier and I didn't want to bother you, so I came and sat out here. It's so peaceful."

"You wouldn't have bothered me. Never think that," he says, tucking my windblown hair behind my ear.

"Okay," I whisper, just as Jake braces himself on the arms of the chair and kisses me, soft and sweet. Pulling away, he holds his hand out for me to take.

Placing mine in his, I stand up, but he only takes two steps before stopping and nodding at the boat in the water. "Step in," he says.

"The boat?"

"Yes, the boat." He smirks.

Using him for balance, I step off the dock and into the boat, letting out a little scream when it starts to rock under my weight. But I just laugh it off, letting go of his hand to sit on one of the benches.

Jake is way smoother than me when he steps in and unties the rope attaching the boat to the dock. Pushing us off, he sits across from me and grabs the oars. When he starts to row, my eyes are glued to his arms as they flex with his movements, and I clench my thighs together, thinking about those same strong arms wrapped around me – holding me, lifting me, touching me.

Taking a deep breath, I tear my eyes away and look out around the lake. Squinting, I stick my hand in the water and let the freezing temperature jolt me away from my thoughts of Jake's sexy arms.

Distracting myself, I run my fingers over the vine pattern

weaving its way around the boat. It's as if I'm looking at the real thing. The details are so intricate.

Glancing back at Jake, I find his eyes already on me, watching me.

"This is beautiful, Jake. The boat, the water, the day," I tell him, smiling.

His face softens just the slightest. "Good."

We fall back into a comfortable silence, and I watch as the boat cuts through the water seamlessly. Closing my eyes, I lean back onto the bench behind me and listen to the swishing of the water around us.

I love it out here. It's so peaceful.

I usually hate being in small boats like this out on a lake because I have no idea what's lurking beneath the surface if I happened to fall in. The last time I was in one was when I was at Girl Scout camp and the other girls thought it was funny to rock the boat like we were going to fall in because they saw how scared I was of it. But that water was gross.

This is heaven. Plus, I have Jake to rescue me if fall in.

Enjoying the silence for a few more minutes, I open my eyes and sit up. "Tell me something."

"Like what?" he asks.

"I don't know. Anything. Tell me about your family."

"We all live here in Pine Cove. My dad is the town doctor and my mom is his receptionist. I have an older brother and two younger brothers."

"How old are they? What do they do?"

"Ryan is 34 and is the Sheriff. Tyler's 29 and a fireman in town. And then Chris is 27, and he's an Army doctor. He's overseas right now."

Damn, they all have impressive jobs.

"What about you?"

"Are you asking me how old I am, darlin'?" He smirks.

"Maybe." I smile.

"I'm 33. Is that okay with you?" He smirks again.

"I guess." I smile, biting my lip. "So how did you end up being the fine wood worker that you are?"

"Is that an appropriate thing to ask a man after he just showed you his woodworking skills?"

"Oh my god." I laugh. "I didn't mean that."

"I know." He laughs, giving me his first real smile. And holy sweet baby Jesus, a dimple pops out of his left cheek and I want to faint. I didn't think he could get any sexier.

"What?" I ask, forgetting what we were talking about, and that just makes him smile wider, flashing me his sexy straight, white teeth. Can teeth be sexy?

"You asked me about my woodworking."

"Oh, yeah, um, how did you start? With boats, not your penis," I add, still mesmerized by his smile.

"I always liked making things with my hands. And one day I was in the hardware store and Dottie's husband saw me looking a little lost, so he asked if I wanted to learn a unique skill."

"You've been doing it for a long time, then?"

"Sort of. But it's only in the past five years that I've created my business."

"What did you do before five years ago?" I feel like I'm taking a risk by asking him so many questions, but I can't help it, I need to unravel him.

"I went to college. And then I joined the Navy."

"Because you love boats?" I smile.

"Something like that," he says, but his demeanor starts to

shift.

"Why didn't you just start your business from the beginning? Or did you always want to join the Navy?"

I watch his face harden and his jaw flex tight. I clearly asked the wrong question. Looking away, I leave him with his thoughts, and give him the time to relax again. I knew my questions were going to hit a wall at some point, I just didn't realize asking him about the Navy would be such a sensitive subject.

When I feel us starting to gain speed, my eyes dart back over to him, and I see him staring off at nothing, a blank look in his eyes. I don't think he realizes what he's doing.

"Hey, Jake." I try to get his attention, but he doesn't hear me. "Jake," I say a little louder, but still nothing. "Jake!" I yell, finally getting his eyes on mine. "Come back from wherever you are. You're here with me, okay?"

His jaw ticks, and he slows his pace, his eyes becoming clearer the longer he looks into mine. Blinking a few times to refocus, he looks around, and then starts to direct us back towards the dock.

Tying the boat up, Jake steps out and holds his hand out to help me. I try and let go when I'm safely on the dock, but he tightens his grip, and my eyes find his.

"I…" he trails off.

"It's okay," I say, squeezing his hand. "You don't have to tell me." His eyes soften a little, but I know his mind is still somewhere else, so I decide to give him an out. "Do you mind taking me home? I have a few things I have to take care of." Relief flashes in his eyes, and I know I made the right choice.

He nods and starts walking us up and around his house to his truck. The ride back to the cottage is a little strained, but I know he needs his space right now to sort through whatever is going on in his head. I just hope he'll feel comfortable enough to tell me one day.

When he parks, I lean over the middle console and kiss his cheek, smiling softly. "See you soon."

Hopping out, I quickly climb the front steps and retreat inside, heading straight to the kitchen. I need a glass of wine, or a whole bottle.

I seem to be taking one step forward with Jake, and then five steps back.

Chapter 10

Walking into work Monday morning, I'm exhausted. After my day with Jake yesterday, I drank wine and watched TV until I was tired enough to sleep. But even then, I didn't sleep for more than an hour before I started tossing and turning.

"Morning, Courtney," I say, putting my purse away.

"Hey, Ally," she says, putting her hand on her hip. "Please tell me you were as hung over as me yesterday. I was miserable for hours. I don't think I've drank that much since college."

"Uh, not really. I was when I first woke up, though."

"What does that mean?" she asks, a confused look on her face until she smiles wide. "Oh, shit, wait! Jake brought you home! Did he take advantage of the fact that you were drunk?"

She winks. "That kiss was hot by the way. Thanks for doing it right in front of me."

"Oh my god," I groan, slapping my hand to my forehead. "I'm glad you enjoyed it. And no, he carried me inside and put me to bed. And then I made him stay with me."

"Oohh, tell me more!" She beams, and I give her a quick rundown of yesterday's events.

"I just hate that I upset him. I didn't know if, or how, I could help, so I thought it was best to leave him be to deal, you know?"

"Ally, it's not your fault. You wanted to get to know him and asking him about his life is normal."

"Yeah, I guess." I shrug.

"No, listen. Jake obviously has some things to work out that he's struggling with. But you just keep being you. You can't force anything."

"Yeah, I guess," I repeat. I have nothing else to add.

I've been thinking about all of this since I got home yesterday and I just can't anymore. My brain is going to explode if I don't find something to occupy myself with. I brew the coffees and set up the creamer station, just trying to go through the motions of normalcy.

Customers come and go all morning and I'm thankful, but surprised, with how busy it is.

"Is it usually this busy on a Monday?" I ask Courtney when there's a little break.

"No, they're here to check you out," she says, like it's such an obvious answer.

"What do you mean they're here to check me out?"

She laughs lightly. "Yeah, well, you made out with Jake Taylor Saturday night in a bar full of people. That's big news around here.”

“I wasn’t really paying attention to the people around us.”

“I’ll say,” she scoffs. “And the people of Pine Cove haven’t seen Jake take an interest in anyone in a very long time. Not since I got here anyway.”

“And before? Do you know?”

“No.” She shakes her head. “But you have to realize that Jake doesn’t go out in Pine Cove. *Ever.* So, the fact that he was even at The Rusty Anchor, let alone making out with you – the new girl no one knows anything about – is a big deal. That’s a lot of hot gossip for us townies.”

“Great, so I’m the subject of gossip.”

“You’re doing great so far! Everyone’s coming in to check you out and you’re being really nice and friendly. Just keep it up and pretend you don’t know what’s happening.”

“I’ll try,” I say sarcastically, rolling my eyes.

The rest of the day goes by so slow, with what seems like the whole town coming in to check me out. I could tell that’s why they were here, too, because they were staring at me as if inspecting me, and being extra friendly. Some even started asking me a whole host of personal questions. But instead of saying what I was thinking, I made sure I put on my Miss Manners hat and didn’t let them think I knew the little game they were playing.

“That was exhausting,” I sigh, wiping the tables down at closing.

“You’re good for business.” Courtney laughs. “I’m glad I hired you.”

“Gee, thanks. I’m glad our friendship has brought you a monetary gain.”

“Oh, shut it.” She smiles as we both finish our cleaning

and head out.

"See you Thursday," I say as I walk to my car.

"See you then." She waves.

Making a stop at the grocery store before going home is a must. Dottie left me the basics to start me out, but I'm in desperate need of actual food and ingredients to cook with. Walking around the store, I decide on a whim to pick up what I think I'd need to make homemade blueberry pie. I have the next two days off, so I may call Dottie and see if she can come over and teach me how to make her famous pie. Then I'll be able to pay Jake for his services.

HA. That makes him sound like a hooker.

And if I know how to make his favorite pie, then I can bribe him with it if I ever might need to.

Putting my groceries away at the cottage, I find Dottie's number on the fridge and call her straight away. "Hello?"

"Hi, Dottie, it's Ally."

"Ally, dear, how are you? Are you settling in fine?"

"Yes, I am, thank you. How are you liking living with your daughter and her family?"

"It's an adjustment with all of the constant noise and activity around me." She laughs. "But I love them dearly."

"That's good. I was actually wondering if you were free tomorrow or Wednesday? I thought maybe you could come over and teach me how to make your blueberry pie?"

"Do you need to pay Jake already?" She chuckles.

"Yes, something like that." Oh, if she only knew.

"I can be there Wednesday at eleven if that's good for you?"

"Yes, that's great. Thank you so much."

"Of course, dear, I'm glad you called. I'll see you then,

have a good night."

"Bye, Dottie."

I hang up and smile. Pie can fix anything, right?

Deciding to have a lazy day on Tuesday, I sleep in and catch up on some of the sleep I've lost due to a certain man who's invaded my life since moving here. I do a little cleaning and organizing, and spend some time sitting out on the back porch, sipping iced tea and reading. This is the first relaxing day I've had in a long while, even before moving here.

I take a midafternoon walk around the property to stretch my legs and enjoy the fresh air, and find myself standing in front of the cottage, staring at it. I take in all the bursting colors and flowers that are spilling out and overflowing from everywhere, and I have the sudden urge to paint it.

I'm only just getting used to this feeling again, and I've missed it.

Setting up an easel and a kitchen chair out in front of the house, I go back for one of the larger canvases I purchased, and all of my supplies.

Taking a seat, I smile up at the little blue cottage that I've grown very attached to. I have to mix together a few shades until I finally capture the perfect robin's egg blue I need, and when I make that first brushstroke on the canvas, I feel my body relax.

It's different than the other night with Jake. Then, I was driven by lust filled, all-consuming emotions that I couldn't shake. While now, all I'm feeling is peace and gratitude. I do know, though, that I wouldn't be sitting here painting at all if it wasn't for him. Jake woke me up. One touch from him, and everything I thought I had buried into oblivion came rushing to the surface.

Minutes turn to hours as I sit out here and let the world fall away. I haven't felt this calm in a long time.

When the sun starts to disappear behind me, I blink out of my daze, realizing how late it's gotten. Putting my brush down, I stand and stretch, stepping back to look at what I've done so far. I love it.

Gathering my supplies, I bring everything inside and then carefully the still wet painting into the spare bedroom, leaning it against one of the walls where I know it won't be seen or disturbed.

Waking up early the next day, I want to make sure I'm ready for Dottie's arrival. I want her house to look as good as she left it, so I dust from top to bottom, water the plants outside, sweep the front and back porches, and then make sure the kitchen is spotless for our baking today.

I have just enough time to shower and change before I hear a knock at the door. Rushing to open it, I find Dottie with a big smile and an armful of bags. She's sporting a classic grandma look today with a pink tracksuit and white sneakers, and I freaking love it.

"Hi, Dottie. I'm so glad you're here."

"I'm glad you called so soon, dear. I was hoping I wouldn't have to wait a month or two."

"Of course not! I'm dying for more of your company. Making pies was just an excuse," I tell her, reaching for the bags in her hands. "Here, let me take those."

We walk into the house, and she stops to look around. "Oh, I've missed this place. But you've taken good care of it so far."

"Did you think I'd ruin it in a week?"

"No, dear. I just mean you haven't changed anything really."

"Of course not, I love this place. I wouldn't change a thing."

She places her hand on my arm and looks at me with glassy eyes. "That's very sweet of you, thank you. I had a good feeling about you from the beginning, and I'm glad to know I was right."

"Thanks, Dottie." I smile. "Now, should we get started? Then we can sit and have some tea after. If you have time?"

"That sounds lovely, dear. I have all the time in the world today."

For the next hour, we work side by side making our pies. Her secret ingredient she says, is love. So, while I combine and roll the crust out, I try and convey to it that I love it more than anything in the whole wide world. If that will come through in the end, I have no idea. It's freaking dough! Or crust? I don't know, but I know it doesn't have feelings.

Dottie said she lost her original recipe decades ago, so she's been making it by memory ever since.

"Is it okay if I write it down?" I ask.

"Hmm, yes, I suppose you may be privileged to it now." She jokes, smiling warmly at me.

"Thank you, that means a lot. I miss my grandmother and her baking, so this reminds me of that. Plus, I think I'll have to make Jake a few of these in the near future for helping me out so much."

"He's had to help you already?" she asks, a small smile on her lips.

"Well, yes, sort of. My first night, I called him at like 2am to come and help me because I heard loud noises and growling outside, and I didn't know what to do. Turns out it was a bear out on the porch that broke a few flower pots, and then Jake came over the next morning and fixed everything. It was really nice of him to come in the middle of the night to help a complete stranger, and all I had to offer him was a slice of pie. Now, though, I can make him a whole pie."

I look over at Dottie and see her smiling, a twinkle in her eyes. "So, he was nice then?"

"Yes, he was. He didn't talk much, but he was nice," I tell her, not mentioning the fact that he basically hypnotized me that night, and now I can't get enough of him. I don't think that would be good for her elderly heart.

We put our pies in the oven, and I make us tea before we go and sit out on the back porch.

"Now, tell me everything, dear," she says, patting my knee, "About you and my Jake."

"What do you mean?" I ask, trying to play it cool.

"Come now. Just because I moved an hour north doesn't mean I don't get the gossip at my front door."

"Uh, um, what?" I stutter.

"You were seen out with Jake, dear. Catch up." She laughs.

Oh my god.

"Well, yes, I guess we were seen out. He and I are…I don't know."

"He's handsome, no?"

I feel my cheeks heat as she studies me. "He is, yes." I smile. But handsome doesn't even begin to describe him.

She chuckles softly. "Yes, he's a nice young man. Jake's a bit stoic and reserved, and doesn't let many people close to him. But he's always a sweetheart to me. My husband and him met in the hardware store when Jake was just a teenager, and then after that, he was around all the time. He was always asking questions and wanting to learn, so my husband decided to take him under his wing. There used to be a workshop here next to the cottage, but I gave it all to Jake when my husband passed." The look on Dottie's face shows the love she has for Jake. "I just want him to be happy. I love that boy like he was my own."

"You don't think he's happy?" I ask, curious.

"No, not for many years now."

"Why?"

"I think he should be the one to tell you that."

"Right, of course." I nod, wishing she'd just tell me, even though I know she's right.

"Oh my, did you paint that?" Dottie asks, looking at the sunset painting I did. Shit, I forgot I had left it out here, leaning next to the chair she's sitting in.

"Yes, I did that the other day," I tell her, looking away. Please don't ask me about the couple in it. Please.

"It's beautiful, Ally. You captured the colors perfectly. I feel as if I was there. And this couple – so romantic."

I clear my throat, not feeling comfortable with the praise.

"You're very good, dear. A true artist," she adds, a wistful tone to her voice.

"Thank you," I say shyly.

"Do you have any others?"

"No. That's my first one in a very long time. But I'm working on a larger one that I just started yesterday."

Reaching over, she puts her hand on my knee. "It's this place, isn't it? It inspires the soul and shows the truth in your heart."

I look into her light blue eyes and see a wise old woman who's seen and done a lot in her life to know the truth of her own heart.

Swallowing, I look down into my cup. "Yes, I felt it right away. I think I was meant to come here. I feel like I can breathe for the first time in a very long time."

"I'm glad." She smiles sweetly at me. "Now, let's go check on our pies."

Chapter 11

I really hope this doesn't blow up in my face.

I'm driving to Jake's house to bring him the second pie I made with Dottie this afternoon, and I'm seriously second guessing myself. He hasn't called or come over since he dropped me off on Sunday, and I don't know what's going on in his head or if he even wants to see me.

But as I turn into his driveway, I think about how he let me into his home and into his space when he said he doesn't ever do that. It gives me a little more confidence in what I'm doing, but not much.

Parking, I pull the mirror down and check my makeup. I can do this.

Grabbing the pie, I get out and head up his front steps.

I'm so nervous, my hands are shaking. When I knock tentatively, the door swings open only a moment later like he already knew I was here.

Damn, he looks good in his jeans and t-shirt. It's only been a few days, but looking at him now, it feels like much longer. His hair is messier than usual, like he's been running his hands through it all day, and his beard is longer. I like it, though. He looks all rugged and mountainy.

"Ally," he says, his voice a little rough, and his eyes distant.

"Hi." I smile nervously. "I wanted to bring you this." I hold the pie out to him. "Dottie taught me her secret recipe today."

"She did?"

"Yeah, so uh, here." I shove the pie at him and turn to walk back to my car. He doesn't look happy that I'm here.

"Wait." He grabs my hand before I can even take a step away from him. "Where are you going?" I turn back and meet his eyes, seeing that they've gone softer. "Are you hungry? I was making dinner."

"What?"

He tugs on my hand and I step towards him. "I said are you hungry?"

"Yes."

"Come in, then." He tightens his grip on my hand and pulls me inside. "Thank you for this," he says, looking at the pie.

"You're welcome." I take a few steps into his house, and a delicious aroma fills my senses. I hold back a moan, my stomach grumbling on cue. "Oh my god, Jake, it smells amazing."

Putting the pie down on the counter, he goes over to the

stove to stir something in a pot. "It's my mom's famous sauce. I'm making spaghetti and meatballs."

"That's one of my favorites." I smile.

"Good." He nods. "Do you want a drink?"

"What do you have?"

"Water, whisky, wine."

"I'll have wine," I tell him, and watch as he opens a new bottle and pours me a glass. Taking a sip, I let it calm me. Just being near Jake makes me nervous and excited, and right now, all I can think about is ripping his clothes off.

I need to shake those thoughts away. I have to focus. I came over to talk to him, not jump him.

"Jake?" I say tentatively, taking a deep breath.

"Yeah, darlin'?"

"I…um…never mind." I chicken out.

Turning fully to me, he studies my face. "What's wrong?"

"Nothing." I shake my head, staring down at my wine, really hoping he'll drop it. I was going to apologize for Sunday and upsetting him, but I can't seem to get the words out.

"Let me take you out this weekend," he says, saving me from explaining myself.

I look up at him. "What?"

"Let me take you out on a date."

"Okay," I say instantly. Like I'd say no?

Smiling slightly, he returns to stirring the sauce. "I'll pick you up Friday at seven. Now, come and taste this, let me know if it's good." Looking over his shoulder at me, he holds up a spoon with sauce.

Hopping down from my stool, I walk over to him and take a tentative lick, and an explosion of flavor bursts in my mouth.

"That's amazing," I moan, licking my lips and watching his eyes go dark as he stares at my mouth.

Jake swipes the spoon across my lips, and I go to lick it off, but he shakes his head no. Leaning down, he slides his tongue over my mouth, licking the sauce off before kissing me softly.

Sighing, I sway on my feet, grabbing the counter to steady myself.

"Yup, it's good," he says, stepping away. "Sit down, and I'll make you a plate." In a dazed state, I walk back to my stool and sit, watching him dish out two plates of spaghetti and meatballs for us.

We eat in comfortable silence for a few minutes before Jake clears his throat. "You look beautiful tonight."

Caught off guard, I start to choke on the meatball I was chewing, and cough violently. Grabbing my wine, I take a huge gulp to wash it down, sucking in ragged breaths.

"Are you okay?" he asks, a hint of a smile on his lips.

"Yes. You just surprised me."

He smiles wide, his dimple making an appearance. "I surprised you by saying you look beautiful? Darlin', that's a fact the world already knows. I was just pointing it out."

"Oh." I feel a blush creep up my cheeks. Damn, he's smooth.

"What did I do to earn Dottie's blueberry pie?" he asks.

"I owed you one for helping me. And she taught me this afternoon, so now I can make you one for every time you have to rescue me. Which seems to be quite often for some reason." I laugh.

"I may just have to come over and break some stuff so you can call me to fix it."

"That's not necessary, I'll make it for you whenever you want. All you have to do is ask."

His eyes go dark again, and I don't think he's thinking about pie anymore. A blush creeps up my neck and into my cheeks. Looking away, I tuck my hair behind my ear.

When we finish eating, Jake clears the dishes and serves up two slices of pie, but I wait for him to take the first bite. I really hope he likes it. That freaking crust better have received my love.

"Darlin'," he groans after a forkful.

"Yeah?" I answer, unsure which way this will go.

"It's amazing, babe. I'll be coming to you for this all the time now. Dottie only gave it to me when I helped her."

"I'll give it to you whenever," I say without thinking.

Oh my god.

"Good to know." He smirks. "I'd love for you to give it to me whenever." Smiling, he finishes his pie and leans back in his chair, running his hands through his hair. I watch his arms flexing with the movement, and I'd love to give it to him right now. My eyes rake over his body and I feel my core clench, needing him.

"You can't look at me like that, darlin', unless you want me to strip you down and lay you out on this counter." His voice is deep and gravely, and shoots through me like lightning.

Holy fuck. I want that.

My eyes meet his and he has a wicked smile playing on his lips. "Is that what you want?" he asks.

My mouth has gone dry and I take a big swig of wine, licking my lips, hoping 'yes' will form. But it doesn't.

Standing, Jake walks around the counter and pulls my stool out so I'm facing him. With heated eyes, he steps between my legs and slides his hands up my thighs as I wrap my arms around his neck, pulling him down to my mouth. I need his kiss like I need my next breath.

The moment our lips meet, a fire rushes through my veins and I instinctively wrap my legs around his hips, pulling him as close to me as I can. Using that to his advantage, Jake lifts me up and sets me on the counter, deepening our kiss.

He kisses his way across my jaw, finding the sweet spot behind my ear that has me begging him for more. His hands come between us to roughly pop the button open on my jeans and slide the zipper down, shoving his hand inside.

"Darlin'," he growls, feeling the effect he has on me with a simple touch, before thrusting two thick fingers inside of me.

A strangled moan is torn from my throat, and I claw at his neck, needing him to do more. Capturing my lips with his, Jake takes every sound I make as he moves inside of me, his thumb making circles on my clit. I can feel the storm building in me, but I still need more, I still need more of him.

Answering my unspoken pleas, Jake inserts a third finger, and I go blind. He pumps in and out of me, over and over. Pressing hard on my clit, he curls his fingers inside of me and I scream, exploding into a million pieces, coming apart on his kitchen island.

My body goes limp and I cling to Jake's neck, breathing hard. Peppering him with kisses, I slowly make my way up his jaw to his lips, showing him how I feel because I can't find my voice.

Jake slowly removes his fingers and wraps his arms around me, pulling me close. There's a shift in how we kiss each other. I curl my fingers in the ends of his hair, and he spreads his hands out on my back as we both moan into the kiss.

He has to feel it too.

"Darlin'…" Jake breathes against my lips, resting his forehead against mine. I feel like my heart is going to beat out of my chest. "Go for a walk with me?" he asks.

I lean back and look into his beautiful ocean eyes, seeing something new there. "Sure. I may need some help standing and walking, though." I feel my cheeks flush, and a wicked grin flashes on his face as he buttons and zips my jeans back up for me.

Helping me down from the counter, Jake takes my hand and intertwines our fingers, walking us out the back door. It's dark, but the moon and stars light our way down the stone path to the dock. The night air is filled with the gentle lapping of water against the dock and crickets talking to one another as the moon illuminates a reflected path across the water to us.

Jake takes a seat in one of the Adirondack chairs and pulls me down onto his lap, wrapping his arms around me — shrouding me in his warmth.

"You know, I'm fully capable of sitting in my own chair," I say, tilting my head back to smile up at him.

"I know, but then I wouldn't be able to hold you," he answers, tightening his arms around me.

"Aren't I too heavy?" I ask, slightly self-conscience.

"Not at all, baby. That ass feels like a pillow."

"Okay, whatever you say, mountain man." I laugh. "I guess your big muscles can hold me up."

He kisses my cheek and I snuggle back into him, letting myself get comfortable. Staring out at the water, I lose myself in thought. It's so calm here. The ocean at the cottage is beautiful, but there's something about the still waters of this lake that makes me feel centered.

"What're you thinking?" he asks after a minute.

"Just that I feel so calm here."

"That's why I picked this place. The moment I walked out here and saw the lake, I knew this was where I needed to be. I bought it when I came home after my last deployment. I needed my own space. And since then, this place has given me what little peace that life can offer me now."

"I see that. You belong out here in the forest and in your workshop."

"Yeah, I can be a bit of a recluse sometimes."

"That's how I used to be with painting. When I was in school, I would shut myself in my room or the studio, put on some music, and just let myself go. I didn't want to be bothered by anyone. I just wanted to be."

"Why did you stop?"

"Life," I say, shrugging my shoulders. "When you heard me say artists feel deep because they have to…well, I think I felt *too* much. And what I was feeling wasn't good. It was a dark place I found myself retreating to more and more often, and I had to stop. I had to put myself back together and know I wouldn't go back there if, and when, I tried again."

"Why were you in the dark, darlin'?" he whispers in my ear.

"I just was. I was made up of only pieces of myself. And there came a point where I had to be the one to save myself and mend the pieces back together. It took me seven years, but here I am."

Tightening his arms around me, Jake doesn't say anything, he just holds me. I don't want him to say anything. There's nothing to say. The quiet strength he's giving me resonates more than any comforting words ever could.

We stay quiet for a long while, just listening to the sounds of the night.

"There are so many stars," I whisper. "I've never seen so many."

"Another reason why I love it here," he whispers, sending a shiver down my spine. Feeling it, he squeezes me, shrouding me in his warmth.

As the minutes pass, I start to feel my eyes droop, and I sigh. "I should probably get back. I have work in the morning."

Kissing my hair, Jake stands and places me on my feet. Taking my hand, we walk back up the dock and into his house. "You know," he says, "I may like your pie better than Dottie's."

"I know you're just saying that so that I'll be flattered enough to make it for you again."

"Oh, you'll make it for me again," he says seductively, pulling me in for a quick kiss. "I see myself saving you a lot in the future."

"Is that so? I'll have you know I am plenty capable of saving myself, thank you very much."

"Of that, I have no doubt. But it's always nice to let us men think you need us every so often."

I smile and lean up on my toes to kiss him goodnight. "Deal, mountain man," I whisper.

Jake opens the front door for me, and when I reach the bottom of the stairs, I turn back, a flirty smile playing on my lips. "I'll let you earn your pie, don't worry."

Jake's deep laugh fills me, and follows me as I get in my car and drive back to the cottage. It's wrapped around me as I lay down, falling asleep to images of Jake saving me. Because sometimes a girl needs a break from saving herself.

Chapter 12

Digging through my closet on Friday night, I try and find something to wear for my date with Jake. All day yesterday and today, I've been on edge wondering how tonight will go. Where is he taking me? Should I dress up? Dress down? Will we do an activity? Just go to dinner?

I haven't been on a date since college, and I'm freaking out. Going on a date is official. It's public.

Grabbing my phone, I quickly send out an SOS text in the group chat, and hope one of them is free to help me.

My phone rings a few seconds later, and I see Elizabeth's name flash on my screen. "Ally, what's up?" she asks right away.

"Ellie, I need help! I have a date with Jake tonight." I'm

about ready to go into full panic mode.

"Whoa, calm down." She laughs. "Ally, it's just a date. You two aren't strangers."

"I know that. It's just that–"

"No. Don't think about all of your horrible dates and guys from college. This is different. Relax. It's just you and him, okay?"

"Okay, but what do I wear?"

"Oh, that's the problem?" She laughs. "Go with something simple but pretty. How about that short flowy skirt with the blue flowers on it, a white tee, and your jean jacket if it's cool out? Then wear a pair of cute sandals."

"How did you do that? You're like, hundreds of miles away."

"I know your closet, bitch. We're best friends. Now go get dressed. And you should curl your hair in waves and do your makeup natural, but play up your eyes. Let those baby blues seduce him."

"I'm glad you know me so well." I laugh.

"Duh."

"Thanks, you're the best."

"I know. And I expect a full report later."

"Of course. I wouldn't dream of not telling you how it goes," I say, sarcasm dripping from every word.

"No need to be bitchy." She laughs. "I just hope Jake knows how wonderful you are. He should know that you giving him the time of day is rare and special."

"Thanks," I say softly.

"Alright, go get ready and have fun. And don't do anything Ashley wouldn't do," she says, and I can hear the smile in her voice.

"Oh, lord. That really gives me free reign then, doesn't it?"

"That's the point. Now, go get ready!"

"Okay, okay. Love you, bye."

I hang up and return to my closet with a new purpose. I dig out everything she told me to wear and put it on. And I can't believe it. It's perfect. She's a miracle worker from six hours away.

I finish up with my hair and makeup just in time for the doorbell to ring at seven sharp. Walking slowly down the hall, I take a couple of deep breaths to prepare myself.

Opening the door, Jake is standing there looking all too handsome in dark rinse jeans and a light blue button down that makes his eyes seem bluer. He even shaved. I can see every sharp plane and angle of his jaw and cheekbones.

Unable to resist, I reach up and run my fingertips over his smooth skin, smiling. "You shaved for me?"

He smiles, his dimple even more prominent on a smooth face, and even more effective. I'm such a goner.

"I did." Leaning down, he kisses me, and I feel the electric current zap through me like it does every time our lips touch – sparking me alive.

"I also brought you these," he says, holding out a big bouquet of tulips for me.

"Jake," I breathe. "I love tulips. Thank you, they're beautiful."

Holding them up to my nose, I breathe them in, loving the bright colors he chose. He smiles softly at my reaction, and I quickly go to the kitchen to put them in a vase.

Taking my hand when I return, we walk out to his truck and he opens the door for me.

"You look beautiful, darlin'," he says when he gets in behind the wheel. Threading his fingers with mine, he kisses my knuckles, and my cheeks grow warm at the compliment.

"Thank you. You don't look so bad yourself," I tell him, and he flashes me a sexy grin.

I hold his hand in my lap as he drives. After only about twenty minutes, Jake pulls into the parking lot of a restaurant called The Sea Spray. What a cute name.

Inside, the hostess guides us through the dining room and out onto a deck, my eyes widening instantly.

It's beautiful.

The deck extends out over the ocean, and all I see is endless water. Strings of white lights line the railings and are strung up overhead, crisscrossing above our heads. Wooden tables and chairs cover the deck for eating, and there are a few couches at the end for sitting and enjoying the view.

I squeeze Jake's hand and he looks down at me. "I love it. It's so pretty."

"I thought you might think that."

I'm happy we're seated close to the end and along the edge so I have an unobstructed view for the coming sunset.

Jake holds my chair out for me and I smile my thanks. Sitting across from me, he opens his menu, and I take the time to appreciate him. I want to spend hours memorizing every plane, angle, slope, and curve of him.

"Like what you see?" Jake asks, lifting his head to smile at me, showing off his sexy dimple.

Deciding to own the fact that I was staring, I smirk and take a sip of my water. "Yes, I do. Very much."

He lifts an eyebrow and stares back, his eyes burning heat into mine. "Me too."

Smiling, I pick up my menu and study it for a minute. "I think I'll will go with the lobster mac and cheese. It sounds amazing."

"Good choice." When our waitress comes by, we order our dinner and drinks. "Tell me about your life back in New Jersey."

"It was good. I have three best friends that I love to pieces. We've known each other since we were freshman in high school."

"Do you miss them?"

"I do. I talked to Elizabeth today, but we all conferenced together last weekend. It was hard leaving them, but they knew I needed to do this."

"Why?"

"Life was being lived all around me, and time kept moving, but I felt like I was stuck. I wasn't really living. I was just going through the motions of life."

"I know what you mean."

"You do?"

"When I retired from the Navy, I was different. Everyone knew. I knew." He swallows hard, but continues. "My family and friends were moving forward in their lives, but I couldn't. I spent most of my time in my workshop. It was the only place that gave me any clarity. But lately," he says, pinning me with his eyes. "I've started to feel alive again."

"Jake," I start, trying to find the right words. "You made me paint for the first time in seven years. You gave that back to me without even realizing it." He doesn't know what that means to me.

Taking my hand in his, he brushes his thumb across the back of my knuckles. Squeezing it, he reaches across the table with his other and tucks a wayward strand of hair behind my ear. Lingering, he caresses his thumb over my cheek, and I lean into his touch, the look in his eyes spreading warmth through me.

When our food is delivered, the heavenly scent of cheesy goodness fills my nose and I dig in. It's the most delicious mac and cheese I've ever had. The sweetness of the lobster pairs well with the cheesy macaroni.

The sun is starting to set, and it frames Jake in the most breathtaking way, making him look almost ethereal. And as the sky darkens, the string lights above our heads start to shine like stars in the night.

After dinner, Jake pays the bill, and we decide to sit on the couches at the of the deck to finish our drinks.

We're sitting close, our bodies touch from knees to hips. He wraps his arm around me, and I lean into him, looking out at the dark water.

"Do you want to come home with me?" Jake whispers, kissing me behind my ear, sending shivers down my spine. "We could sit outside and make a fire."

"Yes," I sigh, and he stands, taking me with him. We abandon the rest of our drinks as he guides me back through the restaurant and out to his truck.

The ride back to his house is a quiet one, with just the low melodies of the radio filling the cab of his truck.

I hum along to the slow country song playing, and I lose track of time, thinking of how much I want to kiss Jake right now. His lips first, but then I want to strip him naked and run my hands all over his rock-solid body, kissing my way down to his…Oh my god, I need to think of something else.

Growing hotter by the second, I clear my throat and

squirm in my seat. Jake's eyes shoot to mine, and then back to the road, his grip tightening on the steering wheel.

Finally getting to his house, he walks us right around to the back and I settle into one of the couches around the fire pit. Jake grabs wood from a pile under the deck and gets a fire started.

With the light dancing across his face, he looks dangerous and sexy as hell. I crook my finger out, needing him to come here.

He braces his arms on the back of the couch on either side of my head, his lips just a breath away from mine. "I need you," I whisper, grabbing his shirt and closing the distance between us.

I kiss him hard, with everything I have, and with everything I want. Pulling him against me, I need him to feel my racing heart that's ready to beat out my chest. He needs to know what he does to me.

Deepening the kiss, our tongues slide together in a dance I'll never get tired of.

But as much as I want to give in, I push him away. Standing on shaky legs, I curl my fingers into his shirt and turn him, pushing him down to sit. Giving him a coy smile, I straddle his hips, and feel how hard he is beneath me. I rock my hips gently, watching as his eyes darken into the stormy blue seas that only happen when he's turned on.

Placing my hands on his shoulders, I lean in and kiss his neck – sucking, licking, and biting my way up his jaw and over to his mouth. Taking his bottom lip between my teeth, I nibble gently before licking away the sting.

He tries to kiss me, but I pull back, shaking my head. "Not yet, mountain man. I'm in control right now," I tell him, and his eyes darken even more.

I unbutton his shirt slowly, kissing the skin I expose with every button I release. Tugging the hem out of his jeans, I spread his shirt open and push it off his shoulders, enjoying the glorious expanse of his chest.

Sliding my hands from his shoulders to his waistband, his muscles contract under my touch, and I love that I have that effect on him.

Leaning forward, I kiss his chest, swirling my tongue around each of his nipples as I unbuckle his belt, sliding the button open and slowly unzipping his jeans.

Stripping off my jean jacket, I lift my shirt up and off of me before unclasping my bra, freeing my breasts.

Jake's hands immediately grab my waist as he leans forward to take my left nipple into his mouth. I sigh loudly, thrusting my chest at him as I rock against him. He bites down, and I cry out at the pain, but moan when he flattens his tongue to quickly take the sting away.

Moving over to my other breast, he pays equal attention to it while still kneading the left, rubbing his thumb over my sensitive flesh.

Gripping Jake through his jeans, I slide my hand up and down his length, and he groans into my breast, biting down harder than the last time – a strangled scream torn from my lips, loving the pain mixed with pleasure.

Lifting us, Jake shoves his jeans down just far enough to where he frees himself, and I grab him, stroking his length, loving the groans he makes into my skin as he kisses his way across my chest and up my neck.

Jake slides his hands up my bare thighs and under my skirt to grip my ass, grinding me into him. "Reach in the pocket of my jeans, baby. Put it on me." He sounds like he's barely holding on to his sanity.

Stumbling around, I find the condom in his pocket, and with shaking hands, I rip it open and roll it down on him. He places his hand on top of mine to steady me, and guides our hands up and down his length, letting me feel what I do to him.

"I need you, darlin'. Lift up."

Holding the back of the couch, I keep my eyes on his as do as he says. Reaching between us, Jake grips my lace panties in his fist and rips them off, positioning himself at my entrance.

Slowly, I start to lower myself down, taking every glorious inch of him inside of me. Feeling the heat of the fire on my back, my head falls back as I let out a groan, low and long. Pulling me towards him, Jake grazes his teeth along the exposed flesh of my neck until he's fully seated inside of me.

I gently rock back and forth, feeling him in me at this angle, and feeling him reach a spot I didn't even know existed.

Placing one hand on his chest and the other on his shoulder, I lift myself up, and then back down on him.

I find a rhythm, and with every downward stroke, he hits me perfectly, the sensation making my legs shake.

Jake lets me have this control at first, feeling him, and taking from him. But when he can't hold back any longer, he grips my hips hard enough to leave marks. Lifting me up, he pulls me down hard, and we both moan loudly – filling the quiet of the night with the sounds of our passion.

Jake keeps control over me. He moves me with him—over and over, faster and faster—until I feel my inner muscles start to flutter, and Jake pulls me down on him with everything he has. I cry out, exploding around him. Groaning, he holds me to him as I squeeze him into me, milking him for all he has.

Breathing hard, Jake wraps his arms around me, and we hold on to one another. The cool night air starts to chill our overheated skin as the fire crackles behind me.

Jake brushes his lips against my neck and lightly traces patterns on my back as I stroke his hair. My heart rate starts to settle back down as I'm lulled into a dream-like state.

I don't know how much time passes, but it's too soon that Jake grips my ass and stands, still keeping himself inside of me.

I wrap my legs around his waist and rest my head on his shoulder as he starts to walk. With every step, I feel him grow inside of me again, and I rock my hips, already needing him all over again.

Without breaking contact, Jake lays me on the edge of his bed and kisses me deep into the mattress, slowly starting to pump in and out of me again. With my legs locked around his hips, he looks down at me with heated eyes, his grip on my ass tightening as he steadily moves faster and faster until I'm fisting the sheets next to me and arching off the bed, my mouth open in a silent cry.

I've never desired a man, or felt so desired by a man in my life. Jake Taylor is going to be the downfall of everything I am and everything I used to be.

Chapter 13

The light streaming through the window wakes me out of a deep, sex induced sleep. Groaning, I turn away from it and curl into the warm body next to me.

Smiling, I open my eyes and look up at Jake, happy that he's still here this time, and still sleeping.

Studying his relaxed face, I reach up and lightly trace the planes of his jaw, cheeks, forehead, nose, eyes, and lips. I want to memorize his features so I can paint them one day. He has a face worthy of immortalization on canvas.

"What're you doing?" he grumbles, still half asleep.

"Memorizing you," I whisper back.

"Why?"

"So I can paint your perfect, handsome face someday."

"Hmm, perfect and handsome?" He smiles, his eyes still closed.

"Yes." I stretch up and kiss him softly.

"Glad I can be an inspiration for you, darlin'."

"You are, mountain man," I confess, pulling away gently.

Slipping out of bed, I silently walk across his room to the bathroom. And while I planned on just sneaking back into bed, I look at the shower longingly, my body wanting the hot water. I feel used in the most delicious of ways, but I'm sore from being taken so many times, and in so many ways all night. Jake is insatiable. But then again, so am I when it comes to him.

Starting the water, I go and grab a fluffy towel from the closet and leave it on the vanity before stepping under the hot stream of water, my muscles relaxing on impact. But then a cold burst of air hits my back as a naked Jake joins me.

"Jake, I'm freezing here. You're stealing all of the hot water," I huff, my skin breaking out in goosebumps.

"Then come closer, darlin'," he drawls in his sexy morning voice.

Wrapping his arm around my waist, he pulls me flush against him as he steps back so the water hits both of us now. My skin flushing with goosebumps for a completely different reason.

Starting at my shoulders, Jake runs his soapy hands all over my body, making sure to clean every inch, taking extra care and time on my breasts and between my legs. I moan low and long, leaning into his body.

I'm still sensitive from last night, so it only takes a few strokes of his fingers against my core to make me fall apart in his arms. I honestly didn't think I had anything left in me to give him, but I'm starting to believe that Jake knows my body better than me.

Breathing hard into his chest, I lather my hands, ready to return the favor. I start with his shoulders, chest, and arms – worshiping every inch I touch. Turning him around, I rub his back, massaging him as I go, feeling him relax beneath my touch.

Bending, I run my hands down each of his legs and back up, saving the best part of him for last. Standing in front of him again, I lean forward and kiss his chest, letting my hand stroke him. Increasing my pressure, Jake leans in and braces his hands on the glass behind me, caging me in.

Breathing hard, he kisses my neck. "Faster, darlin'," he groans in my ear.

I pump him faster, feeling him harden and lengthen in my hand with each pass, reveling in the fact that I can bring this man pleasure. Every grunt and groan that escapes his lips gives me a sense of power and confidence that I've never had.

Squeezing him, I reach down and grip his balls, making Jake jerk in my hand. And with a deep groan, he releases ropes of white all over my stomach.

Reaching down, I swirl my fingers through it, spreading it around further. Looking into his eyes, I bring my hand up to my mouth and lick my fingers clean. He tastes like pure man – musky and salty. A heady combination.

"I've never seen anything sexier," he says, his voice strained.

Smiling, I do it again. "You taste good, mountain man."

Pressing me back into the glass with his hips, Jake slams his mouth down on mine, plunging his tongue between my lips. Tasting, sweeping, taking, and claiming me.

I've never wanted, or needed, anything more in my life

than to be claimed by this man.

"I don't know what you're doing to me," Jake whispers against my lips.

"I was thinking the same thing," I whisper back, kissing him hard.

Pushing myself against him, our bodies slide against one another as the water continues to beat down on us.

It isn't until the water starts to get cold that Jake turns it off and we step out. Grabbing the towel I had left on the counter, he pats me dry before doing the same to himself. Taking my hand, we walk out of the bathroom and over to his dresser where he pulls out sweat pants and a t-shirt for me. They're huge, but I don't care.

Smiling, I run my fingers through my hair, trying to untangle it. The happiness I feel is unreal.

"What're you smiling about?" he asks, smirking.

"Oh, nothing. I'm just happy. I forgot how that felt."

Stalking over to me, Jake presses me into the wall, kissing me senseless. I don't think I'll ever get used to the way he kisses me. Sometimes it's soft and gentle, and other times it's hard and bruising. I love it all. The unpredictability keeps me wanting more.

"Let's go downstairs. I'll make breakfast," he says, tearing himself away from me.

"Good, I'm starving." I start to walk towards the door when I feel a slap on my ass and I jump, looking back at smiling Jake.

"Lead the way, darlin'."

Smiling, we head down to the kitchen and sit at the island, leaning forward on my elbows and placing my chin in my hands.

"So, what are you making me?"

"French toast?"

My stomach growls in anticipation. "Sounds perfect."

Nodding, he gets to work taking out a bowl, a loaf of bread, milk, eggs, vanilla, and cinnamon. I watch him closely, noticing everything about him. The effortless way he whisks the eggs, his forearm flexing in the process, and the intense look on his face. His perfect lips are pursed and his jaw is set. I could watch him all day long, memorizing how his body moves.

My hands are itching to hold a paintbrush so I can capture him on canvas. I want to paint everything he does, and I've never painted portraits before. But then again, he seems to defy everything I'm used to.

"What are you thinking about?" he asks.

Snapping out of my thoughts, I look up to find him studying me. I tuck a piece of wet hair behind my ear and decide to answer him truthfully instead of being embarrassed. "I was thinking about how I want to paint you, and how I would do it first." He stops plating the food and looks at me, an odd look on his face. "You asked, mountain man." I smile softly. "I was just being honest."

"I always want you to be honest with me," he says, placing a plate of fluffy French toast in front of me.

"I am." I pour maple syrup over my stack, and the scent of vanilla and cinnamon makes my mouth water. And with one bite, I moan instantly. "Oh my god, Jake. This is so good."

I'm distracted momentarily by how good of a cook he is, but when I take a sip of the coffee he just handed me, I look up at him seriously.

"I want you to always be honest with me, too. I can take

whatever it is you want talk about. I'm not a weak woman."

"I know you're not, darlin'. I've never thought that," he says, taking the seat across from me.

"Okay." I nod, looking him in the eyes so I can see the truth. Picking up my fork again, I keep eating until I've all but licked the plate clean. "You're seriously an amazing cook. I've never met a man who could cook before."

"Good. I don't need the competition."

"Oh, please," I scoff. "There's no competition."

"With you, there will always be competition."

"What does that mean?"

"It means that there will always be a man I'll have to fight off if I want to keep you."

Um, what?

"Jake." I roll my eyes. "First of all, I get to decide who I'm with. Always. And second, you have no idea what you're talking about."

His eyebrows shoot up. "I don't?"

"No, you don't."

"Then tell me."

"I'm just saying that you don't have to worry. You're all the man I need." I look away nervously and take a sip of coffee.

But hearing his stool scrape on the floor, I look up and see him rounding the counter, a wild look in his eyes. He's on me in less than two seconds, kissing me hard, and pushing me back into the island.

"You're damn right I'm all the man you need. I'm all you'll ever need."

Kissing me hard again, I throw my hands around his neck, raking my fingers through his wet hair. His lips are bruising against mine, his tongue penetrating my mouth like he can't get close enough. It's hot, dirty, and sexy.

Pulling away just as abruptly as he started, I suck in air like I've been underwater and am getting oxygen for the first time in minutes.

"Are you sore?" he asks, smoothing his hands up my thighs.

"Yes, but I can always take what you give me."

He smiles wickedly. "I know you can, darlin'. But I don't want to hurt you, so I'll have to wait until later."

He kisses me softly and untangles himself from my embrace. Too distracted by this man, my eyes widen when they see the time on the microwave clock.

"Oh my god, is that the time? I have to be at work soon and I need to go home and change."

"I'll take you back. I didn't know you had work this morning."

"Yeah, I kind of got distracted and forgot."

"I guess that's my fault." He smiles smugly.

"It is. You're a bad influence."

"Can't say I'm sorry about that, darlin'."

"I don't want you to be. I don't mind at all."

Walking towards the front door, Jake grabs his keys, and I'm about to follow him when I look down at his clothes on me.

"Wait," I say, stopping him. "Should I go and find my clothes first?"

A possessive, heated, look comes over him. "No. I like you in my clothes. You look sexy." Kissing me, he grabs my hand and pulls me outside, closing the door behind me so I can't question him.

I look sexy? And he's saying that while I'm in his baggy

sweat pants and t-shirt with no makeup on? That's a first.

"But my clothes…" I try and say.

"Get them later. Don't worry about it."

Alright, but I hope he knows he's not getting these back now. I'm putting these on whenever I'm alone and want to feel wrapped up in him.

When we pull up to the cottage, I'm reluctant to let go of his hand, loving the warmth and comfort it gives me. "I'll see you soon?" I ask, my hand on the door handle.

"Of course," he says, bringing my hand to his lips and gently kissing my knuckles. "Soon isn't soon enough."

Releasing me, I smile softly, and slip out of his truck. I really wish I didn't have to go into work.

"You're late, missy," Courtney says the second I walk through the café's doors. "You better have a good reason. Like perhaps you've been up all night banging a certain hottie?" Wow, she sure has a way of greeting a person in the morning.

"Yes, maybe that is why I'm late." I smile.

"Holy shit!" she exclaims. "Tell me everything!"

"Fine," I sigh, pretending it's a chore, when really I'm dying to tell her. "We went out on a real date last night. He took me to this beautiful waterfront restaurant called The Sea Spray."

"I love that place," she says, nodding her approval.

"Jake was such a gentleman, and the food and drinks were good. Then we went back to his place and he made a fire outside where I then proceeded to seduce him. And that's where it starts, but it ended many, many times later up in his bed. And shower." I fan my face, feeling hot all of a sudden.

"AHH, I'm so happy!" she yells, pulling me in for a giant hug.

"Me too," I say, laughing at her excitement.

"How did you break the weird silence you had going after Sunday? You never told me."

"I had Dottie come over on Wednesday and we made her blueberry pie together. Then I took the extra one we made over to Jake that night because I know it's his favorite."

"Oh, he ate your pie and loved it, did he?" She winks.

"Shit, Courtney. Your mind is in the gutter today. Has your husband not been taking care of you?"

"No, he has. That's why my mind is so dirty."

"Okay, well, keep that shit to yourself." I laugh. "I don't need any more fuel for my fantasies about Jake."

"Is that so?" a deep, rumbling voice says from behind us.

Turning, I'm face to face with my fantasy inducing man himself. I really need to pay more attention to what I say in the café, and listen when the bell rings on the door. This is the second time now that Jake's snuck up on us.

His eyes are sparkling in the morning light that's streaming through the front windows, and I'm momentarily transfixed. I could stare into them all day long and still find a reason to keep looking.

I smile, happy to see him even if I was just with him less than an hour ago.

"Yes, it is," I finally answer, owning up to the fact that I have dirty fantasies about him.

"Maybe you'd like share some of them with me?" His voice drops an octave lower, and my body hums alive, feeling the vibrations course through me.

I'm standing speechless in front of him, and before I can think of something to say, Jake steps closer to me, leaning across the counter. "I'll tell you mine if you tell me yours, darlin'." I can't breathe or form words, so I just nod, and he smiles, giving me a glimpse of his sexy dimple. "I'll take a coffee, please. Strong. I didn't get much sleep last night."

"Is that so?" I ask, finally finding my voice. "What a shame."

"I'm not complaining. I'll take never sleeping again if it means I get to relive last night over and over again."

My hands slip, and I spill some of the coffee I was pouring. Did he just say that out loud? In front of Courtney? I look over at her and see that she's busying herself placing trays of cookies in the case, pretending not to listen.

"You okay there, darlin'?" he asks.

"Uh, um, yes, I'm fine." I hand him his coffee, and his fingers wrap around mine.

"You sure?"

Swallowing hard, I nod. "Never better," I manage to squeak out.

Pulling on my hand a little, he forces me forward as he leans in. "I'll see you later." Closing the distance, he kisses me fast and hard, releasing me too quickly.

Taking his coffee from my hand, he leaves a couple singles on the counter and walks out as quietly as he came in.

A throat clearing next to me brings me back to the present. "Uh, Ally? That boy is so falling for you. He looks at you like you're the last drink of water in the desert."

"Oh, please." I roll my eyes. "He does not."

"He does. Trust me."

Smiling, I turn back to the coffee pots and pour a cup for

myself, sipping it black.

The rest of the day goes by in a blur, and all I can think about is seeing Jake later. It's like I'm a teenager crushing on the most popular boy in school. I really should get a grip, but the truth is, I honestly don't want to. Jake makes me feel alive in every sense of the word. My body, mind, heart, and soul have all felt more alive since meeting him.

Driving home, I have my windows down and my sunroof open, enjoying the warmer weather as summer approaches. Memorial Day Weekend is only two weeks away, and I need to see if Ash, Mel, and Ellie can get away from work to come up and visit for a few days.

When I pass the lake, I smile, thinking about seeing Jake in a short while. I can't believe he heard me this morning. I don't know if he's going to hold me to what he said earlier, but I will more than likely pass out from being turned on so much if he whispers every dirty thing he wants to do to me.

Chapter 14

Changing out of my work clothes, I put on a short flowy dress that I know Jake will appreciate, and pair it with nude wedges. I can't wait to feel his hands skim up my bare calves and thighs before disappearing under my dress.

Dresses and skirts are definitely way more fun than jeans.

As I'm touching up my hair and makeup, I hear a knock at the door, and hurry to finish. Fluffing my hair, I flip it over a couple of times to give it volume and a freshly wind-blown look.

When I open the door, a smile overtakes me when all I see is a big bouquet of flowers.

"You just gave me flowers," I tell him. Reaching for them, I hold the bunch close to my chest and inhale the sweet scent.

"You deserve flowers every day," Jake states matter-of-factly, and a warmth spreads through me.

"They're beautiful. Another favorite flower of mine. How are you guessing? Tulips yesterday, and peonies today."

He shrugs. "I just picked the ones that remind me of you. Tulips are bright and colorful, and were once the most desired and coveted flower in the world. Peonies are delicate, classy, and timeless."

Swooning, I take a minute to let that sink in. No one has ever said such a beautiful thing to me before. "Jake…I…thank you. I love them." Placing them close to my face, I relish in the fact that this big Viking man in front of me picked these flowers out because they reminded him of me.

Grabbing his shirt, I bring his mouth down to mine. His soft, strong lips mold to mine, and the floor beneath me shifts. Sighing, Jake's tongue slips into my mouth, and the slow dance I've been craving since this morning begins. My body hums as his hands find my waist and slide up my back, holding me to him.

Losing myself in Jake is the easiest thing in the world. I'm pulled to him like a magnet, never wanting to separate. My body simmers with a raging fire only he can ignite, and only he knows how to control.

Slowly untangling from each other, our lips stay just an inch away as we catch our breath. Looking into his eyes, I'm immediately caught in the swirling waters.

His five o'clock shadow tickles my palm as I smooth my hand over his cheek, and I suddenly wonder what it would feel like against my body as he kissed his way up my thighs – rough against smooth.

Lost in thought, I trace his lips with the tip of my finger, and he catches it between his teeth. Biting down on the pad of my index finger, he sucks on it gently, and I feel the pull all the way to my core.

My eyes close briefly, and when they open again, I see his have gone molten – a fire burning just for me.

A soft smile plays at my lips as I take my finger away and step out of his reach. Lightheaded, I let my feet carry me to the kitchen so I can find a vase for these beautiful flowers. I feel him behind me though, watching everything I do.

"Let's go, darlin'," he says, his voice strained. "Unless you want me to lift up that short little dress you have on and shove myself inside of you, I suggest you march that sexy ass out to my truck."

My knees buckle at his words, and I brace myself against the counter. "What if that's exactly what I want?"

Stepping up behind me, Jake leans against the counter, his body so close to mine, but not touching me. "I know it is," he whispers in my ear. "But I want to take you out first."

He steps back, and I try and focus on why I even came in here. Oh, right, the flowers. Trimming the stems, I put the bouquet in water and place the vase on the kitchen table.

On shaky legs, I walk back into the living room and grab my purse before stepping out onto the porch, trying to take in as much fresh air as I can. But it does nothing to clear my lungs of Jake's sweet, musky scent, or my head of the images he created.

Jake closes the front door, and we walk to his truck. He opens the door for me, but lets me hop up inside on my own. I know if he even touches me in the slightest way, we'll never make it to dinner.

Without looking at me, he starts the truck and heads out

onto the road. Glancing over at him, I see him flex his hands on the steering wheel, his jaw set tight.

"I was thinking," he says, eyes straight ahead. "I want to take you somewhere this week."

"You do?" I ask, surprised.

"Yes." He nods. "When do you have off?"

"Monday through Wednesday."

"Good. I'm taking you somewhere then."

"Where?" I'd honestly go anywhere he wanted to take me, but I'm curious.

"Just on a short road trip."

"Okay, Mr. Mysterious, I'll go with it." I smile. "I'm down for an adventure."

He relaxes at my response, loosening his death grip on the steering wheel. "Good. I knew you'd be."

"Any hints?" I probe.

"We're going north."

"*More* north?"

"There's a lot more of Maine above us, darlin'."

Tucking a strand of hair behind my ear, I tap my finger to my chin. "Alright, so we're staying in Maine and going north. A moose park, maybe?"

His laugh fills the cab of the truck – a deep melody filling my heart with joy. "No, babe. We don't have those here. But it is a park, and you might see a moose on the way."

"Are you taking me to Acadia?" I smile, excited at the thought. From all the pictures I've seen, it looks gorgeous.

He nods, smiling at my excitement.

"Really? It's on my list of places to go," I tell him.

"Good," he says, taking my hand and lifting it to his mouth, kissing my knuckles sweetly.

Placing our joined hands on my lap, I gently trace patterns on the back of his hand with my free one.

"Where are we going tonight?"

"Do you not like surprises?" He laughs.

"I do. I love them actually. I just didn't think dinner was a surprise."

"It could be."

"Fine," I huff. "I'll just wait and see."

Looking out the window and away from him, I hear a low chuckle as the hand I'm holding vibrates. Looking back at him, I see Jake trying to contain himself.

"Is something funny, Mr. Taylor?"

"Nope." He coughs, smiling. "Nothing's funny, babe."

"That's what I thought," I say haughtily.

Reaching over to adjust the radio dials, I switch around, and stop when I find a country station to sing along to one of my favorites. It reminds me of drives to the beach back home.

I love that music can take you back to a time and place in your life, letting you relive it. And I love all genres – country, pop, hip-hop, R&B, rock, classical, jazz. I think there's a song for every mood and every feeling.

"So, she can paint and sing? Anything else you're withholding, Miss Rose?" Jake asks when the song is over.

"I have many talents. You'll have to wait and see what you discover next."

"I look forward to that," he says, and when the next song starts, Jake looks over at me with a sexy grin before he starts to sing along.

My jaw drops.

Jake's voice is smooth like honey and feels like velvet caressing my skin. Singing the next line with more emotion, his voice gets a little raspy while still remaining smooth somehow. I've never heard anything sexier, and I feel it resonate deep into my bones while my skin breaks out in goosebumps.

I can't look away from him. I watch his throat work and his lips move. Glancing at me, he smiles, and sings the next line about riding with his baby directly to me.

Have I died and gone to Valhalla? Because in what real life scenario does this big, tall, strong Viking of a mountain man also have the ability to sing?

When the song ends, Jake brings our joined hands up to his mouth and kisses mine.

"Jake," I breathe. "I want to kiss you so fucking bad right now. You have no idea."

His laughter is just more music to my ears. "I'll have to sing more often then."

"You better. But only for me. I don't want to have to fight off women when they try and jump your bones after hearing your voice."

"Darlin', trust me, I'll save it just for you." He smiles.

"Pull over," I command in a soft voice.

"What?"

"Pull the truck over. Right now."

He seems confused by my demand, but does as I say and pulls over onto the shoulder of the dark side road.

The second he puts the truck in park, I unbuckle my seatbelt and throw myself at him. Straddling his hips, I grip his face between my hands and slam my mouth down on his.

I moan instantly, sliding my tongue against his and running my hands through his hair, loving the feel of it gliding through my fingers. Gripping hard, Jake groans into my mouth, and I feel it vibrate through my whole body.

When I feel his hands start to slide up my legs, though, I use every ounce of strength I have to pull away from him. I untangle myself from his grip and crawl back over to my seat and buckle myself back into my seatbelt again.

I had just wanted to give him a taste for later, but now I just want all of him.

"Darlin', why did you stop?" he asks, breathing hard.

Smiling sweetly, I pat his chest. "You were taking me to dinner. Aren't you hungry?"

"Yes. For you." Reaching across the middle console, Jake rests his hand on my thigh, slowly sliding it upwards. "I love this dress. You tease me with your long legs and soft skin, and all I can think about is how they'll look wrapped around me." Moving his hand up a little more, it disappears under the skirt of the dress, but stops near the apex of my thighs. "And how easy it is for me to slide my hand up and under here. If I wanted to, I could feel how wet you are for me. I could take care of you so easily if you needed me, darlin'. You just have to ask."

My breath starts to come in short, rapid intakes. Why does he have to say things like that?

I risk a quick look at him, and if I had any chance of winning this battle of wills, I just lost. Jake's eyes are shining with so much need and desire, and it's all for me.

Moving his hand off my thigh, he unbuckles my seat belt again, and I don't waste another second before I lift myself up and over onto his lap.

"You win," I whisper, right before Jake shuts me up with his lips.

Melting against him, I go straight to undoing his belt and jeans, needing him to put out this fire burning inside of me. Lifting up, I give him the room he needs to shove his jeans and boxers down, freeing himself.

Digging in his pocket, I pull out a condom I know he keeps there, and rip it open. He watches my hands tremble as I roll it down on him, his eyes blazing with need as he slides his hands under my skirt to smooth his palms over my ass.

Gripping me hard, he groans. "Darlin', this ass will be the death of me. When I get you in my bed later, I'm going to lay you out and trace every curve of your body. First with my hands, then with my mouth. I want every inch of you imprinted in my mind so that when you're not around, I can still feel you."

Moaning at his words, Jake's mouth leaves a path of flames up my neck, his teeth grazing the sensitive flesh behind me ear.

I can't even think straight anymore.

Pushing my panties aside, he slides his fingers between my folds. "Always so ready for me," he rasps.

Positioning himself at my entrance, he slams up into me in one stroke, and I scream out at the sudden invasion, my body feeling like it's being split in two.

Every sound we make echoes back at me in this small space, drowning out all thought.

Jake grips my ass to the point where I think he'll leave permanent hand prints, and I brace myself on his shoulders. Over and over again, Jake lifts me up, and I slam back down on him, filling me completely.

It feels primal and unhinged, and it's not long before my legs are shaking and my vision blurs.

With one final stroke, I let go, my body not my own as it shatters around him.

He owns all of me.

Trying to drag in breath after breath, I close my eyes and rest my head on Jake's shoulder, breathing in his musky, woodsy scent.

When my head stops spinning, I lean back and look at my sexy mountain man. His hair is all wild from my hands, making his overgrown golden locks look like a fierce lion's mane.

Smiling softly, I lean in, kissing his swollen lips.

With that simple touch, my heart swells with a feeling I'm too scared to label. My head is trying to tell my heart to slow down, but I don't think that's even an option anymore.

Lifting myself off of him, I move back over to my seat, smoothing my dress down. Looking back over at Jake, I bite my lip nervously.

"So, dinner then?" I smile shyly, not wanting to give away what I'm thinking.

Jake flashes me a wicked grin and laughs. "Yeah, darlin', dinner."

After adjusting himself, he pulls back out onto the road and continues on towards wherever he was taking me. I don't even care anymore. All I can think about is the fact that I just had sex in his truck on the side of the road.

"You realize anyone could have driven by and seen us?" I laugh lightly, realizing what we just did.

"Yes, but you didn't care, did you?" he asks, already knowing my answer.

"Nope, it didn't even cross my mind actually." Smiling, I see a satisfied little gleam in his eyes. "I'm starving."

"We'll be there soon," he says, squeezing my hand.

True to his word, a few minutes later we pull into the parking lot of a little dive bar.

"I know it looks kind of shitty from the outside, but it's not on the inside, and they have good food."

"Good. Because I could go for a big, juicy burger with fries and a cold beer."

"My kind of woman," he says, getting out of the truck and coming around to open my door.

"I know." I smirk, taking his hand again as we walk inside.

Looking around, it's actually not as bad as I thought it'd be. It's a country bar, with the walls covered in saddles, hats, ropes, and pictures of different artists. The floor and tables are both a dark brown wood that's been worn down and scratched from years of use, but gives it more of a homey feel. A small stage sits unoccupied on the far back wall with a dancefloor in front of it that's probably used for live music or karaoke.

Jake walks us over to a booth, and a waitress comes over almost immediately.

"Hey, Jake, how're you doing tonight?" she asks, practically eye fucking him.

She has long brown hair, brown eyes, pouty lips, and a tight little body with big boobs. Please, honey, you're not fooling anyone with those balloons on your chest. I thought I left all the fake and superficial bitches back in Jersey, but I guess they're everywhere.

Not even bothering to acknowledge me, she flips her hair over her shoulder and thrusts her boobs out, as if that was necessary. Her tight, low-cut t-shirt is enough for anyone, girls included, to zero in on her honkers straight away.

"Hey, Amber. I'll have a bud draft. Ally?"

Amber, really? Sounds like a stripper. Looks like one, too.

She reluctantly turns my way when Jake addresses me, and narrows her eyes. Okay, bitch.

"I'll have a Stella, thanks," I say politely, making sure I keep my true feelings to myself.

"Sure, I'll go get those," she replies, smiling seductively at Jake before walking back to the bar – my eyes shooting daggers at her the entire time.

"You okay?"

"Yeah, just peachy," I say, forcing a smile.

Tilting his head to the side, he studies me with a small smile playing on his lips.

"Fine," I sigh. "I didn't like her thrusting her boobs out at you and giving you sex eyes while I'm sitting right here."

"And if you weren't sitting here, that'd be okay?"

Is he joking?

"No, it wouldn't be okay, but at least I wouldn't have to see it."

"You're sexy when you're jealous."

"I'm not jealous." Liar. "I just…never mind."

Smiling like he's won the lottery, Jake leans back in his seat, that damn dimple mocking me because he knows I *am* jealous. Possessive of him might be a better way of putting it, though.

When Amber returns with our beers, she makes sure to bend over when she places them on the table so Jake has a full view of her cleavage.

Why don't you just shake them in his face while you're at it?

Shifting my eyes back to Jake, I notice he's not even looking at her. Instead, he's watching me with a knowing smirk.

"Do you need time to look at the menu?" She practically purrs at Jake.

"No, we're ready. I'll have the cowboy burger and fries, medium rare."

"I'll have the same," I say, smiling as I shove my menu back at her.

Huffing, Amber flips her hair and walks away, putting a little sway in her hips this time. Oh my god, she's relentless.

"I think Amber has a crush on you. Just letting you know in case you didn't catch any of her blatant come-ons."

"I come here with my brothers sometimes, and she always serves us." He shrugs, like that's supposed to reassure me or something.

"Are you and your brothers close?" I ask, trying to get my mind off the tramp.

"Yeah." He nods, drinking his beer. "All our lives, really. I can count on them to always be there if I need them."

"That's how my sisters and I are. Especially when we were growing up. No matter what was ever happening, we stuck together. And when things got particularly bad, we'd have sleepovers in each other's rooms and stay up late talking about the dumbest stuff. It made the world of difference to me."

"Bad?"

"Yeah, my dad. He, uh, wasn't the greatest," I confess, clearing my suddenly dry throat.

"Did he hurt you?" Jake asks, his voice hard.

"Not physically, no. But I always had my sisters. A lot of the times I'd run into their room just to know that we were all together. Marissa is the oldest, then Kelly, and I'm the youngest. They're both married to great guys now. I'm glad they found their happiness." They have men who stand with them, not against.

"What about you?"

"What about me?"

"Do you get to find that?"

"Um…" I look down at my drink, not wanting him to know that I've started to think of him as my happy. "I haven't really thought about it in a long time. I've been on a self-proclaimed man hiatus for the past seven years."

He tilts his head slightly, studying me. "You haven't been with a man in seven years?"

"No, I haven't," I confess, looking him directly in the eyes.

Something flashes in his, but it's gone before I can figure out what it is. "Tell me more about your dad."

Swallowing hard, I take a few sips of my beer. "He's been an angry, unhappy man, for as long as I can remember. He never treated my mom well, and he was never someone that I could count on or look up to. He disappointed me more times than I can count, until I just gave up believing he'd ever be the father, or man, I needed him to be.

"My mom is the best woman in the world, hands down. She always made sure my sisters and I knew we were loved, and she always encouraged us to chase after what we wanted. It was her who pushed me to study art. My dad thought it was a stupid and useless skill. So, to get a degree in it was *definitely* something he deemed useless.

"I haven't spoken to him since my parents split up a few years ago. He hasn't ever even tried to contact me. My sister's reach out to him on occasion, but I never do. They never had to live alone with him and my mom like I did, so they don't really understand why I don't try."

"What was it like?" he asks gently.

"I was the one left at home to deal with all of the fighting, yelling, and criticism when they left for college. They have no idea what I had to endure. But I'd also never tell them either. They were living their lives and were happy. I envied them for escaping, but I could never leave my mom alone there."

Feeling the tears sting the back of my eyes, I take a deep breath to relax.

I'm better. My mom is better. We're all fine now.

Jake reaches across the table and takes my hand. "Darlin', I'm sorry. I can't even imagine what it was like to grow up having a father you couldn't depend on." His voice is both angry on my behalf, and comforting to soothe me. "Why did your mom stay with him? Didn't she see what it was doing to you?"

"They only stayed together as long as they did because they thought it was better for us. I asked her once, not long after they split, why she even married him, let alone had a family with him, and she told me he wasn't always like that. She said he used to be a good man, and he used to be good to her.

"How am I supposed to deal with that? I already had mistrust and disillusions towards men, and now she tells me he used to be good? So, a man can marry a woman, lover her, have a family, and then completely change and be horrible?" My voice breaks as I look to Jake for the answers I know he can't give me.

"Ally, he wasn't a man. A real man would never tell a woman he loves her when he doesn't. And a real man wouldn't marry a woman and have a family when he's not capable." The fierce tone of his voice keeps my tears at bay. "The fact that that asshole mistreated you makes me angrier than you can even imagine." Shaking his head, he squeezes my hand and rakes the other one roughly through his hair.

"Every time I've ever given a piece of myself to a guy, it's been returned to me broken, if returned at all." His eyes shoot to mine, and I let him see the dark pieces inside of me. "I've already put myself back together too many times, and I don't think I can do it again."

"Ally…" he says, his voice strained.

"I just need you to know where I'm coming from. And to know that this"–I motion between us–"is new for me."

Nodding, he rubs soothing circles across the back of my hand. And when he opens his mouth to say something, Amber is back with our food.

"Anything else I can get for you, Jake?"

A little laugh escapes me, and she snaps her eyes to me, glaring. Coughing, I try to cover it up, but she's not buying it.

"I'll have another beer," I tell her, sliding my empty glass to the end of the table.

Giving me major side eye, Amber pouts and turns back to Jake.

"Me too," he says, handing her his empty glass.

When she's far enough away I start laughing, happy that the tension from what I was talking about has dissipated. This girl is ridiculous. Jake's on a date with me, and yet she's flirting with him like he's going to just dump me and go after her.

"Something funny, babe?" Jake smirks.

"She's trying to take you from me, in front of me, and I think that's funny."

"Not happening," he says firmly.

Smiling, I pick up my burger and take a huge bite, moaning and closing my eyes. This is the best burger I've had in a long time.

Jake freezes, his burger halfway to his mouth. "Darlin', you can't make noises like that. It makes me think about how you'd sound with something else in your mouth."

Coughing, I start to choke, and I practically grab the beer out of Amber's hand when she returns, taking a few big gulps to clear my throat.

Of course she doesn't seem fazed at all by my choking, and she walks away smiling, probably wishing I would have just suffocated so she could comfort Jake all the way to her bed.

"You good there, darlin'?" He smirks.

"Jake, why did you say that?" I ask, trying to calm my heart.

"Just being honest." He winks, biting into his own burger. Imitating me, Jake moans, and holy hell he was right. I start to think about this mouth devouring a certain part of my body.

Squirming in my seat, I pop a fry in my mouth and stare at him while he eats. He opens wide to take a big bite, and I watch as his mouth and jaw move, and his throat bob as he swallows. When the juices start to run down from the corner of his mouth, his tongue darts out to quickly lick it away.

"Something you want to say, darlin'?"

My eyes shoot up to his, and he's looking at me like he knows exactly what I've been thinking.

"Um…"

"Didn't we agree that I'd tell you mine if you told me yours?"

"Here?" I bite my lip and look around.

"We can revisit it later," he says, even though his eyes are telling me that he wants me to tell him every dirty thought I have in my head right now.

Nodding, I pick up my burger again and force myself to eat. But I'm not really hungry for food anymore, just the man across from me. And with both of us staring at the other while we eat, I can't take the tension for very long.

Excusing myself, I go to find the bathroom, and as I walk past the bar on my way, I see Amber flirting with the bartender. She's curling her long brown hair around her finger and leaning towards him so he can get a good look at her boobs. Yeah, this girl needs to relax.

Shaking my head, I keep walking past the bar to the ladies' room that's on the other side. And as I'm washing my hands, I look in the mirror to see someone I don't recognize staring back at me. I've never seen myself look so…happy. My cheeks are flushed, my skin is glowing, and my eyes are shining with something new.

"Well, well, well. Look who we have here."

Glancing behind me, I see Amber standing by the door. Great.

"Hi." I smile, reaching for a paper towel to dry my hands. What did she do, follow me in here?

"Cut the nice girl act."

What a bitch. "It's not an act."

"Listen, I don't know why you're here with Jake, but he's mine," she says, anger flaring in her eyes.

Turning to her fully, I all but laugh in her face. "You're delusional if you think he's yours. Flipping your hair and pushing your tits out at him doesn't make him yours. If it did, you'd probably have a claim on every man you've ever talked to."

Her jaw drops – a position I'm sure she's probably used to. "Excuse me, what are you saying?"

"Are you dense?"

"Excuse me?"

"Oh, lord," I say, rolling my eyes. "Look, Amber, is it? I'm with Jake, and Jake is with me. It's that simple."

"For now, maybe. But he'll come around."

This time I really do laugh in her face. "Honey, that will never happen. Even if we weren't together, I can guarantee you he still wouldn't be yours."

"And you know this how?" she scoffs, putting her hands on her hips.

Walking towards her, I lean in close, not intimidated by her in the slightest. "He'd have to want you in the first place. A tramp with fake tits that she thrusts at every man that moves doesn't do it for a man like Jake." I hold eye contact for a few seconds so what I said can sink in, and then I push past her and out the door, ending this conversation.

Back at the table, Jake is finishing his beer, totally unaware that there's a bitch trying to sink her dirty claws into him. Good thing I'm here now to save him from that.

Smiling at that thought, I sit back down in front of my man.

"You ready to go?" he asks.

"Yeah, I'm ready, babe." I smile, winking.

Standing, he throws a few bills down on the table and pulls me close, kissing me below my ear. "I like you calling me that," he whispers, guiding me towards the door.

"I can think of a few other names as well," I say when we get outside.

"Like what?"

"Let's see…There's hot stuff, sexy, Thor, man of steel, sweet cheeks. But I'd have to say my favorite is mountain man.

It makes me think of climbing you like a tree."

Pushing me against his truck, Jake claims my mouth in a hard, bruising kiss. I can feel every inch of his hard-muscled body pressed against me. Plunging past my lips, he swirls his tongue against mine, making me all but lose consciousness.

I moan into him, feeling his hard length against me as I dig my fingers into his back. I try and move my hips against his, but he just presses me harder against his truck, not letting me.

Nibbling on my lip, Jake pulls away and opens the door behind me. Lifting me up, he practically throws me inside before jogging around to his door. Starting the truck, he tears out of the parking lot, kicking up rocks and leaving a dust cloud behind us.

Staring at his hard face and tight grip on the steering wheel, I let out a little laugh.

"Something funny?" he asks, his eyes darting to mine.

"You tore out of there like–"

"Like I can't wait to be inside of you?" he finishes, cutting me off.

Sobering up, I see nothing but desire for me written all over his face. Desire that's for me, and only me.

Jake breaks every speed limit to get back to his house in record time, and when he parks, he jumps out of the truck, coming to my side as I hurry to unbuckle my seat belt. Hopping down to meet him, I step on a rock funny and stumble forward, but Jake is right there to steady me. He picks me up and runs inside – ever the impatient man.

Throwing me down on the nearest couch, he presses me deep into the cushions, kissing me breathless.

Grabbing my hips, he pulls me into a sitting position and

kneels in front of me. "I've been dreaming about how you'd taste since I first kissed your lips."

"Jake, I…um." Fidgeting with the hem of my dress, Jake puts his hands on top of mine.

"Has no one ever tasted you before, darlin'?"

Shaking my head no, he moves my hands away and slides his up my dress until it's bunched around my waist, exposing my red lace panties.

"Good," he says, gripping my hips. "I get to be the one to show you what you've been missing."

Looking into his stormy blue eyes, I find something there that I've been needing for a very long time. "Kiss me," I whisper, needing him desperately.

Kissing me soft and slow at first, just tasting and savoring, Jake leans into me, deepening the kiss. A slow burn builds in my chest with every second that passes. My heart wants more of Jake. I want all of Jake – mind, body, heart, and soul.

Kissing his way down my neck, he pulls away to look at me, seeing that I'm flushed and ready for him.

Placing his large hands on my thighs, he slowly spreads his fingers out, hooking them under the red lace I wore just for him. Slowing dragging them down my legs, a shiver runs through me.

He kisses the insides of my knees, spreading my legs farther apart and looking straight at me like I'm a dessert made just for him.

Kissing, biting, and licking his way up my inner thighs, his scruff rubs against me. My breathing becomes shorter and my head spins, but I keep my eyes on Jake, not wanting to miss anything.

When he finally gets close to where I need him most, he

pulls away. "Jake, please," I beg.

Tightening his grip on my thighs, he pulls me to the edge of the couch and lifts my legs up and over his massive shoulders, exposing me fully.

I feel his hot breath on me first, inhaling and exhaling, taking in the scent of my arousal.

Looking up at me from between my legs, he flashes me a wicked grin. "Enjoy, baby. I know I will."

Fuck.

Blowing cool air on me, a shiver racks my body before he dives in, and the second his hot tongue spreads me open, I'm lost. Arching off the couch, my loud moans drown out every other sound as I search for something to grip.

He licks me from my entrance to my clit, and my mouth falls open in a silent scream. Making the same pass again, he sucks on my tight little bundle of nerves before pressing down on it with his tongue, my head thrashing from side to side. I can't handle everything I'm feeling.

Swirling his tongue around my entrance, he circles it slowly, teasing me before thrusting it inside of me. I scream out, my hips automatically lifting off the couch, but Jake tightens his grip and pulls me closer to him, giving me no room to move.

It's all too much. I'm feeling too much.

He sweeps back up my folds and bites down, sucking on my clit as hard as he can.

My throat closes, and I let out a strangled cry as my body shakes, almost at its breaking point.

Grabbing his hair, I pull hard, not knowing if I need him to stop before I pass out, or if I need him to keep going until I reach oblivion.

I feel Jake groan into me, and the vibrations bring me even closer to the edge as he continues to taste me with reckless abandon.

His tongue tortures and teases me, bringing me close to the edge and then sweeping down and away.

"Jake…Jake…Please!" I yell, needing to let go.

Releasing my hips, he shoves two fingers inside of me at the same time he presses his tongue flat against me. And I'm a goner.

Screaming, I thrash my head from side to side, sucking his fingers deep inside of me as I grind into his mouth, shattering into a million pieces.

I feel like I'm floating. Flying.

When my body goes limp, I release my grip on his hair and stare at him blankly, my eyes glazed over.

Slowly sliding his fingers out of me, he brings them up to his mouth and licks them clean, humming. "Never tasted anything so sweet. You may be my new favorite flavor, darlin'."

Closing my eyes, I feel Jake over me, kissing my forehead, cheeks, and nose before sweetly kissing my lips. Opening for him right away, I taste myself on his tongue.

When I start to regain my senses, I push Jake off of me and onto the couch. Straddling his hips, I kiss my way across his jaw and down his neck, fully intending on returning the favor.

Scooting backwards, I undo his belt. "Now I want to taste you, mountain man," I whisper, taking his earlobe between my teeth, making him groan against my neck.

Shimmying off his lap, I kneel in front of him, pulling his boots and jeans off before dragging his boxers down, springing free his huge, rock-solid cock that's begging for me to have a taste.

Biting my lip, I look up at Jake, seeing his hooded eyes heated and dark, watching everything I do.

I have no idea how that monster will fit in my mouth, but I want this to be good for him.

Gripping him at the base, I squeeze gently, stroking him all the way up and swirling my thumb over the tip. Jake's head falls back against the couch as he lets out a long and low groan.

Without his eyes on me, I lean forward, making the same pass with my tongue. I suck just the tip into my mouth and taste the musky manliness that is all Jake.

Another loud groan from him fills me with a new confidence as I rake my nails across his hips to grip his base, knowing I'll never be able to fit all of him in my mouth. I take in as much of him as I can, and use my other hand to slide up the other half.

I look up at Jake and his eyes blaze down at me, his jaw clenched. He's watching my every move.

Relaxing my mouth, I take a little more of him until he hits the back of my throat. Swallowing, Jake fists the back of my head and grunts out a muffled moan.

I love the power I have over him right now, and I slide back up, swirling my tongue around his crown, sucking hard.

I don't think I've ever enjoyed bringing a man pleasure as much as I do with Jake. I thrive on being the one who makes him moan and groan and shake with need.

Rubbing my thighs together, I try and relieve the ache I feel building inside of me again, but it doesn't work.

"Suck. Harder," he growls.

Hollowing out my cheeks, I feel him grow even harder

and thicker in my mouth as I pick up my pace. His grip tightens on my hair to the point of pain, but I don't care. All I care about is giving him this, giving him me. Anything he wants, I'll give him.

Grunting, Jake holds my head still as he lets go, shooting everything he has down my throat. Swallowing, I take it all.

When his hand relaxes, I slide up him, licking every drop.

Grabbing my chin, he tilts my head up, needing my eyes. "Stand up," he commands, he voice rough.

Standing on shaky legs, Jake pulls me down so I'm straddling him again, and he kisses me until I start to lose my mind as my hips rock back and forth against him, needing him again.

Smoothing his hands down my back, he squeezes my ass before sliding his fingers to my core.

"Sucking my cock made you this wet, baby?"

"Yes," I moan, gripping his hair hard as he shoves two fingers inside of me and strokes my clit with his thumb. Working his fingers, he adds a third one, and I shove my face in his neck, groaning.

I rake my teeth up his neck as he pumps in and out of me, knowing the pressure building in me is about to explode.

"Let go, baby," he says, my inner muscles fluttering on command as I free fall, biting down on his shoulder, my body trying to swallow his hand.

I collapse into his arms and suck in ragged, uneven breaths as Jake holds me against him, stroking my back.

He stands with me in his arms and I wrap my legs around his waist as he carries us up the stairs to his bed. Curling into him, I lay my head against his chest and fall asleep to the sound of his steady heartbeat.

Chapter 15

Waking up in Jake's arms, I spread my hand over his chest, feeling the smooth expanse beneath me as I breathe in the woodsy scent of his skin.

"You awake, darlin'?" he whispers.

"Mhmm," I manage to answer.

"Do you have work?"

"Mhmm."

"Do you need help getting up?"

"Mhmm."

His chest starts to shake under me and I muster the strength need to turn my head and look at him.

"Is that all you can say right now?" He smiles.

Nodding my head, he hooks his thumbs under my arms

and drags me up his chest to kiss me. A soft sigh escapes my lips and I melt into him, not even caring if my breath isn't minty fresh.

Rolling us over, Jake presses me into the bed and I can feel him growing against me. Pulling the sheets away, he reaches into the nightstand and pulls out a condom. Quickly sheathing himself, he settles between my legs and enters me in one swift motion.

Scratching at his neck, my head falls back into the pillows, moaning, loving the feeling of Jake inside of me.

We move together like we've known each other's bodies for a lifetime despite just only beginning to learn one another's rhythm.

Wrapping my legs around his waist, I meet his every stroke, his every breath, and his every moan.

Slick with sweat, our bodies take from each other until the pressure in me builds to a level I can't contain.

"Jake…I…"

"Let go, baby," he growls. "Come with me."

And with one final slam, I scream out his name as we finish together, my body imploding with too many sensations.

Kissing my closed eyelids, Jake slowly pulls out and rolls onto his back. "Waking up with you is definitely something I could get used to."

"Me too." I smile, unable to move.

"You snore, you know."

I suck in a sharp breath. "No I don't!"

"You do." He chuckles. "But it's soft and cute. Like a sleeping baby tiger."

"A baby tiger?"

"Yeah. Looks all cute and innocent, but will still bite you

nonetheless."

"Is that how you see me?"

"Well, you did bite my neck last night," he says, and prop myself up on my elbow to look down at the mark I left on his shoulder.

"Oh, I did bite you. Hard." Running my fingers over the red marks, I smile, loving that he has evidence of me on his body.

"You like that you left your mark, don't you?"

I nod my head. "It looks good on you," I whisper, leaning down to kiss it.

Rolling back on top of me, he kisses me hard. "Alright, we have to get up before I take you all over again. You have to get to work soon."

"I forgot! You keep distracting me with your mouth and body. It's not fair."

Smiling, he stands and holds his hand out for me. Walking into the bathroom, he starts the shower and grabs two towels from the closet.

"Jake, we can't shower together. We'll just end up being in there too long and I'll be late."

"I promise not to touch your sexy body if you promise not to touch mine." He winks, stepping under the hot stream of water.

Shaking my head, I join him, already knowing I won't be able to resist running my hands all over a dripping wet Jake.

Reaching for the body wash, he grabs it first and holds it out to me. When I go to take it, though, Jake doesn't let go. Instead, he pulls it towards him and I stumble into his wet, solid body, his arm wrapping around my waist to steady me.

"You're breaking the rules, mountain man," I say right

before his lips crash down on mine.

"Sorry, couldn't resist," he answers, a smug smile on his face.

Releasing me, he takes the body wash back and squeezes some out for himself, rubbing it all over his arms and chest. I can't look away. Watching him lather his body is one of the sexiest things I've ever seen, and I wish he'd do the same to me, but sadly I have work.

Taking the soap from him, I quickly rub my skin clean and rinse off, my restraint miniscule.

Stepping out, Jake wraps a fluffy towel around me and kisses me sweetly. He gives me another pair of sweat pants and a t-shirt to put on before driving me back home.

"I'll wait for you, darlin'. You go get ready and I'll drive you to work."

"Are you sure?"

"Yes. I'm not ready to let you go yet."

Feeling a blush creep up my cheeks, I jump out of the truck and hurry inside.

Changing quickly, I throw my damp hair up into a bun and apply a light layer of makeup, not needing much with how much my skin is glowing with my newfound happiness. It's weird, but it's like it's literally radiating out of me.

Hurrying back outside, I find Jake leaning against the passenger side door, ready to open it for me.

"You look beautiful as always," he says, kissing my cheek before I climb back into his truck.

Jake takes my hand as soon as we get on the road, and I smile as I look out the window, watching the trees pass in a blur as we head into town.

Pulling into a spot right in front of the café, I unbuckle

my seatbelt and lean over to kiss his cheek. "Thanks for the ride, mountain man." Hopping out, I look back before pushing the café's door open, and see Jake with a small smile on his lips. I really hope the days goes by quick.

"Someone's happy this morning," Courtney says as I'm putting my purse away, making me jump. "Could it have something to do with the hunk who just dropped you off for everyone on Main Street to see? Hmmm…Did someone spend the night together?" She smirks, her hands on her hips.

"Yes, and yes," I answer to both questions.

She squeals and jumps, clapping her hands together. "This makes me so happy! You guys are so cute together!"

"You're awfully chipper this morning," I say, eyeing her.

"Are things going good with you two, then?"

Starting the coffees, I sigh blissfully. "Yes. He's really amazing."

"You're falling in love with him, aren't you?"

Turning around, I fidget with the hem of my shirt and look out the front window. I can see the hardware store from here, and like my mind conjured him, Jake steps out onto the sidewalk, a paper bag in hand. I watch him cross the street, the sun hitting his golden hair like a halo framing his ruggedly handsome face.

"I am," I whisper, not meaning to admit that out loud.

Following where my eyes are looking, she laughs lightly and heads back into the kitchen when she sees Jake getting closer to the café's door.

With the jingle of the bell, he floats inside like a warm summer breeze. "Hey, darlin'," he greets, smiling at me like he hasn't seen me in days.

"Hi," I manage to say back, my mind a mess.

"I'll have a coffee, please."

Nodding, I pour him a cup, and when he goes to pull out money, I shake my head. "It's on me, handsome." I smile.

"Oh, is that another perk of being your man, darlin'?"

"One of many, yes."

"Yes, let's see," he says, holding his hands up to count off on his fingers. "I get to see you naked, kiss every inch of you, fill my hands with your luscious ass, feel you squeeze me inside your tight, hot–"

"Oh my god, you need to shut up," I say, leaning across the counter to cover his mouth with my hand. "Courtney is in the kitchen and I still have to make it through a whole work day."

Smiling behind my hand, he pulls it away. "Feeling hot for me, babe?"

"Yes," I hiss. "Now put some damn cream in your coffee and leave before I do something that will break a million health codes."

Jake throws his head back and laughs. "Oh, darlin', how I'd love to put some of your cream in my coffee."

Slapping my hand to my forehead, I groan. "I meant…never mind. Please hurry and go."

"Alright, I'll stop." He laughs, and I watch him pour a little half and half in his coffee as I walk around the counter to see him out.

Pulling me in close, he whispers, "If only we were alone in here, we could break all the health codes. I'd lift you up on the counter and spread you open, licking your sweet cream."

Moaning at his words, Jake kisses me hard, sliding his tongue across the seam of my lips. I open for him and he dives in, making me forget where we are until a throat clears somewhere in the room and I pull away, my cheeks flushing instantly.

"Well, if only we all could get a kiss like that with our morning coffee." Looking around Jake, I see Alex standing there with a cocky smile.

"Not happening," Jake growls, already knowing who the voice belongs to.

"Hey, just saying. I don't know if she's giving them away to the first customers of the day. If so, I'll have to get here earlier tomorrow."

With a murderous look on his face, Jake turns to Alex. "Stay the fuck away from Ally, got it?"

"What are you, her keeper?" he scoffs.

"No, I'm her man, now order what you want and get out."

"Jesus, Jake, relax. I'm just joking around," Alex says, holding his hands up. "Ally, I'll have a coffee and a Danish, thanks."

"No problem," I say, rounding the counter to make him his coffee and grab a Danish from the case.

Paying, Alex smiles sweetly at me. "Have a nice day, beautiful." He winks, making Jake growl. "Jake, you too," he adds, laughing as he walks out.

"That guy is just asking to be punched in the face."

"Jake, it's fine. He's harmless. So, you're picking me up later?" I ask, trying to change the subject.

Shaking his head, he turns back to me. "Yeah, what time should I be here?"

"She'll be done at six," Courtney answers, coming back out from the kitchen carrying a tray of fresh cookies.

"Alright, see you later, beautiful."

Leaning across the counter, I kiss him quickly. "See you

later, handsome."

"Bye, Jake. You're distracting my employee from her opening duties," Courtney scolds.

Laughing, he backs up until he reaches the door, throwing me a dimpled smile before walking out.

"That boy is so falling for you, too. It's obvious."

"It is?"

"Yes. And that kiss was hot, by the way."

"You were spying?"

"Of course," she scoffs. "You think I'd miss eavesdropping and watching you guys go at it? I wish Jack would stop by so I could jump him. That's how hot it was."

"You're crazy." I laugh, shaking my head.

"Do you have any plans for your days off? Maybe you'd want to go shopping with me?"

"Oh, I'd love to, but I can't. Jake is taking me somewhere."

"Hold up. What? Where is he taking you?"

"He's taking me to his family's house in Bar Harbor for a few days."

"Holy shit, seriously?"

"I was pretty surprised, too. I mean, isn't it too soon for that?"

"Not if you don't think it is."

"I don't know." I shrug. "I'm just really excited to be alone with him for three days."

"I would be too if I were you." She laughs. "Just enjoy yourself. Bar Harbor and Acadia National Park are two of the most beautiful places I've ever been."

"Really?"

"Yeah, you'll love it," she says, fixing the pastries in the case.

"This day needs to go by fast, then." I laugh, heading over to clean the tables.

Thank goodness we were busy today and the day flew by. At six sharp, I see Jake pull up in front of the café, and my heart flutters at just the sight of him.

"Looks like your man is here."

"Mhmm," I hum, picking up the pace of my cleaning so I can run out there and kiss him. I've been thinking about it since he left this morning.

"I can finish up. You go on."

I perk up. "Are you sure?"

"Yes." She laughs. "Don't leave him waiting."

"Thank you, thank you!" I run over and hug her before grabbing my bag and hurrying out the door.

"Have fun!" she yells as the door closes behind me.

Smiling, I open the door of his truck and jump inside. Leaning over the middle console, I cup his cheek and kiss him straight away.

"Miss me?" He laughs.

"Yes," I sigh. "I thought about you all day. I messed up a few orders because I was thinking about kissing you," I confess, caressing his cheek. "And touching you." Leaning in, I plant another chaste kiss to his lips and then sit back in my seat.

"Glad to know I'm not the only one. I almost cut myself while carving because I was thinking about running my hands all over the soft curves of your body, hearing your soft breathy moans in my ear."

"Jake!" I gasp. "Please don't do that. I don't want you hurting yourself."

"Don't worry, darlin'." He smiles. "I won't. I can't help that you're always on my mind, though."

"Sorry I'm so irresistible," I joke, batting my eyes and flipping my hair over my shoulder.

"You are, though," he says, backing out of the spot.

When we pull up to the cottage and get out, Jake reaches into the back seat and takes out a duffle bag I hadn't noticed before.

"What's that for?"

"I'm staying the night with you. I thought we could get an early start tomorrow."

I put my hand on my hip, trying to act offended. "So, you decided to just invite yourself over? That's quite presumptuous, Mr. Taylor. Do you take me for an easy woman?"

"Not at all, darlin'," he says, kissing me quick. "I just knew you wouldn't turn me away."

"Okay," I start, opening the front door. "Just because I can't resist you, doesn't mean—"

Dropping his bag as soon as we enter, Jake spins me around and slams the door closed, pinning me against it.

"It means everything," he states, cupping my cheek and kissing me hard.

Stepping back just as abruptly, Jake picks his bag back up and heads into my room. When I'm able, I peel myself off the door and follow him.

Pulling out my small suitcase, I lay it open on the bed. "What should I pack for our trip?"

"Anything you want. Do you hike?"

"That'd be a firm no."

"Alright, then." He laughs. "Pack whatever you want."

I've never heard a man not tell a woman to pack light. He really is perfect.

"I'll go see what you have in the kitchen and I'll make us something for dinner."

"You're perfect," I say, the words just slipping out before I can catch them.

Laughing, he turns to me before walking out. "I'll make sure to remind you that you said that."

I really need to watch my mouth. I can't be giving away everything I'm thinking.

After packing my suitcase with everything I think I'll need, I head into the kitchen, finding Jake bent over as he puts something in the oven. Mmm, what a sight.

"What did you make?" I ask, walking up behind him and placing my hand on his back.

"Something good, don't worry," he says, kissing my cheek. "Let's sit outside until it's ready."

"Okay." I smile, pouring myself a glass of wine. "Do you want some? I have bourbon, too."

"You do?" he asks, lifting his eyebrows in surprise.

"Yes, mountain man. Us girls do enjoy a nice glass every so often."

"You do? I'll keep that in mind." He smirks as I pour him a few fingers of Maker's Mark.

Settling into the chairs on the back porch, I sip my wine and let it slide down my throat, warming my veins.

Looking out at the water, I see the sky is starting to change colors with the sunset. Good. We're just in time for the show.

When the sun has disappeared below the horizon, and the delicious scent of melting cheese wafts its way out to us, I sigh. "Jake, what did you make? It smells like cheesy heavenly goodness."

Smiling, he stands and takes my hand. "Come on, it should be done."

"But what is it?" I ask eagerly.

Opening the oven, he grabs two pot holders and removes a casserole dish, placing it on the stove.

"Oh. My. God. You made me mac and cheese?!" Jumping up and down, I throw my arms around his neck and kiss him hard. "You really are perfect!" I exclaim.

"You're easy to please." He laughs, shaking his head.

"Yes, I am." I smile. When it involves Jake, it doesn't take much to make me happy.

Grabbing forks from the drawer, I sit at the table while Jake serves up two big plates of his steamy, melty, extra cheesy mac and cheese, and as soon as he puts it down in front of me, I dig right in, not caring if I burn my mouth.

Right away, my eyes roll back and I moan. "Jake, this is sooo good."

I don't even realize how sexual I sound until I hear the clanging of his fork as it falls to his plate.

"Ally, Jesus," he says, voice strained.

Opening my eyes, I see the struggle he's having trying to contain himself, and I wink, going in for another mouthful.

Picking up his fork again, he shakes his head. I can't help that it's so good. He knows I love my food.

I finish my plate in no time, and wait for Jake to be done before I clear the table and wash the dishes. Putting the leftovers in the fridge, we go and sit on the couch to watch some TV.

It almost feels like we've done this a thousand times, and I snuggle into his side and Jake drapes his arm around me. I rest my head against him, and it feels like a space carved out just for me.

I feel my eyes start to droop, and the next thing I know I'm being carried to bed by two strong arms.

Jake places me under the covers and kisses my forehead before leaving the room. Returning a minute later, he gets in on the other side and I throw my arm around him, resting my head on his chest.

Sighing, I fall asleep instantly.

Chapter 16

Waking up in Jake's arms is the best feeling in the world. His big, strong body wrapped around mine makes me feel protected. As much as he riles me up, he also comforts me with his touch.

Sliding his arm off of me, I try and sneak out so I can go to the bathroom, but his arm reaches out and brings me back in. Turning my head, I see that he's not even awake yet.

Smiling, I kiss his arm. "Jake," I whisper, really needing to get up. But he doesn't move.

"Jake," I try again, shaking his arm lightly.

"Mmm," he hums, bringing me even tighter against him. "Don't leave me," he mumbles.

"Jake," I say a little louder, shaking his arm. "I have to get up."

His eyes open slowly, blinking a few times before he focuses on my face.

"I need to get up, Jake," I whisper.

"Oh, sorry," he says in his raspy morning voice.

Scurrying out of bed, I shuffle down the hall to the bathroom and cringe when I see myself in the mirror. I didn't get a chance to take my makeup off last night so now I have raccoon eyes. It's a miracle Jake didn't just get scared when he saw me.

After using the bathroom, I go through my morning routine, and then head into the kitchen to make a pot of coffee.

Pouring two mugs, I add a little cream to both and then head back to my room. Sprawled out on my bed, Jake has one arm behind his head and the other out to the side, the sheets barely covering him. I almost trip, taking in all of the muscles and smooth skin that's just begging for me to touch them.

If I wasn't awake before, I definitely am now.

As I approach the bed slowly, one of Jake's eyes pops open and he smiles sleepily at me. "You made me coffee, darlin'?"

Trying not to spill any of it, I smile and hand him one of the mugs. "I did, handsome."

Taking a sip, he smiles. "It's perfect, babe, thank you."

"You're welcome. What time did you want to head out this morning? It's six now."

"Whenever we're ready. It's about a three-hour drive."

"Okay, I'll finish packing after my coffee."

Sitting back down on the bed, I lean up against the headboard and stretch my legs out, closing my eyes. Reaching out, Jake places his warm hand on my leg, absentmindedly caressing my thigh.

When I finish my coffee, I go to get up, but Jake gently squeezes my leg, stopping me.

"Not yet," he says, sliding his palm up further.

"Jake. I have to get ready."

"Not yet," he repeats, spreading his fingers out.

"We don't have time," I whisper, kissing his cheek and moving his hand off of me.

Swinging my legs over the edge, I stand up and feel a sting flash across my right cheek.

Gasping, I spin around. "No time, Jake! But try that again later and we'll see what happens." I wink, blowing him a kiss as I sway my hips a little extra as I walk out of the room, hearing his low laugh follow me.

I find my phone on the coffee table in the living room and check my messages. Damn, there's twenty-five new texts in the group chat. Reading through them, I laugh out loud at the absurdity of my friends. Ashley was texting all about her latest dating disaster where the guy was supposed to be a tall and hot businessman, but turned out to be a below average balding accountant. This is probably the fifth date that's turned out horrible for her on that app.

Texting back my sympathies, I also tell them that I'm going away with Jake for a few days and to not be offended if I don't answer them.

To my surprise, my phone starts vibrating in my hand and I see Melanie's name flash on my screen. Swiping to answer, I walk out onto the porch for privacy.

"Hey, Mel, you're up early."

"My shift starts at 7 so I'm about to leave the house." Ah, yes, nursing hours. "But then you dropped that little bomb on us and I had to call you. You're going on a trip with him?"

"Yes," I tell her, the smile evident in my voice.

"Ally, that's a big deal."

"He's amazing, Mel. He's all I think about, and I want to spend every free second I have with him. I know that sounds crazy and fast, but…"

"It's not crazy, Ally. I'm so happy for you. I called so I could hear it in your voice that you're good. I hope we get to meet this man of yours soon. We need to make sure he's good enough."

"I think I can judge that by now." I laugh. "But yes, you guys can meet him soon. I was thinking, if you can get off of work for MDW, I'd love for you to come up here."

"I actually have that weekend off on my schedule already, so it works for me."

"Yay! Okay, I'll message the group and see if Ash and Ellie can get off too."

"Sounds good. Alright, I have to head out now or I'll be late. Love you, see you soon."

"Love you, too."

Hanging up, I send out a group text about next weekend and then text my mom as well, letting her know everything's going well up here and that I'll call her later.

I miss her. I really hope she's doing okay on her own.

Sitting back in the chair, I listen to the rain that's gently falling. Hopefully the weather will be nice a little more north, but I also don't mind the rain. It's calming.

I head back in after a few minutes, and almost run smack dab into a shirtless Jake.

"I was wondering where you went," he says, looking me over like I might be hurt.

"I just went out to talk to Mel and text a few people. Why, were you worried I was carried off by a bear?"

"No." He smiles, wrapping his arms around my waist.

"I would have called for you to save me anyhow."

He kisses me softly, nibbling my bottom lip between his teeth. "I'd save you from anything."

Swooning, I brace myself on his arms and lean up on my toes to kiss him fully, pressing my whole body into him.

Pulling away slightly, I spread my hands out on his chest and look into his swirling ocean eyes. "I'd save you, too, you know. You're not invincible, even if you look like you are."

He stares at me with a look in his eyes that I can't decipher. Kissing me again, I feel it all the way down to my toes.

"Okay, okay, let's hurry and get on the road, no more kissing." I smile, pushing him away playfully.

"We'll see." He slaps my ass as I walk past him, and I rub the sting out, shaking my head with a smile.

After gathering the rest of my things, Jake takes our bags out to the truck while I walk through the house to make sure all of the windows and doors are lock before meeting him out front. I doubt there's much crime here in Pine Cove, but the Jersey in me has me being extra cautious. This is still Dottie's house after all.

"Ready?"

"Yes, road trip!" I exclaim, clapping my hands.

Laughing, he opens the passenger door for me. "Are you a fan?"

"Of road trips? Yes. Just give me the open road, good music, and snacks. The snacks are vital."

"Hmm, good to know."

"But I've also never gone on one with a handsome man before, so I'm guessing it's even better."

"Flattery will get you all the snacks you want, darlin'."

"I'll rain compliments on you all day then."

"Not necessary. I already know you think I'm perfect."

Laughing, I lean over and kiss his cheek. "Okay, I'll limit my praises for you. But I'll still need snacks."

"I wouldn't dream of denying you anything." He smiles, pulling out of the driveway. Jake takes my hand like usual, and I'm struck with an overwhelming feeling.

I've gotten used to him.

I've never, not once, in my life been completely comfortable, or myself, around a man. But with Jake, I am. I don't think twice about reaching out to touch him or leaning in to kiss him. With every other guy, I always did. I second guessed everything and was hesitant to initiate anything. But with Jake, it feels like the most natural thing in the world. It feels right.

Looking out the window, I watch the raindrops slide down the glass, blurring the world outside.

The first two hours pass, and true to his word, Jake has supplied me with all the snacks I wanted when we made our first rest stop.

"Have you been painting?" he asks, his eyes darting to mine.

"Yes. I actually started one last week that's coming along pretty well."

He squeezes my hand. "That's great, darlin'."

"It's of the cottage. Ever since I first saw it, I knew I had to paint it. The colors are so vibrant, and it radiates the feeling of home. Wherever I go after, I want to always be able to look at the painting and remember how being there made me feel."

"Do you plan on leaving?" he asks, his hand tightening on the steering wheel.

"No. I just mean that I'm only renting from Dottie. Her or her family may want to sell it one day."

"True." He nods, his body relaxing.

"I love it here. In Pine Cove, I mean. Everyone I've met has been so nice and I feel more myself here than I ever have before. It's freeing – moving to a new place and not knowing anyone."

"Well, Pine Cove definitely got a hundred times more beautiful when you arrived."

"Was there no one before me to make it beautiful for you?" I was only joking, but his body tenses, and his hand on the steering wheel tightens to the point where his knuckles start turning white.

"No. There wasn't."

Okay, that was a lie.

"You can talk to me, Jake," I say in a calm voice, but he just tightens his hand further, to the point where I think he's going to cut off all circulation. "Hey, Jake, relax. You don't have to talk about it. Just forget I asked," I tell him, smoothing my hand up and down his forearm.

I watch as his hand starts to loosen its grip on the wheel, the color slowly coming back to his fingers. Thank God. I thought he was going to break the damned thing.

Slowing down, Jake pulls the truck over to the shoulder of the road we're on.

"What's wrong? Is the truck okay?"

Unbuckling his seatbelt, he reaches over and does the same to mine.

"Jake?" I ask, confused. I look into his eyes, but I can't read them. The blue is darkening, swirling.

"Come here," he rasps.

Tucking my legs up, he grabs my waist and helps me over the console so I'm straddling him. Brushing my fingertips across his cheeks, I lean down and press my lips against his. Soft at first, until he pulls me tighter against him and I sigh into the kiss, our tongues coming together in that slow dance we do so well.

He needs this. He needs me to make whatever he was thinking about go away. He may not be ready to talk, but I can give him this. I can give him me.

Resting my forehead against his, I try and catch my breath. "Are we far?" I whisper.

"Ten minutes."

"Hurry." Kissing him hard, I press my whole body against him.

Tearing myself away, I climb back over to my seat and buckle up so I'm not tempted to jump him right here and now.

Pulling back out onto the road, Jake hits the gas and gets us there in only eight minutes.

Throwing the truck in park, we both jump out together. I'm definitely not waiting for him to open my door this time. Jake grabs my hand and pulls me towards the door, fumbling with his keys until he finally gets it open.

Pushing me inside, he slams the door closed behind us and hoists me over his shoulder, running up a set of stairs and down a hallway before throwing me down on the bed. Bouncing once, I watch as he whips off his clothes.

"Darlin', you're going to have to strip right now or I'm ripping those clothes right off of you."

"You distracted me with your nakedness."

Flashing me a wolfish smile, Jake places his hand on himself, stroking once, twice. "Hurry, I need you, darlin'."

Peeling my top and bra off as fast as I can, Jake reaches out and slides my sneakers off before pulling down my leggings in one swift motion.

He grabs a condom from his jeans, and I sit up and take it from him. "Let me." Ripping it open, I roll it down his length, loving the sharp intake of breath I hear the moment I touch him.

Pushing me back onto the bed, Jake climbs on top of me and I open for him immediately. He slides into me in one swift move.

Grabbing a fistful of sheets, I arch off the bed and Jake takes my left nipple into his mouth, sucking hard. I let out a strangled cry, feeling the pull all the way to my core.

I dig my nails into his shoulders, needing more from him.

Going back and forth between my breasts, Jake sucks my nipples deep into his mouth, bites down, and then smooths them out with his tongue.

My breathy moans turn to cries as I grab a fistful of his hair, pulling as hard as I can to bring his lips to mine, needing to taste his sweet mouth.

Wrapping my arms around his neck, I hook my legs around his waist and use all of my strength to roll us over. I smile down at Jake as I brace my hands on his chest, spreading my fingers wide. I can feel his heart is beating faster than I've ever felt before, and I look into his eyes, seeing his emotions swirling around.

Lifting myself up as far as I can, I drop back down, feeling every single thick inch of him stretching me. I lose myself in him, keeping my pace slow so I can savor every jolt of electricity that runs down my legs and up my spine with every stroke.

My body shudders, my nerve endings frayed.

My legs are shaking, but I keep pushing myself up, meeting Jake on my way down. With one last drag, I fall onto him with all of my weight, feeling the sparks fan out across my skin before my body explodes around him and my eyes roll back.

Somewhere in my bliss, Jake rolls us over so he's on top. "You looked so fucking sexy taking everything you needed from me, baby, but now it's my turn."

Pulling out, he flips me over and lifts my hips, slamming back into me. Moaning, I grip the comforter as Jake pounds into me with an uncontrolled passion.

Another orgasm builds in me as he takes what he needs from me, holding nothing back.

Bringing me closer to the edge of a cliff with every stroke, Jake keeps pushing me until I'm suddenly thrown off. My screams are muffled as waves crash over me – the most beautiful of storms dragging me under to where all I see is black.

Chapter 17

I start to come to when I feel something slide up and down my arm. Rolling towards the heat next to me, I curl up against a solid wall of muscles.

Fingers dance up and down my spine and I arch into it like a cat, purring and moving closer to the source.

"Ally," a husky voice whispers in my ear.

"Mmm?"

"It's time to get up."

"Mmm."

"I want to take you somewhere."

"Take me somewhere?" I mumble.

"Yeah, come on, we need food."

Kisses pepper my face and I sigh. "Yes, please feed me.

I'm famished."

Jake slaps my ass and my eyes shoot open. "I knew that'd wake you right up." He smiles, rubbing the sting out of my cheek.

"You just love my ass, don't you?"

"What's not to love? It's like a round, juicy peach that's just for me – ripe and ready to bite into."

"Jake, if you bite my ass, I swear I'll do the same to you."

A mischievous gleam in his eyes comes right before he flips me over and licks my left cheek, biting into it. My muffled moans are swallowed up by the pillow in my face, my body automatically arching into him, demanding more.

Smoothing his palms over my round globes, he kneads the flesh, groaning.

Turning my head, I look back at him just in time to see him lick my right cheek before biting into it. Moaning even louder, his eyes meet mine with a burning fire.

"The sweetest peach I've ever tasted." He hums, slapping each of my cheeks again so they're stinging with his marks.

Wiggling out from his reach, I sit up and crawl over to him, pushing him face down on the bed. "When I called you to come and fix my fake broken oven, I watched you walk into the kitchen, and all I could think about was how sexy your ass looked in your jeans. Now here I am," I say, smoothing my palms over his rock-solid globes. "And it's even better than I imagined."

Squeezing him, I return the same lick and bite on each of his cheeks, hearing him groan into the pillows. Jake tries to lift himself up, but I push him down again. I'm not finished yet.

Kissing my way up his spine, I massage his back as I go. Jake sighs with every muscle I loosen, and groans after every lick and kiss I give him.

Straddling his hips, I continue to massage his back, feeling him relax under my touch. I run my fingers through his hair, scratching my nails against his scalp, and tugging on his ends.

"Baby," he mumbles into the pillow. Turning his head, I meet his eyes. "I knew your hands were magic."

Smiling, I kiss the center of his back and crawl off of him. "Now you need to feed me. Your peach wasn't ripe enough. Too hard."

His deep, throaty laugh fills my ears. "Alright, darlin', go get ready and I'll meet you downstairs. If we shower together, we'll never leave. I'll go get your bag and leave it on the bed for you."

"Thanks." I smile, blowing him a kiss before I close the bathroom door.

Stepping out of the bathroom after a hot shower, I find my suitcase sitting on the bed. I have no idea where we're going, but I look out the window and see sunshine, so I decide to put on a pretty maxi dress and wedges.

Drying my hair, I twist it up into a high bun and apply my makeup. I add earrings and a necklace and give myself a small smile in the mirror before heading downstairs, stopping when I reach the bottom and come face-to-face with an extraordinary view.

I didn't see this when Jake was running me up the stairs earlier. Sliding glass doors lead out onto a deck that extends out over the water where I can see islands in the distance and mountains lining the horizons to the left and right.

Pulling my eyes away, I turn and walk through the kitchen and into the living room where Jake is sitting and watching TV.

When he looks up, his eyes slowly rake up and down my

body. "You look beautiful," he praises, standing up and kissing my cheek.

"Thanks." I smile. "You don't look so bad yourself."

"After you, darlin'." Placing his hand at the small of my back, he leads me outside and opens the passenger door for me.

"This house is amazing, Jake," I tell when he gets in behind the wheel. "Has your family always had it? Did you come here as kids?"

"My parents bought it before they had us, and then slowly updated it over the years. I always loved coming here. I'd go on hikes with my dad and brothers in the park, or we'd go fishing and then cook up what we caught for dinner."

"Sounds fun." I smile. "For people who like those things, I mean."

"Fishing's not your thing either?"

"I've never been, but the thought of touching fish is gross."

"Well, we'll just stay away from hiking and fishing then. I can think of a better use of our time anyway." He grins.

"Me too." I smile. "So, where are we going?"

"To my favorite local. The food is good and they have all this Maine and fishing stuff on the walls. They're always packed."

"They better not be. I could eat a cow."

"Don't worry. They shouldn't be tonight."

On the drive into town, we pass a lot of inns and bed and breakfasts that really sell me on the quaintness of Bar Harbor. Driving along one of the main streets in downtown, I look out at the people walking about and the different shops and restaurants that line both sides of the road.

Coming to the top of a small hill in the road, I'm able to look straight out at the harbor in front of me. The sun glints off the surface of the water where boats of all sizes sway in the current, and islands covered in pine trees sit not too far offshore.

"This would make such a beautiful painting," I tell him, trying to take it all in.

"See over there?" He points. "They charter boats for whale watching."

"I love whales." I smile.

"And next to it is another great restaurant. I thought we could go there tomorrow." He points to a restaurant that rests on a pier that extends far out into the water. Half of it is enclosed, and half is outdoor patio seating with a small ramp that extends off the side, leading down to a dock where a few picnic tables sit. It looks like the perfect place to sit for an afternoon lunch on a nice day.

"I'd love to go there, Jake. Eating on the water is my favorite."

"Did you want to go tonight?"

"No, no. I want to go to your favorite place," I assure him.

Parking near the water, Jake takes my hand and leads us back up the main road. "It's just right up there." He points to a place with a giant light up moose on its roof and lobster claws coming off the front façade.

"Oh my god, Jake, it looks so cute!" I exclaim, squeezing his hand and leaning into his side.

"Great. I'm glad you find it cute," he says sarcastically.

"Oh, shut it."

A sign hangs off the side of the building that reads The Claw. Cute name, too. Jake opens the door for me, and I step through, smiling right away. This place is definitely cute. The walls are covered in license plates, signs, surf boards, lobster traps, and all kinds of other Maine themed stuff.

"Definitely not cute. It's very masculine," I tell him, fighting a smile.

Shaking his head, I see his lips twitch as he walks up to the hostess stand. "Table for two, please."

"No problem, follow me." Grabbing two menus, the young girl leads us through a sea of tables, past the bar, and over to the back corner. The windows to our right showcase a small hidden alley with shops, and to the left is an open view into the kitchen. Line cooks stand laughing and moving about as they plate food.

I can already see why it's Jake's favorite place.

Opening the menu, I see what I want straight away, so when the waiter comes, I order a blueberry mojito and fish and chips.

Jake and I spend the whole dinner talking about his family, and I'm happy he's actually sharing with me. I do make sure to stay away from all topics involving women, though. I'm not ruining our trip by prying into his past when he's not ready to talk about. I know no one could ever force me to talk about my past if I didn't want to.

When it's time for dessert, my choice is a no brainer, and I order a slice of fresh, warm, blueberry pie and ice cream with an Irish coffee.

"I seriously love everything blueberry," I say, moaning as I eat another forkful of pie. "And I love how every place in Maine has it on their menus."

When our waiter comes by to check on us, Jake says something to him that I can't hear and asks for the check.

Looking at me, he just smiles and winks. "I ordered something to-go so I can hear you make those noises again."

Blushing, I finish my pie. "Well, that's embarrassing."

"Babe, you're sexy no matter what. I love how much you love food."

"Jake!"

The waiter comes back quickly with the check and hands Jake a bag. Standing, he holds his hand out for me to take. "Come on. Let's walk a little. I promise I won't bring up your expressive eating again."

"You better not," I say sternly.

Weaving our way back through the crowded restaurant, we step out into the warm evening air. The sky is still light with the sun not yet set.

Crossing the street, we go right, and I stop at the pretty fountain on the corner. Digging through my purse, I try and find a coin to toss in.

"What are you doing?"

"Looking for a coin so I can make a wish."

Reaching into his pocket, Jake pulls out a quarter for me. "Thanks."

Letting go of his hand, I turn around so my back is to the fountain, and toss the coin over my shoulder, making my wish. Ever since I was young, I've always wished for the same thing whenever I had to. Birthdays, 11:11, fountains, going over train tracks. I've only ever wanted to be happy. Truly happy.

When I open my eyes, I look over at Jake. "Did it go in?"

"Yes." He nods. "What did you wish for?"

"If I tell you, then it won't come true."

Leaning down, Jake gives me a soft, sweet kiss that leaves my stomach in butterflies. Maybe my wish is finally starting to come true after 28 years.

Walking on, we stroll through a small park that's on top of the hill that overlooks the harbor, and then down the sidewalk past a few more shops before crossing the street to walk along the water.

Passing the whale watching and waterfront restaurant Jake had pointed out earlier, he leads me over to a ramp near where we parked that extends down to a freestanding floating dock.

"Jake, that doesn't look safe." The ramp is long, thin, and swaying in the breeze as the dock rocks back and forth in the water's current. "I think I'd fall right in."

Stepping onto the ramp, he turns around and holds his hands out to me. "Trust me?" he asks, his eyes serious, showing me that he means more than just right now.

"Of course, I do. But–"

"No buts. I'd never let anything bad happen to you, Ally."

He called me Ally.

Looking into his eyes, I search for the truth in his words, and I don't have to look far. It's written right there. I know he'd never let me fall, and I know he'd rescue me if I did.

I do trust him, and that's not easy for me.

Placing my hand in his, he envelopes mine and holds tight. "Just take one step forward. I'm here to keep you steady."

Nervous, I take a small step onto the shaky ramp. Facing me, Jake walks backwards as I take small steps with him, clinging to his hand.

This is definitely not safe. The ramp is moving around with the current, and if it weren't for Jake, I know I would have lost my balance and have fallen into the water already.

"Jake," I say, my voice shaky.

"I got you," he whispers when we finally reach the dock,

wrapping his arms around my waist.

Looking up at his handsome face, I trace his cheek with my fingers, feeling his smile. Running my finger over the dip in his cheek, I circle it, loving his sexy dimple.

Leaning down, Jake captures my lips with his, and a fire immediately spreads through me. Running my hands through his hair, I wrap my arms around his neck and pull him as close as possible.

But I forget where we are and I feel the dock beneath me rock, our kiss broken as I start to lose my balance. I let out a little scream, and Jake steadies me, laughing.

"Jake!" I yell, slapping his chest. "Oh my god, we're going to fall in! Why is this thing so freaking small?"

"I told you I got you, darlin'," he says simply.

"I know, but I don't want to distract you and then we fall in."

"And how would you distract me?"

"With my amazing kisses, obviously," I say, making him laugh, the sweet sound vibrating through me.

He smiles down at me, and I melt into his arms. "I'm going to turn you around so you can see the view. But I've got you, so don't worry."

Slowly, Jake spins me until I'm facing the harbor and I gasp. "Wow," I breathe. "It's different down here. I feel like I'm a part of the water. Like I could just reach out and touch that island over there."

Holding me tight against him, Jake rests his chin on top of my head. We stand here for a long while as the sun slowly disappears behind us.

"We should go," he says, loosening his hold on me.

Gripping my hips from behind, he guides me back up the

ramp to the safety of solid ground.

Back in the truck, Jake pulls out of the lot and drives down another main street so I can see the different shops and restaurants on this one, too. I hope we can walk around tomorrow so I can look in a few of these places.

The drive back to the house isn't long, and when we park in the driveway, Jake turns to me, a nervous look on his face.

"What's wrong?"

"Nothing," he says. "I just want to show you something." Getting out, he comes around and opens my door.

Walking into the house, Jake takes me over to a closed door off of the living room. "Open it," he urges, letting go of my hand.

Tentatively, I place my hand on the knob and twist. Pushing the door open, I freeze when I see what's behind it.

My mind races with a million thoughts before it all clears away, and only one thing repeats over and over.

I'm in love with Jake Taylor.

"Jake…" I whisper, stepping into the bedroom.

He doesn't say anything as I walk over to the bed and run my fingers over one of the new canvases laid out on top. There are all different sizes here, along with a new palette, brushes, and what looks like twenty tubes of paint. An easel and stool are set up by the window with a view of the mountains and water.

"Jake…" I whisper again, feeling the soft bristles of the new brushes.

Turning around, I look up at him, and tears I didn't even know had formed start to fall from my eyes.

He walks over and brushes them away gently. "Did I buy the wrong supplies?" he asks, thinking I'm crying because he got something wrong.

"No." I shake my head. "It's all perfect. I can't believe you did this. When did you do this?"

"I brought it all with me and set it up when you were getting ready earlier."

Grabbing his shirt, I pull him down and kiss him hard. I need him to know how I feel, but I can't say the words yet.

I can't tell him I love him, but I can show him.

And that's exactly what I do for the next few hours.

I show him over and over again how I feel without saying the words. I've never felt my heart swell to this capacity before and know that there's still more room to love.

At some point during the night, Jake opens the to-go box from dinner and pulls out a blueberry whoopie pie. Breaking it in half, he holds a piece up to my mouth and I bite into it, moaning instantly.

"My favorite sound," he says, licking the filling left behind on my lips.

Chapter 18

Kisses pepper my face as I slowly blink my eyes open in a dark room.

"Time to wake up, darlin'."

"What time is it?" I mumble.

"Four."

"In the morning?"

"Yes."

"Then it's not time to wake up. The sun's not even up."

"That's the point," he says, pulling the covers back.

"Jake!"

"Come on, I want to take you somewhere."

"Where?"

"To see the sunrise. I promise you'll love it."

"Okay, fine." I pout, sitting up and throwing my legs over the side of the bed. "But you better be making me coffee."

"Of course, darlin'. Do I look stupid?"

I give him a look. "That's debatable."

Taking a quick shower to wake myself up, I throw on yoga pants, a t-shirt, and a sweatshirt. Brushing my hair out, I make a long braid down my back and dab some concealer under my eyes to look a little more human. But that's it. I don't have the energy to do anything more.

The smell of fresh, strong coffee starts to waft upstairs, and I quickly grab my sneakers before following the scent of my soul.

Walking into the kitchen, I find Jake pouring coffee into two thermoses with a mug already waiting for me on the counter. Taking a sip, I sigh, letting the caffeine spread through my body.

"So, where are we going?"

"You'll see."

I take a few more gulps of earth's greatest crop and put my empty mug in the sink. "Alright, I'm ready," I announce, and we head out.

I shove my hands into the pockets of my sweatshirt to try and keep the chilly morning air away as Jake tosses a duffel bag into the back seat.

"What's in there?" I ask, climbing up inside.

"Just a couple of blankets."

"We'll need blankets?"

"Yes, we're going to the top of a mountain."

"Jake," I groan. "I told you I don't hike."

Chuckling softly, he shakes his head as he starts the truck and makes his way down the dark roads. "We're not hiking up a mountain. And if we were, we wouldn't do it in the dark, or even be there in time for sunrise."

"Okay, good. And don't be a smartass." I slap his arm. "You just woke me up in the middle of the night and my mind isn't awake yet."

"My apologies, darlin'." He smiles.

We drive for a few minutes before coming up on the Acadia National Park entrance sign, and I sit up a little straighter, wishing it was light out so I could see everything that's out there.

Winding through the darkened park, we eventually come upon a sign that has an arrow pointing to the left for Cadillac Mountain.

"We can drive up the mountain?"

"Yes. I told you we weren't hiking, but you'll still be joining the Cadillac Sunrise Club."

"Okay?"

"The top of Cadillac Mountain is where the sun's rays first touch the East Coast in the morning."

"Really?" I ask, excited.

Nodding, he squeezes my hand and then lets go so he can focus on maneuvering up the mountain.

"I didn't know mountains have parking lots," I say with a laugh when we reach the top.

"This one does. Along with a bathroom and gift shop."

"Seriously?"

"Yeah, that way everyone can enjoy the view, not just hikers."

"Well, thank goodness for that."

Grabbing his duffel from the back, Jake guides us with a flashlight up onto a small path that we follow until he finds the perfect smooth rock outcrop.

Spreading a blanket out, he sits and pats the spot between his legs for me. I settle against him, and Jake pulls out the other blanket and drapes it over our legs.

He hands me one of the thermoses, and I take a sip of the hot, delicious coffee. "You've thought of everything," I say, snuggling into him when the wind blows, his arms tightening around me.

I rest my head against his chest, feeling safe in his arms. I close my eyes briefly, soaking up the warmth of Jake.

"It's starting," he whispers, kissing my hair.

Opening my eyes, I smile, seeing the sky start to lighten with predawn. And with the sky lightening, I'm able to see down the mountain and out across the Atlantic Ocean.

It's breathtaking.

When the first sliver of the sun emerges from the horizon, its rays shoot out across the ocean to us.

"And there you have it," Jake whispers. "The first rays greet us. Your beautiful face is the first thing they get to touch this morning."

Smiling, I tilt my head up and kiss his chin.

The sun continues to rise, lighting up the world around us and bringing color to everything it touches.

"This is amazing, Jake. Thank you."

"Anything for you," he says, kissing my hair.

Smiling to myself, he can't see the tears that prick my eyes at his words. "I need to paint this," I sigh.

"That's why I made you a little setup in the house. I want you to always be able to paint whenever, and wherever you want. If you want to, you can."

"Thank you," I whisper. "You have no idea how much

that means to me."

"I don't want you to ever feel like you can't let yourself be free to feel and create," he says, his arms tightening around me.

He just wants me to be me, and I just fell a little more in love with him.

Sitting for another twenty or so minutes, we watch the sun fully emerge from the ocean and greet us good morning. I take in everything I see, memorizing it for later.

Standing up, we walk around the paths, seeing the view from every angle. The north side has an amazing view of Bar Harbor and the circular islands that dot the ocean, while the east and south views show the rolling hillside of the mountain that bleeds out into the Atlantic. I make sure to take plenty of pictures so I can recreate this later.

"I think I could be up here all day and it still wouldn't be enough."

"Well, I was going to take you to breakfast, but I guess we could stay all day if you want. I think the giftshop has some sweets to keep us going."

"Okay, smartass, I didn't mean literally. I'm starving, actually."

"I know. I can hear your stomach from here."

"Well, come on, feed me."

"Yes, ma'am." Capturing my lips quickly, he starts to lead us back to the truck when a thought strikes me.

"Wait," I say, pulling on his hand so he stops. "Can we take a picture first?"

Smiling, Jake takes a step back towards me. "You want to take a picture with me, darlin'?"

Swallowing, I nod.

"Okay, let's ask someone."

Looking around, Jake goes up to a man and hands him my phone.

"Come here, darlin'." Jake pulls me close and I wrap my arm around him, smiling.

"Thank you," I tell the man after he takes a few pictures and hands me back my phone. I slip it into my pocket straight away, not wanting to look at them yet. I don't want to hate the fact that Jake will look sexy as hell and I'll look like a tired mess next to him.

Getting back in his truck, we wind our way back down the mountain and I all but press my face to the window to take in the view now that it's light out. This place is incredible.

Back in town, Jake parks by the water again and we make our way up the street like last night. Except this time, when we're halfway up, we turn down what seems like a sketchy alley, but then it opens up into a courtyard of businesses.

"Whoa, that's not what I was expecting," I say, looking around.

"I know. It's a hidden spot you have to know is here." Jake points to the wall of windows behind me. A breakfast café called The Wild Blueberry.

"Well I love the name." I laugh. "I hope there's blueberry pancakes."

"I'd say that's a safe bet."

Walking in, I smile. It looks just like Luke's Diner from Gilmore Girls, one of my favorite shows.

The smell of coffee and syrup makes my stomach grumble, and Jake looks down and smiles, hearing it himself.

"Table for two," he tells the hostess.

"Follow me," she says, grabbing two menus and leading us to a small table by the window. "Your waiter will be right over."

"Thank you."

Opening the menu, I see the holy grail of blueberry breakfasts. Pancakes, muffins, French toast, waffles, and even syrup.

"Hi, I'm Dan," the waiter says. "Can I start you off with something to drink?"

"I'll have coffee, please."

"Same," Jake adds.

"I actually know what I want to eat, too," I tell him, but look over at Jake. "Do you?"

He nods. "Go ahead."

"I'll have the blueberry pancakes with blueberry syrup. And then a toasted blueberry muffin on the side, please."

"And I'll have blueberry French toast with a toasted blueberry muffin as well."

"Okay, I'll be right back with your coffees."

"Thank you."

"They're famous for their muffins, actually," Jake tells me when the waiter leaves.

"Well, I could eat the whole kitchen right now, so I hope they're quick."

Laughing, he shakes his head and the waiter comes back with our coffees. Taking a sip, I sigh, letting the hot liquid warm my insides. The top of the mountain was surprisingly cold, and I finished the thermos Jake made me within the first few minutes.

Thankfully, our food only takes ten minutes to come out, and I practically inhale the plate.

"This is so good," I moan around a full mouth.

"Hey, babe. Let's keep the moaning down."

"Shut up," I tell him. "And you said you wouldn't mention my expressive eating again."

"I forgot." He shrugs.

"No, you didn't. You just love making fun of me."

"It's not making fun, darlin'. I told you it's sexy. It makes me think of sex."

"Okay, be quiet." I laugh. "Not here."

Finishing everything in record time, I sip my coffee and wait for Jake – the one of us who actually eats at a normal pace.

"Can we walk around a little when you're finished? I'd like to maybe buy a souvenir or something."

"Of course. Anything you want."

"Hmm, good to know," I say, lifting my mug to my lips to hide my smile.

When Jake is done, I steal the check and go up to the register to pay before he can protest.

"I said I was taking you to breakfast, darlin'."

"Well, too bad. Now I took you to breakfast." I smirk.

Smiling, he shakes his head and we head outside. Going into a couple of shops, I buy postcards, a shot glass, a t-shirt, and even a Christmas ornament from a year-round Christmas store. Now, that's my kind of store.

Taking my bags, Jake holds my hand as we continue on down the street. Passing cute shop after cute shop, we turn down a side street, but it turns out to only have B&Bs and Inns on it.

"Should we go back?"

"No, there's something down here I want to show you."

Walking to the end of the block, we cross the street, and start down a little gravel road. At the end, there's a little sliver of sand and rocks, and then it's just water. The harbor flowing right in front of us.

"See the island across the way?" he asks, pointing in front of us. "When the tide is low, a path forms from here to the island, and you can just walk right across."

"Seriously? I can't picture that right now."

"Yeah, but you have to make it back again before high tide or you'll be stuck over there for twelve hours until the next low tide."

"That'd be a nightmare. I'd be starving!"

"That would be your first thought." He laughs. "Not shelter or water or a bathroom."

"Well, yeah, but you'd figure that out for us." I shrug, leaning into him.

"Of course," he says, wrapping his arm around me. "We'll drive by tomorrow and see if we can catch low tide."

"I'd love to see that," I say as we head back to his truck.

Reaching it, I turn and look up at him. "Do you mind if I spend some time painting this afternoon?"

"You never have to ask me that, darlin'. I will never mind," he says, placing a finger under my chin. Tilting my head up, he kisses me gently, but I press up on my toes and grab his shirt, leaning into the kiss, and loving the warmth that spreads through me.

Pulling back, I bite my lower lip and smile. "Good."

On the ride back to the house, I keep my window open to feel the fresh air on my face. I can't wait to let everything I'm feeling out on a canvas. I've never seen a sunrise like that.

"I'm going to go out on the water for a little bit," Jake tells me when we're inside the house. "You go do your thing, for however long you want. Call me if you need anything."

"Thanks," I say, kissing his cheek.

Walking into my painting room, I smile. I can't believe he did this for me. Feeling a pang in my heart, I rub my chest. No one has ever given me something so thoughtful before.

I decide on a medium sized canvas and place it on the easel by the window. Digging through all of the paints, I pick out the colors I know I'll need and squeeze out a little of each onto my palette.

Grabbing a brush, I sit on the stool and take a deep breath in. Swiping my brush through the blue paint, I make the first stroke on the blank canvas, and the world around me disappears.

I don't know how long I sit here painting, but minutes turn to hours, and it's only when my stomach growls that I decide it's time for a break.

Putting the brush down, I walk over to the attached bathroom, and wash the paint off of my hands before going in search of Jake. I find him in the kitchen, and I walk up behind him at the stove, placing my hand on his back.

"Grilled cheese?" I smile. "You've discovered my weakness for cheese."

"How's your painting coming?" He asks, kissing my cheek.

"Good. It's coming along well."

"Am I allowed to see it?"

"Not yet. Maybe later."

"Are you hungry?"

"You already know I'm starving. That's why I came out here."

"I guess I can read your mind." Turning off the stove, he wraps his arms around me and leans down. "And your body, too," he whispers against my lips.

Taking my bottom lip between his teeth, he nibbles, and I moan softly into him. Sliding my hands up his arms and around his neck, I pull him down, needing to taste him.

Licking the seam of his lips, he groans and opens for me. Moving his hands down my sides, he picks me up and sets me on the counter, stepping between my legs.

Running my fingers through his hair, I pull on the ends, knowing he loves when I do it. Groaning into my mouth, Jake slips his hands under my sweatshirt, his fingers leaving a trail of fire everywhere he touches.

He unclasps my bra and runs his hands up and down my back, down my sides, and up my stomach to palm my breasts. Kneading my flesh, he pinches my nipples between his fingers and I moan, biting his lip as I throw my head back, not able to focus on anything but how he's making me feel.

"You're so beautiful when you're like this," he rasps. "You give in to me fully. And knowing I'm the one giving you everything you need makes me harder than I've ever been in my life."

Shoving my sweatshirt and t-shirt up just enough to expose my breasts, he replaces his hands with his mouth, and my ears go deaf to the pleas and cries I'm making.

"Jake," I moan. "Please…more…" I can't even think straight, but I know he can give me more.

Then his hand is there, feeling me through my yoga pants.

"Is this where you need me, baby?" he growls.

"Yes," I hiss. I try to move my hips into him, but he holds me still, rubbing circles around me through the thin fabric of my pants until I'm all but ready to explode.

Then he stops.

"Jake! Please!"

Putting his hand back, he tortures me again and again until I'm begging him for release. Lifting me off of the counter, he runs up the stairs and throws me on the bed, immediately stripping out of his clothes and ripping mine off of me.

Climbing on top of me, he spreads my thighs and settles between my legs, kissing me deep into the pillows.

Lifting my hips, I feel him right there, only needing a little push.

"Ally, I want to feel you," Jake whispers, kissing me behind my ear and down my neck.

"Yes," I sigh, needing him.

Resting his forehead on mine, I stare into his beautiful stormy eyes. "Will you let me feel you? With nothing between us?"

"I want to feel you," I whisper.

"Are you–"

"Yes. But I've never–"

"Me either."

"I trust you," I whisper, running my fingers across his cheek, pushing his hair away from his face.

His eyes change at my words, and my heart pounds double-time.

Kissing me slow, Jake starts to push into me. "Ally," he groans. "You feel amazing." Licking up the column of my neck, he bites down as he thrusts forward, giving me all of him.

Arching off the bed, I cry out, gripping his arms.

Pulling out almost completely, he thrusts forward again, filling me to the hilt.

He tortures me with the slow burn until neither of us can take it anymore and he starts to move faster.

I wrap my legs around him and claw at his back, a fire

building in my core that moves up my spine until I can't hold off much longer.

"Not yet," he growls. "Too good."

"Please!" I cry, needing to give in.

Jake kisses me, swallowing my pleas as I rake my nails down his back.

Groaning into my mouth, he pulls back and looks into my glazed over eyes. "Now," he commands.

Letting go, I fall over the edge as wave after wave comes crashing over me, and Jake howls out his own release, my body squeezing him for everything he has.

It's never been like this.

I feel him filling me, claiming me.

Falling on top of me, Jake's weight feels like a blanket of strength. He breathes into my neck and rolls us over so I'm half draped over him. Interlocking our legs, I throw my arm over his stomach and kiss his chest as he runs his fingers through my hair, tugging on the ends.

Rubbing my back soothingly, I can feel his heart beating strong and sure beneath me and I close my eyes, drifting off to sleep as I hold the man I love – the man I never believed existed.

Waking up to arms coming around me, Jake brings me into a sitting position and stands, lifting me in his arms.

"Where are we going?" I ask as he carries me out of the room.

"To eat lunch," he says simply.

"But we're naked."

"And?"

"Well, um…" I have no response.

Laughing, he walks down the stairs and sets me on my feet

in the kitchen. "Take a seat. I'll reheat the grilled cheese."

Sitting at the round table, I lean forward, crossing my arms in front of me to cover myself as best I can as I watch as Jake turn the stove back on, my eyes stay glued to his perfect body.

From head to toe, I take in every muscle, every plane, and every angle. My fingers twitch with the desire to touch and claim every inch of him as mine.

"I can feel your eyes on me, darlin'."

"That's because they are."

Turning his head slightly, I catch his sexy little smirk.

Shutting the stove off, Jake grabs two plates and slides the sandwiches on them. He walks towards me, and my eyes drop to his half-mast state that continues to grow the closer he gets.

Placing a plate in front of me, my eyes snap up, staring into his hooded gaze as he sits across from me. Jake takes a bite of his sandwich, and cheese oozes out, sticking to his lips.

Finishing half of my sandwich, Jake takes his last bite, and his eyes never leave mine. With more cheese left behind, his tongue starts to lick it away but I shake my head no. Standing on shaky legs, Jake leans back in his chair, his eyes burning over my body as I walk over to him.

Leaning down, I don't touch him with anything other than my tongue as I lick the melted cheese from his mouth. Nibbling on his lips, I suck them into my mouth and Jake groans – the sexiest sound in the world.

Kissing him softly, I pull away and smile. "I'm going to go paint for a little bit."

"What?" he asks as I start to walk away "Naked?"

Turning my head back, I wink. "It'll bring me inspiration."

"But now I know you'll be in there, naked and ready for me when I can't have you."

"Sorry." I laugh, closing the bedroom door behind me.

Standing in front of my painting, I turn my head to the side and smile. I can't remember a time in my life when I loved painting more than I do now. It feels like the most freeing thing in the world. I'm inspired by everything around me, and my soul is happy for the first time.

I had loved painting when I was in school, but that was different. It was my way of bringing people into my pain. It came from a dark place inside of me.

I tried to escape my issues with men by using men. I thought love was something it isn't, and that lead to me falling for the wrong guys who took what they wanted and then left me behind. But I dug myself out of that darkness and here I am. I'm smiling, I'm happy, and I'm painting a beautiful sunrise, not a broken heart.

Looking at what I have so far, I see the sky, sun, and ocean reflecting back at me like I'm there again. Picking up my brush, I start to work on Jake. I made the perspective that of someone who was standing a little behind and off to the side of us while we sat on the mountain this morning.

Chills run down my spine as I paint him – his broad back and shoulders, muscular legs stretched out in front of him, and his arms wrapped around me.

Taking a deep breath, I stretch my neck from side to side. Using these emotions, I bring to life the love I feel for Jake. The minutes blend together as I lose myself in the details, only coming back to the here and now when I hear a light knock at the door.

"Is it okay if I come in?" Jake asks.

"Yes."

The door creaks open, and his light footsteps come up

behind me. Placing his hands on my shoulders, he kisses me behind the ear.

"Ally, baby, it's amazing."

"Thank you."

"I'm serious," he says, wrapping his arms around my waist. "I love it."

I love you, I say in my head, wishing I could say it aloud.

Leaning back, I rest my head on his chest. I've never craved the approval of anyone before Jake, but his admiration means the world to me.

"Are you hungry?"

"Mhmm," I hum.

"Why don't you go get ready and I'll clean your brushes for you."

"Do you know how?" I ask, turning in his arms so I'm facing him.

"I can figure it out," he says, dropping his hands down to rub my ass.

"Okay, if you insist." I smile.

"I do."

Reaching behind me for my brushes, I hold them out to him. But before he can grab them, I swipe the whole bunch across his cheek, leaving behind rows of blue, green, and brown.

He takes them from me and I laugh, wiggling my way out of his arms to make a run for it, but not getting very far. Jake grabs my arm and spins me around, slashing the brushes down my chest.

"You weren't going to play fair, darlin'?"

Shaking my head no, I move my hair back behind my shoulders, standing before Jake completely naked while he's fully clothed.

"I'd say the one playing unfair is you, Jake. You're wearing clothes."

"I can fix that," he says, reaching for the hem of his shirt.

But I shake my head again and slowly back up towards the door. "Too late. Game over."

Smirking, he places his hand in my palette and stalks towards me with long strides.

He wouldn't.

Letting out a little squeal, I turn and run, but only make it a couple of steps before I feel the slap of wet paint across my ass. Pushing me up against the closed door, Jake runs his hand up the side of my body, leaving behind a trail of fire and paint.

"Marking you as mine just got easier," he growls in my ear.

"Who said I'd want that?"

"Don't try and play me, darlin'. I know you want to mark me as yours just as much as I want to mark you as mine." Pushing me harder against the door with his hips, Jake runs his other hand up the side of leg. "Every man would know you're mine, and I'd take pleasure in knowing they can't have you."

Panting, I feel the cool wood against my hard nipples with every breath I take.

"I'm the only one who gets to make you moan, and scream, and drip with need."

"Yes," I sigh, right before he shoves two fingers inside of me. "Yes!" I scream, throwing my head back and moaning.

"There's my favorite sound." Jake hums in my ear.

Working in and out of me, he adds a third finger and twists his hand to press his thumb against my clit. And I'm done. I explode around his long, thick fingers and collapse against the door, my limbs numb.

Jake slowly removes his fingers and drags them up my body. "Only I can make you cum that fast and hard," he rasps, sucking my earlobe between his teeth.

"Yes. Only you."

Chapter 19

My trip with Jake has been amazing so far. Last night after we cleaned the paint off our bodies, he took me to dinner at the restaurant on the pier, and then we walked to get ice cream.

My God, that man makes me happier than I ever knew possible. Just by holding my hand he makes me happy.

Pulling on leggings and a t-shirt, I see my phone light up on the nightstand with my mom's name, and I pick it up right away. "Hey, mom, how are you?"

"Hi, sweetie, I'm good. I'm on my way to work, but I thought I'd check in and see how you were."

"Oh, yes, sorry I haven't called in a few days. I've been a little busy."

"Yes, I bet. With a handsome man."

"Mom! Oh my god."

"Oh hush, I'm your mother, not a nun."

"Please stop." I laugh.

"What do you have planned for the day?"

"Oh, Jake actually took me away for a few days. Up to his family's house in Bar Harbor."

"So, you're very taken with him then?" she asks, her voice softening.

"Yes, I am."

"I'm happy for you, sweetie. You deserve to experience something good."

"Thank you," I whisper.

"How is it up there?"

"It's so beautiful. I know you'd love it. I'll have to take you one day."

"That'd be lovely, sweetie."

"We're driving around Acadia today and I'm excited. He took me to the top of a mountain in the park to see the sunrise yesterday, and it was amazing."

"I'm so glad you're enjoying yourself and that your young man is taking care of you."

"Yeah, he's really great, mom." I smile to myself.

"You sound happy, Ally."

"I really am."

"Oh, honey," she says, a catch in her voice. "I've only ever wanted that for you and your sisters."

"Mom, please don't cry." I can hear the soft sniffles coming through the phone.

"I hope I get to meet this Jake."

"You will soon, I promise."

"Alright, honey, I better go before I start to blubber and

my eyes are all red when I go into school."

"Love you, mom. Miss you."

"I love and miss you more. Have a good rest of your trip. Get home safe."

"I will. Bye, mom."

"Bye, sweetie."

Hanging up, I sit on the bed and think about what she just said. Get home safe. Home. Pine Cove is my home now. Smiling, I braid my hair and dab on a little makeup before going downstairs.

When I walk into the kitchen, I find Jake making up two plates of eggs and bacon and placing them on the table.

"You look beautiful," he says, leaning down to kiss me.

"Thanks, handsome." I smile, sitting down.

Biting into a piece of bacon, I close my eyes, savoring the delicious salty crispiness.

When I open them again, I find Jake smiling at me. "Like bacon, do you?" he jokes.

"Mhmm," is all I manage to say as I devour the fluffy eggs next.

How does he know how to make even the simplest foods taste better than I've ever had?

When we're finished, Jake takes our empty plates to the sink and pours two coffee thermoses. "Ready to go?"

"Yes."

"Alright, let's go, babe," he says, grabbing his keys.

The ride to the park is only a few minutes, and when we reach the entrance sign, I have Jake pull over so we can take a picture in front of it, loving that he doesn't mind taking pictures with me.

Driving on, my eyes never stop moving around.

Everything is absolutely breathtaking. Park Loop Road takes us along the rocky coast of Mt. Desert Island with views that leave me in awe.

Along the 27-mile scenic drive, we stop at Sand Beach, Otter Point, Thunder Cove, and Jordan Pond. Sand Beach is definitely my favorite, though. It's a beautiful horseshoe shaped beach nestled between pine tree covered rocky cliffs with a random little island not too far out from shore.

The water was a swirl of blue and green, just like Jake's eyes.

My next favorite is Jordan Pond. It's a small lake nestled in between the surrounding mountains and has a walking trail that goes around the entire perimeter. There's even a café there that's famous for their pop overs, but the line was too long of a wait, so we just continued on.

I've probably taken over a hundred photos so far. I want to remember everything. I even snuck in a few of Jake when he wasn't paying attention. He really looks like a sexy rugged mountain man here in his jeans and plaid button down amongst the trees.

After we spend hours driving and exploring, I'm positively famished.

"Jake, I need sustenance. I'm so hungry I could eat the map they gave us when we entered."

"Me too, darlin'. Don't worry, I'm taking us back into town for food now."

"Thank you. I'd kiss you right now if I wasn't so weak from hunger."

I bite my lip to keep from laughing when I see him roll his eyes. "I know for a fact you're never too weak to kiss me."

"That's true." I smile, looking out the window as we leave

the park. "You're lucky you got to grow up so close to here. And have a house so you can come to whenever."

"I used to escape here a lot after I got my license. And then again when I left the Navy. It was a place I knew I'd never be bothered."

"It's good you had it. I can't even count the number of times I wished I had a place to escape to."

Looking over at me, Jake squeezes my hand and I squeeze back. It's a small reassurance that neither of us needs a place to escape to anymore.

For our last meal in Bar Harbor, Jake takes me back to the restaurant on the pier and we order fresh lobster rolls and cold beers. Choosing to sit out on the floating dock at one of the picnic tables, I take in the last views of our trip.

"Thank you for taking me here, Jake. I love it. I could spend endless days painting everything I see."

"We can come back. Next time you have a few days off in a row, just let me know."

"Really?"

"Of course. I knew you'd love it here."

"Can we do a whale watching tour and walk across to that island at low tide?"

"Anything your heart desires, darlin'."

"Well, my heart desires a lot, but we'll start with those two things." I smile, loving the idea of coming back here.

Taking his hand, I lace my fingers with his as we walk slowly back to his truck, enjoying the beautiful day.

Back at the house, we pack our bags, and load up his truck.

"I just have to get my art supplies and then I'll be good."

"You can leave it all for next time."

"That'd be okay with your family?"

"Why not?" He shrugs.

"Okay, if you're sure." I go back to get my painting, but leave everything else. I love that he's giving me a little place in his family's house.

The drive back to Pine Cove is peaceful. We listen to the radio and I watch the pine trees pass in a blur around us.

It's pitch black when we pull up to the cottage, with the only light coming from the truck's headlights. Looking around, I try and see if there's anything out there, but it's too dark to tell.

"Don't worry, darlin', I'm going to walk you in. I won't let anything get you," he says with a smirk.

"Excuse me for being cautious," I throw back at him playfully. "Not all of us are mountain men with guns."

Laughing, he gets out and checks our surroundings before lifting me out of my seat and carrying me up to the front door.

"I wasn't so scared you had to carry me," I tell him as I unlock the door.

"I know, but I like holding you close," he whispers in my ear, his warm breath sending shivers down my spine.

Fumbling with the key, I finally manage to open the door and step into the living room.

"I'll go get your bag now that I know nothing will attack us."

Smart ass.

Rolling my eyes, I walk over to the couch and flop down, feeling the exhaustion of our trip. Waking up early every day and then having sex all night has my body drained of all its energy.

Drifting off, I hear Jake come back in, and then I'm being lifted by two strong arms again. I curl into his chest, inhaling his woodsy scent, and humming my approval.

Soft sheets greet me as he lays me down, making sure to remove my sneakers before pulling the comforter over me.

"Are you staying?" I mumble.

"If you want me to."

"Always," I whisper, falling into a deep sleep.

Waking up nestled snuggly against Jake's side, I smile, wiggling just a little closer.

I peek over his shoulder to look at the clock on the nightstand and sigh, seeing that it's time for me to get up for work already.

"What's wrong?" he mumbles.

"Nothing, I just have to get up for work now, even though I'm comfortable."

Opening his eyes, Jake kisses my cheek. "I'll go make the coffee."

"Thanks," I say around a yawn, stretching out.

Going through the motions of getting ready for work, I head into the kitchen and make myself a mug of coffee, joining Jake out on the back porch.

"How are your boats coming along?" I ask.

"Good. I have to ship them out in a couple weeks, though, and I'm not finished carving yet."

"Are they for the same person?"

"Yeah, a husband and wife."

"That's so nice." I smile, stretching my legs out in front of me as I sip my coffee. "Okay, I have to head out," I say after a minute. "Do you want to sit out here a little longer, or leave with me?"

"No, I'll go too."

Heading back inside, we place our mugs in the sink and walk out to our cars.

"Hey," he says, grabbing my arm and pulling me towards him. "You're forgetting something."

"I am?"

Pushing me up against his truck, he captures my lips with his, searing me with his heat. "Yes, my kiss goodbye," he says, pulling away.

"Sorry." I smile.

"You should be, darlin'. Have a good day at work. Try not to mess up too many orders."

"Try not to cut off any fingers. I need them." I wink, getting in my car.

When I walk into the café, the strong scent of coffee and fresh baked pastries fills my lungs. I love working here.

"Ally! How are you? How was your trip?"

"Hey Courtney, I'm good. Do you live here?" I ask with a laugh. "Why haven't I worked with Dara yet? Do you not trust me?"

"Okay, slow down, I trust you. Dara was supposed to work today but I told her I'd work so I could hear all about your trip. Come on, tell me everything!"

"It was really good." I smile.

"No, no, I need details. What did you guys do?"

Walking behind the counter to put my purse away, I try and decide if I should filter anything. "Well, we ate amazing food, walked around, went in shops, saw the sunrise from the top of a mountain. Oh, and had lots and lots of hot sex."

"AHH!" she screams. "Thank goodness! I was hoping you wouldn't leave that part out."

"Of course not. It's a vital part of my trip." Smiling like a lovesick teenager, I make a cup of coffee and grab a donut from the case.

"Anything else?"

"Just…on the way there. I was joking about his past relationships and he got all weird and closed off."

"Give it more time. He'll be ready to talk when he's ready."

"I've honestly never felt this way before. I'm a little scared because it's so new for me, but I'm also too in love to care."

"What did you just say?" Courtney asks, her mouth open.

"What?"

"You just said you're in love."

"I did?" Oh, shit. I did.

Shoving the donut in my mouth, I shake my head. "I didn't mean to say that."

"Yes, you did." She smiles. "Have you told him?"

"No. And I don't plan on it. It's too soon. Plus, I don't know how he feels. He's not very big on emotional conversations as I'm well aware of."

"First of all, it's not too soon when you're with the right person. I knew with Jack after our first date. Well, during our first date actually."

"Really?"

"Yeah." She smiles. "He swept me off my feet right away, and I haven't been put down yet. But even though I knew right away, and later on Jack told me he did too, we didn't actually tell each other until about a month in. Then he proposed about a month after that." She laughs.

"Wait, seriously? After only two months together?"

"Yeah, we just knew. Why wait or delay happiness when you can have it all?"

"If you know, you know."

Chapter 20

Getting home from the café around 6:30, I make myself chicken and gnocchi with pesto, and open a bottle of merlot.

I've always loved the nights back home when I got to put my pajamas on early, drink wine, and veg out on the couch.

Throwing my hair up in a messy bun, I tuck my feet underneath me and put on Cougar Town. I love this show. All they do is drink wine and hang out, and it makes me feel justified when I finish a whole bottle myself. Well, sort of.

A few minutes in, though, my mind starts to drift to thoughts of Jake. Licking a stray drop of wine from my lips, I picture him all sweaty and sexy as he works on his boats with that look of complete concentration and focus on his face. I'd distract him by slowly stripping off my clothes until he bends me over one of his work benches and has his way with me.

Suddenly my phone rings on the table, making me jump.

"Hello?" I answer, not even looking at who's calling, still stuck in my fantasy.

"Hey, darlin'," a sexy, smooth voice greets me.

"Hey, mountain man."

"I missed you today."

"You did?"

"I did. I do."

"I miss you, too," I whisper.

"Good, open the door."

"What?"

"Open the door."

Getting up, I put my wine glass down and pause the TV, slowly walking over to the front door. Opening it, I find Jake standing there with daisies, a bottle of wine, and a paper bag.

"I brought dessert," he says, raking his eyes up and down my body. And when they meet mine again, they're smoldering.

I happen to be wearing the same silk pajama set I had on when we first met. The one that shows a lot and only covers a little. Smiling, I step aside and let him in.

Jake walks past me and I follow him into the kitchen. He puts the flowers in a tall glass of water and grabs two wine glasses. Popping open the bottle he brought, he pours us each a hefty amount.

"Trying to loosen me up, mountain man?"

The corner of his mouth lifts in a small smile as he pulls out a plate and knife and sits at the table with me. Opening the paper bag, Jake pulls out a whoopie pie and cuts it in half, pushing one of them towards me.

"You drink wine?" I ask, taking a sip from my glass.

"I sometimes do." He shrugs.

Licking the side of the whoopie, I moan softly when the sugary filling melts on my tongue.

"You know, I was just thinking about you before you called."

"You were?"

"Yes. Your call interrupted a little fantasy I was having."

Eyeing me with a heated look, he lifts his glass to his lips and slowly takes a sip. I watch as his tongue darts out and licks his lips, savoring the taste.

"I was thinking of you in your workshop, all hot and sweaty, concentrating really hard on what you were doing. And since I hadn't seen you all day, I started thinking of how I could distract you so you'd give me what I want."

"And what was it you wanted that I wasn't giving you?"

"You," I say simply, watching his jaw clench.

"And what did you come up with to get my attention?"

Staring into his ocean eyes, they start to swirl when I swipe my finger through the filling and lick it clean.

"I decided to start stripping. Slowly. You finally looked up when you heard me slide my zipper down. Your eyes were glued to me, heating my skin with every pass they made. When I was finally naked, I walked towards you, a little sway in my hips. I bent down so my breasts were right in your face, and I whispered in your ear to take me right then and there, and however you wanted."

Jakes eyes grow darker and darker with every word I say. Lifting his glass to his lips again, I watch his throat move when he swallows. I never realized how sexy a throat could be.

"Stand up," he commands, his eyes blazing into mine.

"What?"

"Stand up," he repeats.

Confused, I do as he says.

"Strip," he demands, sitting back in his chair and drinking his wine.

With my heart beating wildly in my chest, I bite my lip and grab the hem of my silk pajama top, lifting it up and off of me.

Hungrily, Jake's eyes take in my naked breasts, my nipples turning into taut peaks under his gaze.

Slipping my thumbs under the waistband of the matching shorts, I shimmy my hips a little, letting the silk float to floor. Reaching up, I release my hair from the bun, and let it fall down my back.

Walking slowly towards him, I rest my hand on his shoulder and bend over. "I want you to take me here and now, Jake," I whisper in his ear. "However you want it."

Sucking his earlobe into my mouth, he growls and grabs my hips. Lifting me up, he stalks back down the hall and into my bedroom. Tossing me on the bed, he quickly sheds his clothes and looks down at me with hooded eyes.

Flipping me over, he drags me down the bed until I'm bent over the edge with my toes barely touching the floor. Pressing me into the mattress, he kicks my feet open and I groan when the cool air hits my center.

"You're going to take everything I give you."

Nodding into the comforter, Jake tightens his grip on my hips and eases into me slowly, inch by glorious inch. When he's fulling inside of me, I groan and try and move my hips, but he just tightens his grip.

Pulling out almost completely, Jake pauses, then slams into me, my toes lifting off the floor. Every stroke makes my body slide up the bed, my sensitive nipples rubbing across the fabric before he pulls me back to the edge of the bed and does it all over again.

Jake has complete control over me as he steadily moves faster and faster until my body starts to shake and I scream out, my knuckles turning white as I grip the comforter. Hearing a roar penetrate my already deafening ears, Jake slams into me one last time and my body squeezes him with every muscle it has.

Panting, I unclench my hands, letting the blood start to flow through them again. Jake peels his fingers from my hips and pulls out of me. I feel the loss immediately.

He sweeps my hair to the side and kisses his way up my spine, sliding his hands down my arms and weaving his fingers with mine. Kissing my neck, he licks the rim of my ear and swirls his tongue around my lobe before nibbling it into his mouth.

"I've been dreaming of taking you like that since I first laid eyes on you, darlin'." His voice is like soft velvet, covering my skin in goosebumps. "And one day I'll claim your ass as mine too."

My heart rate kicks up and my inner muscles clench as I push back into him slightly.

Chuckling in my ear, he nips my neck. "I know you, darlin'."

Lifting me into his arms, Jake carries me to the bathroom and sets me down on the edge of the tub. Turning the shower on, he waits for it to warm before holding his hand out and helping me in, stepping in behind me.

Grabbing the shower gel, I turn to face him, watching him squeeze some into his hands. As he runs them down my arms, across my stomach, and up my chest, I push into his touch, humming my praise.

Turning me around, he kneads his fingers down my back, loosening my tight muscles. I brace myself on the wall in front of me and push into his touch.

Bending, he slides his hands down each of my legs, and on his way back up, he kisses my cheeks, giving each a little bite. Sighing, Jake snakes his arm around my waist and pulls me under the hot stream of water with him.

When we're both finished, Jake turns the water off and wraps me in a fluffy towel, carrying me to bed. I'm too tired and drained to do anything but curl myself around the comforter and close my eyes.

Morning light streams through my curtains and I groan, rolling over into a warm, hard body. Sighing, I wrap my arm around Jake's middle and curl into him.

"Morning, beautiful." His sexy, raspy, morning voice cuts through the silence of the room.

"Mmm," I answer, snuggling closer.

"It's time to get up, gorgeous."

"Mmm, not yet."

I feel his chest shake with laughter as he sweeps my messy hair out of my face.

Rolling on top of me, he kisses me into the mattress, waking me up in an instant. Pulling away, he kisses my cheeks, forehead, eyes, and nose.

"Now, that's a wakeup call."

"I knew it'd work." He smiles, his dimple popping out.

Rolling off of me and out of bed, I rake my eyes over his

gloriously naked body as he pulls on his jeans.

"I'll make coffee. Don't go back to sleep."

"Yes, sir."

Shaking his head, Jake smiles and walks out of the room.

Throwing the covers off, I yawn and stretch my arms above my head. I hate mornings, but having my man wake me up like that definitely makes them more enjoyable.

Shuffling over to the closet, I pick out an outfit and make my way to the bathroom. My hair is a mess, and it takes me forever to comb out the bird's nest on my head. I need to never fall asleep with wet hair again. It's horrible.

When I finally get it tangle-free, I look at myself in the mirror and laugh. It's still a hot mess, so I spray it with some leave-in conditioner and swirl it up into a bun, calling a truce on the battle of making it work.

After I finish getting ready, I walk into the kitchen where Jake hands me a steaming mug of coffee. I take a sip right away, loving the strong taste a little extra this morning.

"You look beautiful today," he says, and I feel my cheeks heat. No matter how many times he says it, I still blush when he compliments me. Reaching out, he brushes his fingers over my heated skin. "Beautiful," he whispers.

Getting lost in the swirls of blue and green in his eyes, I blink, trying to shake off the spell he casts over me whenever we lock eyes.

Dropping his hand, he picks up his mug of coffee and we head outside to sit for a few minutes.

"I have to work in the shop again all day, but will you come to my house when you're finished at the café?"

"Of course." I smile, looking out at the boats passing by.

Chapter 21

The next week seems to go by in a blur of Jake, work, Jake, sleep, Jake, and repeat. I've woken up next to him every morning, and I've never slept better in my entire life. He makes me feel so safe and cared for when I'm wrapped in his strong arms.

But tomorrow is when Ash, Mel, and Ellie get here, and so I'll have to go without him in my bed for the next four nights. I don't know how I'm going to deal. Maybe we can sneak off and have a quickie or something? I mean, come on, I need my man.

I had told Jake that I needed to get my place ready tonight for them, but now I'm seriously second guessing myself if I have to be separated for the next few nights.

When did I get so dependent on him? Time apart is good. It's healthy.

At least that's what I'm going to keep telling myself.

"Hey, Courtney," I greet as I walk into work.

I've spent the past week mainly working with Dara while Courtney took some time off before the busy weekend, and I've missed her. Working with Dara was different in that I wasn't bombarded with questions about Jake ten times a shift. But she was just as fun, and I spent most of my shifts laughing.

"Hey, Ally. So, do you think you can separate yourself from your hot man and come out with me tonight?"

"Okay, first of all, yes, I can separate myself from him, but I choose not to," I say. "And I can't go out tonight. I was going to go to the grocery store and get the cottage ready for my friends tomorrow. Then maybe work on a painting."

"Is it for Jake? Oh! Is it a portrait of you? Nude?"

"Are you serious?" I laugh. "No, it's not a nude portrait of me."

"I think he'd like a nude." She shrugs. "Just saying."

"Probably." I smile, making myself a cup of coffee.

"Do I get to meet your friends while they're here?"

"Oh my god, of course! You're coming out with us tomorrow night when they get here. Did I not mention that earlier?"

"No, you didn't. But good. I'd be offended if I wasn't invited."

"We wouldn't want that," I say, rolling my eyes. "I'm nervous for them to meet Jake. We've all been friends since freshman year of high school and are really protective of one another. And brutally honest when needed."

"Ally, come on, they're your best friends. They're going to see you two together and know that it's real. Trust me. I don't know if I've even seen that man smile before you came along."

"Really?"

"Yes, so don't worry. Your friends will see how much he cares about you. It's obvious."

"It is?"

"Yes, now stop questioning me. Don't pretend like you don't know he's crazy about you."

"Eh," I say, shrugging my shoulders with a small smile.

"Are they meeting him tomorrow night?"

"Oh, no, not right away. We're having a girl's night tomorrow. Then on Saturday, I thought we'd come into town and walk around, obviously stop in here, and then have Jake meet us for dinner. And then Sunday we're going to a BBQ at his parent's house."

"Whoa, whoa, wait. You're going to his family's BBQ? You're meeting them for the first time at a huge family gathering?"

"Yes? Why? Is that bad? Wait, what do you mean by huge?"

"Well, I mean half the town is invited. His family is amazing, though, so don't worry, they'll love you."

"Great. I'm already nervous, so thanks for adding to it. I'm just glad I'll have Ash, Mel, and Ellie to talk to when Jake goes off with his brothers or something."

"And I'll be there."

"You will?"

"Yeah, Jack has been going since he was a kid, and then I started going with him after we met. The Taylor's house is so beautiful. They live on the coast with a huge backyard that they fill with tables of food, drinks, and games. They even set off fireworks at night. Everyone in town looks forward to the summer because of their parties."

"Oh, that sounds fun. Jake sprung it on me a few days ago and I've been freaking out ever since. But now that I know it's not just me, my friends, and his family, I'm feeling better."

"Glad to help." She smiles. "And I'll definitely be hanging with you. Jack always leaves me to go hang with the boys and then I usually just get drunk and stuff my face."

"Well, we can do that together now." I laugh. "But I probably shouldn't get drunk in front of his family."

"Yes, you should. It's expected of everyone who goes. There will be so many people there they won't even notice."

"Thank goodness for that. I know my friends won't second guess getting drunk and stuffing their faces. But that also means they get super loud."

"I'm excited to ask them a bunch of embarrassing questions about you."

"Ah, true friendship."

"Of course." She shrugs.

Laughing, I start wiping the tables down and prepping everything for opening.

The people of Pine Cove come in and out during the day, always stopping to chat with me for a minute before leaving. Everyone's been so friendly and welcoming towards me, and I find myself starting to feel like I belong here.

After closing up the café with Courtney, I make a stop at the grocery store to stock up on any and every snack and food I know we'll need this weekend.

Starting with booze, I load up on gin, rum, vodka, and a

case of wine. Then I go up and down the food aisles, piling a bunch of our favorites in the cart. If anyone were to look at me right now, they'd probably think I was having a party for fifty.

After spending an exorbitant amount of money, I make a quick stop at Anthony's before heading home and pick up a pizza. I really don't feel like cooking tonight.

Three slices of pizza, two glasses of wine, and two episodes of Cougar Town later, I get up to start cleaning. It's only nine o'clock, but I'm so tired, I already want to go to bed.

Dragging my feet around the house, I take out all of the spare blankets and pillows from the closets and pile them on the bed in the purple room. Eyeing my paintings that I've been storing in there, I decide to move them over to mine for safe keeping. I haven't exactly told my friends I've started painting again, so that will be a surprise for them.

After about an hour of cleaning, I'm even more exhausted, and I know I'm going to pass out cold.

Climbing into bed, I put my phone on the nightstand, but notice a message from Jake from an hour ago.

Hey, beautiful.

I don't know if he's awake still, but I type out a response. **Hey, handsome. I hope you're not going to be too lonely without me tonight.**

He responds almost immediately. **You know I will be. I need your sexy ass curled up against me.**

I'm lying in bed now. I tell him. **But it's cold and lonely without your big, strong arms wrapped around me.**

I can be over there in ten minutes. You only have to

ask.

I'm so tired. I wouldn't be able to keep my eyes open for very long.

I just want to hold you, baby.

Okay.

Be there soon.

Smiling, I get up and shuffle over to the front door to unlock it in my half-asleep stupor.

I left the door unlocked for you. Just come right to my room.

Ten minutes later, my bedroom door opens, and Jake climbs in next to me. Draping his arm over my waist, he pulls me against him, kissing my hair.

Holding his hand in mine, I kiss his knuckles and snuggle into his warm body.

This is what I needed.

We don't even have to say anything.

Falling into a deep, restful sleep, I dream of days filled with painting and nights filled with Jake.

Chapter 22

"Mmm." Jake's hand slides up my shirt to cup my left breast and roll my nipple between his fingertips.

I love my sexy dreams of Jake.

Moving back down my stomach, he slips his hand under the waistband of my shorts.

"Open for me, baby." His voice has the same early morning gravely tone like in real life.

Rolling onto my back, I spread my legs, letting Jake slide his fingers along my already wet slit. Throwing my arm over my face, I moan, biting my wrist.

"Let me hear you," he says, pulling my arm away.

Spreading me open, he circles my clit and thrusts two big fingers inside of me, and my eyes fly open at the intrusion, realizing that I wasn't dreaming at all.

"There are those eyes I love," Jake says, kissing me hard as his fingers work deep inside of me.

Groaning into his mouth, he swallows my sounds and kisses my jaw, neck, and down my chest, yanking my top down.

"So soft. So good," he says, kissing them both.

"Jake," I whisper, barely able to think straight anymore. But then he takes his hand away. "No, no, please, Jake. I need…"

"I know what you need, don't worry."

Pulling my shorts down, he moves on top of me, settling himself between my legs and entering me in one swift push.

Gasping, I grip his arms, my mouth open in a silent cry at the sudden fullness. Looking into Jake's storming eyes, he pulls out slowly, pausing. He leans his forehead against mine and I watch every emotion pass through his eyes as he pushes back inside of me.

Wrapping my arms around his neck, we keep our eyes locked on one another as he rocks into me.

This feels different.

This is making love.

The layers we hide behind are peeled back, exposing our raw emotions.

I kiss him slow and deep – giving him my breath, my heart, my body, and my soul.

Biting my lip, Jake pulls back to look into my eyes again. Tilting my hips up slightly, he starts to hit a spot that only he can reach. His slow pace drags out the slow burn building inside of me, and it's unlike any of the other times with Jake.

"Come with me, baby," he whispers against my lips.

And I do.

Flames lick my skin and my heart burns as I shatter around him, my body not my own anymore. He's finally taken it.

Sighing, Jake peppers kisses across my collar bone, and I reach up, brushing my fingers over his forehead to sweep his wild hair out of his eyes so I can look into the tide pools I love swimming in.

Smiling wistfully, I curl a strand of his hair around my finger and tug. I wish I could tell him how much I love him. The words are there, just out of reach on the tip of my tongue, but refuse to be uttered aloud.

The longer we stare at each other, the more even my breathing becomes, and my heart rate slows.

Cupping my cheek, he kisses me slow and sweet, savoring all that's unsaid between us.

"Thank you for coming last night," I whisper, wishing I could tell him that it was more than that.

"I needed you too, darlin'."

Sighing, I close my eyes briefly, trying not to cry at how much hearing those words means to me. But he sees the emotions swimming in my eyes, and he runs his thumb back and forth across my cheek, kissing me softly.

"I'll make us coffee," he whispers against my lips. Getting up, he walks out of the room – gloriously naked.

The little bubble we were in is broken, and I already feel the walls building back around Jake. Even with everything we've shared, I know there's still something holding him back.

Stretching out my arms and legs, I throw the covers off and take my sleep shirt off, thinking we're having breakfast naked. I slip on my silk robe that barely covers anything and head into the kitchen, leaning on the wall by the entrance.

"I'm going with waffles. How does that sound?" he asks, his back turned to me.

"Where did you get pants?" I wanted to see his sexy ass while he cooked.

"Disappointed?" he asks, amused.

"Yes, I am."

Laughing, he shakes his head and takes out the ingredients he'll need from the cabinets. "I brought a bag. It's in the living room," he says, turning to see me leaning against the doorway. "Fuck." Prowling over to me in two strides, he kisses me hard and fast. "This robe covers nothing," he says, running a finger down the opening between my breasts and circling my visibly hard nipples through the silk. Running his finger down my side and back over my ass, he rubs the skin right below my left cheek where the robe ends.

Smoothing my hands over his bare chest and arms, I bite my lip. "Keep your shirt off, mountain man. I want to see what's mine."

"Whatever you want, darlin'. Everything I am is yours."

Sliding his hand under the silk, he squeezes my ass. "Just like everything you are is mine." Pushing me against the wall, he kisses me hard and bruising.

"Yes," I whisper against his lips when he pulls away.

Leaving me to stare after him, Jake walks back over to the stove and I watch his back muscles flex and move with every step he takes.

Making a mug of coffee, I take a seat at the kitchen table and watch my man cook.

"What time are your friends getting here today?"

"I'm not sure. Let me see if they've left yet." Getting up, I retrieve my phone from my room and then sit back down.

"They texted saying they left a little while ago. So that means they'll probably be here between two and three."

"What do you have planned?"

"Oh, um, well…do you think you could be free tomorrow night to have dinner with us? Tonight is a girl's night, so no boys allowed." I smile. "But they want to meet the man who I broke all my rules for."

"Is that so?" He smiles. "Then I better be on my best behavior."

"What, did you plan on groping me under the table or something?"

"Eh." He shrugs. "It's always an option. You're irresistible, babe."

"That's both sweet and dirty."

"Exactly how I'd describe you."

Smiling, I cross my legs and sip my coffee, trying not to just open them so I can show him just how sweet and dirty I can be.

After breakfast, Jake unfortunately puts a shirt on and I walk him out onto the porch to see him off.

"I'll see you tomorrow?" he asks.

"Yes. I thought we'd go to Anthony's. I'll let you know the time tomorrow."

"Sounds good. Don't go too crazy tonight, darlin'."

"I can't guarantee that." I laugh. "We haven't seen each other in a month."

"Call me if you need me. I can drive you all home."

"Maybe." I smile.

"Just maybe?"

"Yup. We might just meet a nice gentleman who will be so taken with one of my friends that he'll insist on seeing us home safely."

Watching his eyes darken and his jaw flex, I run my hand up his chest and lean up on my toes. "Kidding, mountain man," I whisper in his ear, kissing his cheek. "You're the only man I'd call to save me."

"Don't torture me, babe. Now all I'll be thinking about is how every man in the bar will be trying to take you away from me."

"Like I'd let them," I scoff.

"I know." He smirks. "I'm the only one who's man enough to handle you anyhow."

"Exactly," I say, pulling him down to my lips to kiss him goodbye.

After seeing him off, I go back inside and throw on yoga pants and a t-shirt, looking longingly at the paintings leaning against the wall. Walking over, I squat down to eye level and run my fingers over the Cadillac Mountain sunrise piece, smiling at the memory.

I have a few things left to touch up before it's finished so I pick it up and grab my easel, taking them out onto the back porch. Going back for my supplies, I pour myself another mug of coffee and settle in to work for a few hours.

Putting on some music, I dip my brush into the orange paint and swipe it across the sunrise, brightening the morning with a single stroke.

I lose myself in the painting for a few hours, bringing my memory to life. Adding a few more strokes to the sun's rays, I put my brush down and look at it.

It's perfect.

Being here has really made me appreciate my art. I never fully gave myself over to a piece and let my heart do the creating, but Jake has changed me in that way. My heart is open now. That first night I painted with him was such an emotional and raw ordeal for me. I've never needed to paint or capture what I was feeling so badly before, and it wasn't just about what I was seeing in front of me.

I need *him*.

If I lose him, I know I'll close up again, and definitely for good this time. I rub the sudden pain in my chest at that thought.

Jake has the power to ruin me in a way I know I'd never recover from.

This is too much.

Going inside, I see I only have an hour or so before the girls get here, so I bring my painting and easel back to my room to dry.

After showering, I put on fresh leggings and a t-shirt and change the sheets from my bed.

Checking my phone, I see an update from Ellie saying they're fifteen minutes out.

Ahhh! I can't believe they're almost here!

Making a fresh pot of coffee, I go and sit out on the front porch to wait, and the second I hear the crunching of gravel beneath a car's tires, I jump up and stand at the bottom of the stairs. Mel's car comes into view, and when she parks, they all jump out screaming, running towards me.

"Ally! We've missed you!" Mel yells, throwing her arms around me.

"I've missed you, too!" Ellie and Ash join in, and I'm surrounded by the love of my best friends. "I'm so glad you're here!"

"Us too! And I can't wait to meet your hot new man."

"Oh, okay Ash, I see how it is. You care more about the man than me." Smiling, I push her away.

"No, bitch. I'm just very curious to see who's finally captured you."

"Like I'm some rogue creature on the loose?" I joke.

"Well…" She shrugs. "You said it, not me."

"Ash, shut up," Ellie cuts in. "Ally, this house is so adorable."

"I know. I love it so much. Come on, just wait until I show you the back."

Taking them inside, I give them a short tour of the house before opening the back door. "Okay, now this is my favorite part." We step out onto the back porch, and they all gasp.

"Holy shit, Al."

"This is amazing."

"I'd never leave."

The three of them stare out at the backyard and the ocean beyond with the same look of amazement on their faces that I'm sure I had when I first saw it.

"I know. I sit out here and watch the sunrise whenever I can. Let's go down to the water," I say, and we all take a seat in an Adirondack chair.

"Ally, I can't believe this is where you've been living for the past month. Shit, I would've quit my job and moved up here with you if I knew it was this nice."

"You still can if you want, Ellie."

"Pass. I wouldn't want to hear you and Jake having sex every night."

"We don't always have sex here. I'm at his house all the time too." None of them say anything, so I turn and find all three of them staring at me with smiles. "What?"

"You're at his house all the time?" Mel asks.

"Yeah?"

"Where does he live?"

"He lives by a lake. He actually has a really beautiful home. I always expect guys to live all caveman and dirty, but nope. It's very rustic chic."

"Okay, you'll need to send us pics."

"Ash, that's weird."

"No, it's not. Just take some when he's not around and send them to us."

"Yeah, okay." I laugh.

"Tell us more about him." Mel urges.

"Oh, um, well…" I smile, blushing. "He's amazing. I'm painting again, and it's different than before. Jake treats me like a priority, and I've never felt so close to another person before. I feel completely myself with him. Yes, he's super gorgeous, but it's the way he makes me feel about myself that outweighs his hotness."

"Damn, Ally. I've never seen you like this. I'm so happy for you. You deserve it more than anyone I know."

"Thanks, El."

"And you're painting again? That's huge, Ally-cat," Mel adds softly.

"Yeah, they're in my room if you want to see them later."

"I can't wait to meet him. Will we tonight?"

"No, I thought tonight would be a girl's night. Courtney is meeting us at the bar later."

"We get to meet this Courtney, do we?" Ash rubs her hands together like an evil villain.

"Ash, you're going to be nice. She's my closest friend here."

"Don't worry your pretty little head, we'll all be nice. I just have a few questions for her."

"I'd expect nothing less," I sigh, rolling my eyes.

Laughing, we all relax in our chairs, turning our faces up to the sun for a little while.

"What look are we going for?" Ellie asks when we're in the purple room an hour later, debating what to wear tonight. "Obviously not dancing all night outfits, but what do you think, Al?"

"I think we should go for a summer rooftop bar vibe."

"Okay, perfect." She smiles, searching around her luggage.

Going into my room, I dig through my closet and pull out a short white sundress with embroidered pink flowers on it, and pink heels to match.

"Oh, that's cute, Ally," Mel says when I come back and lay my dress on the bed.

"I've been dying to wear these heels since I bought them, and they match this dress perfectly." Hopping up on the bed with my mirror, I start the makeup process. I haven't really done up my makeup since I've been here. I love keeping it natural and light, but it's always fun to do a little extra once in a while.

Applying my foundation and powder, I add blush and highlighter to give my cheeks a little glow. Playing up my blue eyes, I layer a gold shimmer eyeshadow over a light pink one, then add eyeliner to my top lid, and a few layers of mascara for the finishing eye-popping look.

It's funny how I've always paid more attention to how I look when going out with just the girls. I like looking good for myself, but I love when we're a girl gang of hotness against the world.

I've missed this. Whenever we would go out back home, we'd always meet at someone's house and pregame while getting ready together.

Oh, now that I think of it… "Who wants a drink?"

"Yes!" all three answer together.

"Wine or liquor?"

"Maybe we'll start with wine to get a little happy, and then we'll have the hard stuff when we're out."

"Alright, Ash, you sound like a pro." Laughing, I head into the kitchen.

"Hey, just because I have a drinking game plan doesn't mean anything!" she yells after me.

Handing out glasses, I pour wine into each.

"To a fun night!" Ellie toasts.

"To being reunited with our bestie!" Mel adds.

"And to seeing what hotties this town has!" Ash throws in, and we all laugh, clinking glasses.

Curling my long blonde hair, I slip on my dress and heels and check myself in the mirror. Fluffing my hair, I do a little twirl.

"Damn, Ally, you look amazing," Ash praises.

"Thanks," I say, blowing her a kiss. "I'd say we all look good."

Ash is wearing a short sundress and heels like me, Mel has on a navy floral maxi dress and wedges, and Ellie has on tight skinny jeans and a flowy off the shoulder top with wedges.

Sitting on the bed while they all finish getting ready, I sip on my second glass of wine, my mind drifting to Jake. Grabbing my phone, I decide to send him a quick text.

Hey, handsome. I'm all dolled up and ready for a night with the girls. But don't worry, I'm not showing too much leg...

Smiling to myself, I hit send, knowing it'll drive him a little crazy.

Swigging back the rest of my wine, I smooth on a pretty pink lipstick and turn to my girls. "Ready?"

"Let's go! I'm starving!" Ash whines, hopping off the bed.

We all squeeze into my car and I text Courtney to tell her we're heading out so she can meet us. The drive into town is louder than I'm used to, and I smile, listening to my friends banter back and forth.

I've missed this.

Opening the door to The Rusty Anchor, all eyes turn to us as we make our way to a table near the bar.

"I'm guessing they can tell we're not from here," Mel whispers as we sit.

"Yeah, they knew with me, too." I laugh. "It's a small town."

"And who is that walking sex of a man behind the bar?" Ash asks, practically humming with desire.

"That's Alex. Gorgeous, right? I flirted with him the first time I came here, but Jake came and shut that down, claiming me as his."

"How?"

"I made him kiss me right then and there in front of everyone." I smile, thinking back on that fuzzy memory.

"Seriously, Ally? Damn girl, you're fierce. I'm going to go get the first round," Ash tells us as she fluffs her hair and pushes her boobs out.

"Go get 'em tiger." I laugh, loving her confidence.

"So, what's new with you guys? We talked about me, but not you."

"Well, nothing is new with me." Mel shrugs. "I'm still single and working too much."

"Same," Ellie adds. "The three of us just hang out, order takeout, and watch movies. I mean, it's only been a month, Ally, and we still text each other all the time." She laughs. "How much news do you expect?"

"I don't know. It's just that I'm not physically there and I don't want to miss out on anything."

"Okay, I'm back," Ash says, placing three drinks down on our table. "I couldn't carry yours, Ally."

"That's okay, I'll get it. And I'll grab menus, too."

Walking up to the bar, Alex gives me a wide smile. "Hey, beautiful." He winks. "I see you brought some friends tonight."

"Hi, Alex." I smile, blushing slightly. I can't help it! He's flirty and super good looking, and has this certain charm that makes me blush. "My friends from back home are visiting for the weekend. Ashley said she left my drink here?"

"Yeah, here you go." He pushes a brown drink across the bar to me.

"What's that?"

"Rum and coke."

"Oh." I frown. "Do you think I could have a gin and tonic with extra limes instead? Please?"

"I thought she had it wrong. I'll make you a new drink."

"Thanks." I smile.

Watching him, he muddles three lime wedges at the

bottom of the glass before adding the ice, gin, tonic, and a fresh lime wedge on the rim.

He slides the drink towards me. "There you go, beautiful. I made it a little extra special."

"Thanks, Alex. You're lucky Jake's not here to hear you flirting though," I tell him, smiling slightly.

"Yes, lucky me. And every other man in here for that matter." Smiling wide, he wipes down the bar in front of me.

"Can I have some menus?" I ask, ignoring his previous statement.

Back at the table, I pull my phone out to check if Jake answered me, I see he still hasn't. I might as well torture him a little more then.

Apparently, the men in here are happy that you're not with me tonight, mountain man. But don't worry, I'm prepared to hit them with my purse if they try anything.

"Okay, lover girl, put the phone down. It's a girl's night."

"I know, I know. Sorry."

"Hey, Ally," Courtney says, walking up next to me.

"Hey, Courtney!" Standing, I give her a hug. "These are my friends – Ashley, Melanie, and Elizabeth."

"Hi." She waves. "It's nice to finally meet you. Ally talks about you guys all the time."

"So, what's your deal Courtney?" Ash asks. "Are you dating? Married? Have kids? Hate puppies?"

"Ashley, shut up," Ellie sighs.

Laughing, Courtney takes a seat. "I'm married," she says, holding up her left hand. "His name is Jack, and he's a fireman in town. He's crazy hot and I love him more than anything in the world. No kids yet. And I love all animals."

"Hmm, okay, good answers."

"Anything else?"

"Yes, does Jack have friends we could meet?"

"He does." She laughs. "Both fireman and cops if that interests you."

"Oh, it does," Ash says, fanning herself. "I love a man in uniform."

"Who doesn't?" Courtney laughs. "The first time I saw Jack in his, I wanted to strip my clothes off and offer myself up right there in my shop."

"Oh, that would have been a great meet cute." Mel laughs.

"I was so nervous, I ended up spilling hot coffee all over him."

"Ooh, was he forced to take his clothes off then?"

"Sadly, no." She smiles.

I'm so glad they get along. I knew they would. We order food, more drinks, and laugh the entire time. I haven't laughed this much in a long time, and my stomach hurts.

Peeking at my phone again, I still see nothing. Huh, that's kind of weird. I baited him with the idea that all the men in here were after me so he'd say some sexy possessive shit that'd get me all hot. But there's nothing.

Jakey, Jakey, Jakey. I'm here drinking a lot of gin and tonics and laughing with my girls. We're talking about all sorts of sexy things and I told them you're amazing in bed. And on couches, in cars, and how gloriously endowed you are. I hope you don't mind, handsome...

Smiling, I slip my phone back in my purse and rejoin the conversation at hand.

Alex continues to pour us drink after drink for the next few hours, and we get a steady drunkenness going that has us getting louder and drawing more attention to our table. Then, the same song that got me dancing a few weeks ago with Courtney comes on and I scream, pulling her up to dance.

"This is our song! Remember?"

"Yes!" she screams, laughing.

The others just sit and watch as Courtney and I shake our hips and spin each other.

"Hey, honey, care to shake that ass on me?" a sleazy voice says from behind me.

"No, thanks," I answer, not bothering to look at him.

"Come on, darling, just one dance." His hand snakes around my waist, and I instinctively throw my elbow back into his ribs. "Ow! What the fuck?!" he yells in my ear, immediately releasing me.

Spinning around, I level the douche bag with a nasty look. "Don't call me darling, and don't put your hands on me." My voice is hard and commanding.

"You're the one shaking that fine ass around for all to see. It seemed to me you were in need of a man to take care of you."

Courtney snorts next to me and opens her mouth to say something, but I shake my head no. "First of all, not every woman who dances wants your greasy hands on her. And second, I have a man who takes *very* good care of me, so move along."

"Get out of here, Jason. Ally's with Jake," Courtney adds.

"Shit," he says, looking semi-scared as he turns and walks back to a table full of guys who are all staring at us.

"Don't mind Jason, he's just your typical small-town wash up. You know, peaked in high school and hasn't done much with his life since?"

"Sure, whatever," I say, walking back over to the table.

"What was that about?" Ellie asks, nodding towards the table of guys.

"Nothing. Just an asshole thinking I'm a tramp looking to bed any guy that approaches me first."

"Oh, yeah, sure, just the usual," she replies sarcastically. "Happens to me all the time."

"Shut up." I laugh, finishing the rest of my drink. "I'm getting another one. Who else needs one?"

A resounding round of yeses answer me back, so I head up to the bar and wave Alex over. "Another round for all of us, please."

"You okay?" he asks, looking concerned. "I saw Jason being an ass."

"Yeah, I'm good, thanks. Nothing I can't handle."

"Let me know if he bothers you again and I'll kick him out."

"Thanks." I smile.

"And you're definitely not driving home. Do you girls have a ride?"

"Okay, dad," I say, rolling my eyes.

"I'm serious. Make sure you call Jake or Jack to drive you."

"I will, don't worry. Now, more drinks, barkeep," I say, slapping my hand on the wood.

"Barkeep? Really?"

"Thought I'd try it out." I shrug, sitting on the stool in front of him while he makes our drinks.

"Your friends seem nice."

"Don't go trying to take one of them home with you, slick. Your bad boy, sexy biker act won't work."

"Bad boy, sexy biker?" He smiles.

"Yeah, you know you're hot, don't play dumb. I'm a taken

woman, so it's okay for me to say that openly."

"And you're drunk." He laughs. "So your mouth is a little looser."

"Hey! My mouth is not loose. Just ask Jake."

"Fuck. Okay, don't say shit like that when I know I can't have you."

"Alright." I wink, smiling.

Shaking his head, he pushes the five drinks towards me. "Don't forget to ask for a ride. I can't fit all of you on the back of my bike."

"Ha! Good one."

Taking two trips to carry all the drinks to the table, I sit back down and sip my fresh cocktail. Damn, Alex makes a perfect gin and tonic.

Pulling out my phone again, I see that it's getting late, and Jake still hasn't messaged me back.

"What's wrong?" Courtney asks.

"Huh? Oh, nothing. It's just that I've messaged Jake a few times tonight and he hasn't answered yet."

"He's probably just busy."

"I'm going to see if he can pick us up. I definitely can't drive home."

"Ahh!! Yes!! We want to meet him!!" Ash yells, clapping her hands.

Dialing his number, it just rings and rings until I get his voicemail. "Hey, hot stuff. So, we're a tad on the drunk side and I was wondering if you could pick us up? I'd be willing to do some filthy things to you as a thank you." Giggling, everyone starts making cat calls and dirty gestures. "Sorry, ignore them. Please, please come so I can show you off." Blowing him a kiss through the phone, I hang up and burst out in a fit of giggles.

"I'm going to tell Jack to get me at last call. Shit, wait, it's already midnight?"

"I know! That means we better drink some more then."

"It doesn't, but sure!" She laughs.

Last call approaches fast, and Jake still hasn't answered me. What the fuck? He's never not answered me, especially when I ask for help.

"He hasn't answered me." I sulk.

"Honey, he's probably sleeping now," Ellie says, trying to reassure me. "Courtney, can your man take us home?"

"Yeah, of course. He'll do whatever I ask." She giggles. "Come on, he's outside waiting."

Walking up the bar to close my tab, Alex comes right over to me. "What can I do for you, beautiful? Need a ride? I see your friends are leaving with Courtney."

"Yeah, Jack is taking us. I just need to close my tab."

"Jake's not coming? It's hard to believe he'd have something better to do than take you home."

"I wouldn't know, he hasn't answered me all night."

"I'd never keep you waiting." He smirks, handing me back my card. "See you around, beautiful."

"'Night, Alex."

Walking through the bar to the front door, I have to really focus on not twisting my ankle in my heels. Falling while drunk is the ultimate sign of sloppiness. And I'm a classy bitch.

"There you are! Come on!" Courtney yells from the inside of a big pickup truck.

Opening the back door, I squeeze in next to Ashley. "Hey, Jack. Thanks for taking us. Jake isn't answering his phone."

"No problem," he answers in a deep, rich voice.

Laying my head back, I close my eyes for the short ride back home, and when we pull up to the house a few minutes later, I hop out and almost fall on my face.

Ugh! I forgot that Jake always helps me down from these huge things. And I'm wearing heels. And I'm drunk.

Great. Another thing I needed help with but Jake is apparently too busy to answer me.

Fuck. I'm way too dependent on him. I've been a self-sufficient, independent woman my entire life, and now what? A man finally treats me right and I suddenly need him for everything?

Hell no. Fuck that.

"You good, Ally?" Courtney asks from her seat.

"Yes! I don't need help with everything. I'm fully capable of taking care of myself."

"Okay, I feel like I missed out on an entire conversation, but I'm glad to hear that."

"Never mind. Yeah, I'm good. Thanks, Jack, you're a prince. 'Night guys." Waving bye, I walk up the porch steps and open the door, ushering the girls in before me.

"Who wants to crash with me?" I ask. But before anyone can answer, Ashley collapses on the couch and stretches out, closing her eyes immediately. "Okay, I'm not carrying her, so she's staying there."

"Fine with us. We'll take the spare room. Love you, Ally-cat." Mel and Ellie hug me and kiss my cheek.

"Love you, too. 'Night."

Heading into my room, I flop down on the bed and undo the straps on my heels, kicking them onto the floor. Ahhh, that feels good.

Checking my phone for the tenth time tonight, there's still

no messages from Jake. But there is one from Courtney.

I don't want to be the one to tell you this, but Jack just told me something...

What?

He was out tonight.

Who? Jack?

No. Jake.

Okay...

With his ex.

What ex? Are you serious?

Yeah. Jack saw them having dinner at Anthony's when he went to pick up takeout.

So, the night I go out with my friends, he goes off and has a secret dinner with an ex he's told me nothing about?

I don't know. Maybe it was a coincidence??

How?

I don't know, I'm trying to be optimistic.

Who even is she??

Jack said they were together in high school and college, and then he came back a few years ago alone. That's all he knows.

What the fuck? Is this why he froze when I asked him about his past on the way to Bar Harbor? I just figured he had his heart broken and he was too manly to talk about it. I never thought he could be hiding something like another woman...

Why did he hide this from me? And why hasn't he answered me? Are they back together?

I'm sorry, Ally, I have no idea.

I don't stay with liars or cheaters.

You don't know anything other than they had dinner together, though.

I know enough. Whatever, I'm going to bed. Thanks for telling me.

Of course. See you tomorrow.

Rolling over, I slide my feet onto the cold wood floor and lift my dress up and off of me. Throwing on sweats and a t-shirt, I stumble down the hall to use the bathroom and grab a bottle of water from the fridge before I stumble my way back to bed, flopping down face first.

I will not let Jake break me.

He's not allowed to.

He wants to ignore me all night so he can have a secret dinner with his secret ex? Fine. I'll ignore him right back, and then break up with him before he has the chance to do it to me.

But breaking up would mean we were together, and I have no idea if we ever really were.

Maybe I was just an easy lay for him once he realized I couldn't resist him.

Letting out a frustrated sigh, I roll over and stare at the ceiling, praying for sleep.

Chapter 23

I can't get comfortable. Tossing and turning, I flip my pillow to the cool side, and lay face down on it.

I sobered up pretty quickly after Courtney texted me, and now I can't shut my brain off. Jake went out to dinner tonight. At Anthony's. Where everyone in town would blatantly see him with her. That's a slap in the face to me. He's making me look, and feel, like a fool.

Letting out a frustrated sigh, I punch my pillow and decide to give up on getting any sleep. Rolling out of bed, I head into the kitchen and make myself tea, letting the hot liquid calm me.

Sitting at the table, I look at the clock and see that it's already after four in the morning, and with nothing but the quiet of the night to keep me company, I think about the first time Jake made me tea. I was so surprised he even knew how.

Tears prick my eyes and I blink them away, refusing to cry. I told myself I wouldn't let another man hurt me, but Jake had somehow seemed like an exception. He had found a way to break through the walls I built around my already cracked heart, and filled every broken piece of me with everything that he is.

But now I can feel those same cracks slowly starting to fracture again, a constant ache radiating out from my chest. A few tears escape my eyes and run down my cheeks, splashing onto the table. Shivering, I sip my tea, trying to warm my chilling body.

I let him into my past, and I let him understand me. I handed myself over to him piece by piece until he had everything. He has everything. I trusted him with my past, present, and future. Something I never wanted, or intended, to do.

Looking around the small kitchen that I've grown to call my own, I see him everywhere. Jake and I had our first kiss in here. He lifted me up onto the counter and seared me with his touch. It was in that moment he marked me as his, and I craved him like an addict needing my next fix.

Cradling my head in my hands, a few tears escape my eyes.

Was all of this just some game to him? Was he just buying time until he could be with her again? Has he been talking to her this whole time?

I feel so stupid. It's like the other shoe has finally dropped. It was all too good to be true.

Long after the cup of tea in front of me has gone cold, I see the sky start to lighten through the window.

Fixing myself a fresh cup of tea, I head outside and curl

up in one of the wicker chairs with a blanket. I catch the sun just starting to peek itself up over the horizon, its rays shining out in every direction trying to rid the world of darkness.

I'd like to think that maybe it's a sign I should let the light overpower the dark in me, but it's in the darkness that I've lived my entire life. It's the place that has never let me down. Living in the shadows has let me control my life.

But ever since Jake showed up at my door that first night, I've slowly been losing that carefully constructed control I've held onto.

My tears dry in streaks down my cheeks and I look over at the empty chair next to me. Curling my hands around the mug, I hold it to my lips and let the steam warm my face.

I don't know why I'm so emotional about all of this shit. I'm usually stronger than this. No, I *know* I'm stronger than this. I should just drive over to his house and demand the truth. But I can't. Either I don't want to hear the truth, or I just want to wallow in my own self-doubt and pity.

Probably a little bit of both.

"Hey, Ally-cat," Mel whispers from the doorway. "Do you mind if I join you?"

"Of course not. Come sit."

"Wow, that's beautiful," she says, looking out at the sunrise.

"I know. I've seen a lot of them already, but it never gets old."

"Why are you up so early?"

"I haven't really even been to sleep."

"Why?" she asks, and I just shrug my shoulder. "Come on, tell me. Is it Jake?

Nodding, I take a sip of tea. "Courtney told me that Jack

saw Jake out last night, and that's why he wasn't answering me."

"Okay?"

"He was out to dinner with his ex."

"Are you serious?" she whispers, her eyes widening.

"Mhmm."

"Maybe they were just catching up? Maybe they're friends?"

"No, I don't know. But my mind has already went to the worst."

"I know you've been burned time and time again, but from what you've told us, Jake seems different. Is he dumb enough to screw up what you two have?"

"If you asked me yesterday morning, I'd have said no. But now I'm not sure."

"Why is this morning any different? Do you trust him?"

"Yes. Well, I mean, I did."

"If you trust him, then don't let that waiver before knowing everything. Jumping to the worst conclusions is natural, but don't let them make you think something that isn't real."

I sip my tea, thinking about that. "You're right."

"I know." She smiles softly. "You guys will talk today, and it'll all be fine. I'm sure of it."

"I'm glad one of us is."

Mel has always had the ability to calmly assess a situation from all angles, and help you see that you're not always seeing the big picture. She's saved each of us from looking like idiots a time or two.

Watching the sunrise in comfortable silence, I sip my tea and wrap the blanket tighter around me.

"Are you hungry?" I ask after a while.

"Starving, actually. I was hoping you'd make one of your hangover breakfasts."

"A night out wouldn't be complete without one."

"Exactly."

Mel and I head back inside, and I make banana, blueberry, and cinnamon pancakes with bacon and eggs on the side. Brewing a fresh pot of coffee, we go and sit to eat when a groggy Ashley and Elizabeth shuffle into the kitchen.

"Oh my god, what smells so good?" Ellie moans.

"And why are you up so early?" Ash grumbles.

"I made pancakes, bacon, and eggs."

"And we're up early because we wanted to watch the sunrise," Mel adds.

"Sunrise? Are you freaking kidding me? I can barely open my eyes right now."

"Well, Ashley, some of us can hold our liquor better than others. You know that."

"Whatever, Mel," Ash snaps back as her and Ellie make themselves coffee and a plate of food.

"Mmm, I've missed your hangover breakfasts, Ally," Ellie says around a full mouth.

"Me, too. They're the best."

"Thanks. I miss cooking. I haven't gotten to do that much of it in the past few weeks. Jake always wakes up before me to make us breakfast, and then usually makes me dinner, too."

"Where can I get one?" Ash asks, pausing mid bite.

"I guess you'll just have to move here." I shrug.

"I'll have a look around, first. Maybe sample the options."

"You make it sound like a meat market. You're talking about guys here, right?"

"Oh, Melanie. Sweet, sweet, Melanie. Yes, I'm talking about men."

"Excuse me for not thinking about men like a buffet to sample."

"No one ever keeps my interest for that long, you know that."

"Alright, enough," Ellie interjects. "Can I please eat without thinking about you sampling the taste of men?"

Shrugging her shoulders, Ash bites into her bacon. "What are we doing today?"

"I thought we'd head into town and walk around. Do a little shopping, and then stop in at the café where I work and Courtney owns."

"When do we get to meet Jake?"

"Oh, um." My eyes dart over to Mel's. "I don't know. He might not be available anymore."

"What the hell does that mean? He doesn't want to meet us?" Ashley asks, a surprised look on her face. "Aren't we going to his family's BBQ tomorrow?"

"Okay, calm down. I just haven't heard from him so I don't know what's happening."

"Why are you being shady?" Ellie asks.

"I'm not being shady."

"You are. What happened between yesterday and today?"

Thankfully, Mel comes to my rescue. "Alright, guys. Just let Ally figure some stuff out and then she'll tell us what's happening."

"Whatever. I'm taking a shower," Ash declares, getting up.

"And I'm going to lay down again. We're not done with this though, Ally," Elizabeth adds, pushing her chair out.

When it's just Mel and I, I sigh, covering my face with my hands. "I hate this. I feel so stupid. And you guys are here to see this."

"Ally, we're your best friends. I'm glad we're here for you right now. Do you want me to tell them?"

"No. No, I'll do it. Thanks, though."

I forgot that I left my car at the bar last night, so Mel drives us into town. "This looks like it's straight out of a Hallmark movie." She laughs.

"I know. I thought the same thing my first day here. Do you guys want to stop at the café first?"

"Let's maybe check out a few stores first so it'll work me up into needing a donut."

"Sounds good."

Browsing around the shops, they each buy a few cute things, and I decide to get the jewelry and dress that I had seen on my first day.

I haven't been in the bookstore yet, so when we step through the doors, the familiar scent of old and new books wafts into me. I love that smell.

A half-hour later, I finally decide on a mystery novel for my next read. I definitely can't be bothered with anything involving romance right now.

"Okay, I'm ready for coffee now," Ash sighs. "And to sit down. I'm still a little hung over."

"Alright, let me just pay for this," I tell them, holding up the book.

The café is only a little farther down the street, and when

we reach it, I wave my hand at the sign. "Here we are, The Blueberry Café." Pushing the door open, the familiar bells jingle above our heads, and the scent of coffee and sugar hits us immediately.

"It smells amazing in here," Ellie groans as we walk up to Courtney behind the counter.

"Just so you know, Ally, you've now been the cause for two raging hangovers in less than a month when I went years without one. Thanks so much."

"Nothing one of Ally's hangover breakfasts can't cure."

"Or some of these pastries," I add. "The first weekend I was here, I'm pretty sure I got drunk like two or three times and had to come into work and shove both a donut and pastry in my mouth. Coffee and sugar make everything better."

"True." Courtney smiles. "Now, what can I get you ladies?"

I choose a blueberry crumb cake square, Mel gets a glazed donut, Ash a bear claw, and Ellie goes for the donut of the week – a strawberry shortcake donut with a whipped cream and fresh strawberry filling.

Sitting down at one of the tables, we all dig in straight away. Moaning with every bite, we start to sound like a group of wanton women desperately in need of men. Which, sadly, really isn't too far from the truth.

"You ladies good over here?" Courtney asks, coming over to our table. "I can't help but hear the orgasmic sounds you're making."

"Oh, shit. Yeah, this is amazing." Ellie smiles, licking her fingers, savoring every last bit of filling that's spilled out.

"Ally, can I show you something new I got in yesterday? It's in the kitchen."

"Yeah, sure."

Once we're safely out of view and earshot from the others, she turns and gives me a big hug. "I'm so sorry. I hate that I had to tell you last night after we had such a good time."

"It's fine."

"Did you talk to him yet?"

"No. I'll just have to see what he says. If he says anything at all, that is."

"Weren't you supposed to have dinner together? He has to reach out before then. Why don't you call? Or just go over there?"

"Yeah, we're supposed to meet at Anthony's, but I'm not sitting through a dinner at the same place he took another woman and pretend like everything's fine. And no, I'm not reaching out. He's going to have to come to me."

"Ally, he wouldn't cheat on you. And even if he did, he certainly wouldn't be going out to dinner in town where everyone would see. That'd be fucking stupid. Don't be stubborn. Go to him."

"What else am I supposed to think? I haven't talked to him in over a day. He hasn't responded to any of my messages or calls. I stopped bothering after you texted me. He probably spent the night banging her every which way to Sunday. They had a lot of years to make up for."

"Wow, okay, I see we've jumped to insane conclusions already. I'm just trying to stay positive here. Maybe he didn't want to ruin your night with your friends by telling you about it."

"We'll see." I shrug, not really knowing what else to say.

"Yes, you will. Okay, I have to get back out there before people start stealing shit." Hugging me again, she kisses my cheek. "And look on the bright side. If he really is a complete asshole, we can always slash his tires and drill holes in his boats."

"Sounds good." I smile, that thought actually comforting.

Returning to the table, all three of them turn to look at me. "Yes?"

"What did she say?" Ellie asks.

"Nothing."

"Bull. We let you slide earlier, but something's up. Just tell us."

Sighing, I pick at the crumbs on my plate. "Jack, Courtney's husband, saw Jake last night at dinner with his ex. An ex I know nothing about."

"Ally, what the fuck?" Ash cuts in angrily.

"And I haven't talked to him since yesterday morning. I'm assuming that's why he was too busy to answer me last night."

"Why wouldn't you tell us?"

"Because I feel like a complete fool. Again. I fell so hard and fast for him, and now I'm just…I don't know. I'm usually the one with the 'fuck men' attitude, and the one who never cares. But I care."

"I'm sorry, but no," Ash says. "Ally, we know you. We know you crave love like the rest of us. You're human. You're a woman. Don't be afraid to feel. Please, don't be afraid to feel. You've been living your life by yourself for as long as I've known you, and even if things turn out for the worst, I never want to see you shut yourself off again. You need to live, damn it. You need to love, and you need to feel pain. You can't have one without the other. It's the delicate balance we all deal with every day. It's what you choose to focus on that makes the difference. Choose life, choose happiness, and choose you."

Tears that I didn't even know formed fall from my eyes. I haven't heard Ashley say something so serious since the day I told them all about my dad in high school. She had this fierce, determined look in her eyes when she told me I had them now to help me through anything I needed.

Wiping my cheeks, I take a deep breath and look at my three best friends. They all share the same watery eyes and looks of agreement.

"Okay," I whisper. "I hear you."

"But do you understand me?"

"Yes, I do. I don't want to go back to how I was."

"Good." She nods, wiping her eyes. "Now, let's get out of here before we all have breakdowns in the middle of this café."

Standing, we bring our plates back up to Courtney and say our goodbyes. Mel drops me off at The Rusty Anchor to pick up my car before we head back to the cottage for lunch and cocktails out in the backyard.

"I seriously love it here, Ally. I can't believe you found this place," Mel says, gazing out at the boats sailing by.

"I know, and Dottie is so sweet, too. We sat together on the porch when I first got here and drank tea and ate pie. Then I had her come back a week later to teach me how to make it because I needed another blueberry fix. She's one of those old gossiping biddies, but in the cute, small-town charming way."

"Dottie sounds like a cool old broad." Ash smiles.

"She is. I should call her again to come down for an afternoon. I know she misses her house, and I want her to see she left it in good hands."

"Where is she?"

"She moved in with her daughter and family an hour north of here."

"You should buy this place from her," Ellie says casually.

I can't say that thought hasn't crossed my mind. More times than I can count over this past month, actually.

"I thought about it. But I don't know, that's a lot of responsibility."

"True." She nods.

I want Pine Cove to be my new home, but the truth is, I had a whispered thought in the back of my head that with how good things were with Jake, we'd eventually move in together. Buying a house would be pointless then.

Shaking those thoughts from my mind, I take a huge gulp of my drink and lean back in my chair.

The thought has crossed my mind to ask if they wouldn't mind staying in tonight, but I wouldn't do that to them. The three of them drove up here for the weekend, and I'm not going to keep them holed up in my house just because my heart feels like it's being squeezed by a vice.

I left my phone inside, so when we come in to start getting ready for dinner, I cautiously chance a look at it.

Shit. He texted.

Taking a deep breath, I swipe it open.

Hey, darlin', what time is dinner tonight?

Is he fucking serious right now? Nothing for over a day, and this is what I get?

Nope.

Fuck that.

"Change of plans. We're going to the bar again."

"What did he say?" Ellie asks, nodding at my phone.

Reading them the message, their faces reflect my same reaction.

"I'll go get the wine. You go pick out a hot outfit," Ashley tells me.

"Yup. I'm probably going to need a whole bottle."

"Well, it's a good thing you bought the whole damn liquor store in anticipation of our arrival. I was offended at first, but not anymore." She smiles, heading into the kitchen.

Downing two glasses while we get ready, I decide to go with a little black dress that shows a lot of leg. I curl my hair in big waves that fall down my back, and I do a subtle smoky eye so my blue eyes look even bluer. Finishing off my look, I smooth on a bold, dark red lipstick, and slip on a pair of black wrap-up heels.

Twirling in the mirror, I smile. I look like a vampiress ready to go out and devour her prey. And I fucking love it.

"Holy shit, Ally. You look hot as hell."

"Thanks, El." I smile, pouring myself another glass of wine as the others come into my room. "You all look hot, too. Damn, this town definitely hasn't seen a group like us before," I say with a laugh.

"Well, it's good to see you've relaxed a bit," Mel says, eyeing my glass.

"Yup. This is my third glass, I feel sexy, and I want to dance. And maybe flirt with Alex a little."

"He's hot," Mel sighs, biting her lip.

"Shit, Mel, go for it! I bet he'd give you a ride on the back of his bike if you asked." I wink.

"Yeah, no. That's okay." She laughs.

"Oh my god, Mel, live a little!" Ash yells, throwing her hands up.

"Alright, enough about me. Let's just go. I'm driving since Ally's already on her way to drunk."

"Not drunk. Tipsy. There's a difference."

"Whatever you say, honey."

Pulling up to the bar, I check my phone and see that Jake has called twice and texted three times. Not even opening them, I slip my phone back into my purse and get out of the car.

Walking into The Rusty Anchor, every head turns to us like last night, and I don't blame them for staring because we look hot as hell.

I keep my head held high as I make my way over to the same table we had yesterday, refusing to let anyone think I'm less than fine. I don't know who knows what in this fishbowl of a town, but I'm not letting them see that their precious townie Jake has fooled me. I may feel weak on the inside, but I'm not letting anyone see that. I've had a lot of practice over the years.

"Wow, we sure know how to make an entrance." Ellie laughs. "I wish we got this much attention back home."

"I'll get the first round," I offer, making my way up to the bar, smiling at Alex.

"Well, well, well, two nights in a row. I feel honored."

"Yes, I thought I'd grace you with my presence again." I smile.

"You look beautiful as always."

"Thank you."

"Same drinks as last night?"

"Yes. And please make mine like you did last night, it was the best I've ever had."

"Now, sweetheart, I know I would be, but you haven't

been falling for my good looks or charm."

"What charm?" I scoff.

"Wow, wound me further," he says in mock hurt.

Smiling freely for the first time all day, I take our drinks back to the table and hold mine up to toast. "Okay, ladies, we are here tonight to have fun and forget about boys. Cheers!"

"Let's get fucked up!" Ash exclaims, throwing her head back laughing, getting the attention of the surrounding tables.

And that's how the next few hours go for us. We drink, yell, laugh, and dance. Jake only crosses my thoughts every other second instead of constantly, so I think that's a major improvement.

"Okay, I'm getting another. Anyone need one yet?" I ask.

"No, we're good," Mel answers, pointing to their full glasses.

"'Kay, I'll be back."

Sitting up on one of the bar stools, my dress rides up my thighs, exposing even more of my legs than before. Crossing them, I can feel the eyes all around me slowly raking up my body, eating up my bare skin like it's theirs to have. Too bad for them, though, because it's not.

Leaning on the bar, I wait for Alex to see me and come over. "Another?" he asks, his eyes darting down to my chest in my low-cut dress.

"Yes, please. Just for me, though."

As I'm watching him make my drink, I start to feel a tingling sensation creep up my spine, and the hairs on the back of my neck stand.

Pushing my drink towards me, Alex looks over my shoulder and smirks. "Looks like your man is here."

"I don't have a man," I state firmly, squeezing the lime

into my drink.

"Well, Jake's here regardless."

"What?" I ask, my eyes widening.

Spinning on the stool, I meet his eyes from across the bar and I feel my heart clench in my chest. I can feel his gaze burning into me from here.

Keeping my face neutral, I watch every stride he takes towards me – a wild and untamed aura cloaking him. But the closer he gets, the faster my heart beats, and the harder it is to hide my reaction.

Holding me captive, he weaves through the people and tables separating us, his eyes never wavering from mine.

When he's only a few feet from me, he looks over my shoulder and growls. "Fuck off, Alex."

What the hell is he mad about?

Starting at my feet, Jake rakes his eyes up my body, taking in all of my exposed skin. Closing the distance between us, he leans forward, and cages me in against the bar with his arms.

"You haven't been answering me," he says, a hardness in his voice.

"Neither were you," I shoot back, not willing to give in to him.

"I need to talk to you."

"About what?" I ask innocently, tilting my head to the side.

"You already know about what."

"Oh, do I? If I do, it's certainly not because you told me." My eyes blaze with a new found anger I feel bubbling in me now that he's standing in front of me. "You lied to me. You hid her from me. Do you want her? Just tell me and I'll leave. I don't stay where I'm not wanted."

"Darlin', you don't understand."

"Don't call me that," I spit back. "Not anymore."

Leaning in, his hot, sweet breath sends a shiver down my spine as he whispers in my ear, "You're sexy when you're mad at me, darlin'. It makes me want to run my hands up your smooth legs and under your dress to the place I know is already ready for me."

Holding back a moan, I straighten my spine and push him away. "I'm not playing games with you, Jake."

"Neither am I. Your dress is so fucking short every man in here has already fantasized about lifting it that last little bit to see what color lace panties you have on."

"Stop. Just stop. You have no right to be mad at what I'm wearing." Shooting my eyes around the bar, I see half of the people in here are staring at us. "Everyone's staring. If you want to talk, we can go outside." Pushing him away, I step down from the stool and make my way towards the front of the bar and out the door, all the while feeling Jake's eyes glued to my body.

I walk down the side of the building before I turn to face him, crossing my arms over my chest. "Well?" I ask, waiting for him to say something. But he doesn't. He just stares. "Who is she, Jake?"

"My ex."

"That's all I get?"

"She showed up at my parent's house yesterday looking for me. I refused to tell her where I lived, so I met her in town. We just had dinner."

"HA! Okay, Jake. You *just* had dinner, and chose not to tell me. And then proceeded to not answer any of my messages." Shaking my head, I turn my back to him to take a deep breath. "I don't forgive cheaters, Jake."

Grabbing my arm, he spins me back around. "I didn't cheat on you, Ally. I'd never hurt you like that."

"Well, you've already hurt me. More than I've ever been before."

A pained expression crosses his eyes and he lets go of my arm. "I shouldn't have come tonight," he murmurs, backing away from me.

"No," I say firmly, "you don't get to do that. I've spent the entire night and day wondering if we were over, and wondering if we were ever even together. Do you love her? Are you back with her?"

He barks out a laugh. "I wouldn't get back with her if someone paid me."

"Then why can't you tell me anything?! Why are you always holding back? I've told you things that I've never told anyone, and you won't let me in, not even a little bit. Why won't you ever talk to me?"

"Because she's the one who fucked me up!" he yells, raking his hands through his hair. "She broke me. And I swore I wouldn't let another woman have the power to do that again."

"Then what have we been doing?" I ask, throwing my arms out. "What has all of this been to you?"

"I had to listen to her apologize to me tonight," he says, not answering me. "The person I once loved and gave up everything for, had the fucking nerve to think I needed her apology. Do you want to know why I hate her? Why I'm so fucked up?" He takes another step towards me and I take one back, seeing the fire in his eyes.

"I caught her and my best friend fucking in our bed. I

came home early on leave and decided to surprise her. But it turns out she had the surprise for me. I followed her to Boston after high school. I was pre-law for her. And then when I was too much of a coward to tell her I didn't want to go to law school, I joined the Navy. I gave her everything for eight years. We were going to get married–"

"Married?! She was your fiancé?!"

"And do you want to know why she was apologizing to me all these years later?" he asks, ignoring another of my questions as his eyes burn into mine.

"Why?"

"Because she thinks she finally understands how much she hurt me. But she doesn't know. Going from man to man and never finding love isn't the same as getting your heart ripped out from your chest and thrown into a shredder."

"Why should I believe you? How do I know you haven't been waiting for her to come back? Or just biding your time with me?"

"Are you fucking serious?" he growls. "I don't want her. I want you. I need you. She came here asking for another chance and I said no."

Seeing red, I curl my fingers into my palms, trying to hold in my anger. "Why should I believe you?"

"I'm not your dad, Ally. I'd never lie to you," he says, stalking forward until I'm up against the side of the bar.

"How dare you! You don't get to throw that in my face!" I yell, pushing him away from me. But he just pulls me back and pins me against the wall.

"It's the truth. I'm not your dad. I'm not going to lie to you. I'm not going to pretend I'm something I'm not. I didn't tell you about her because I didn't want you to see me as weak.

I want you to see me as the man you can count on, and the man who would do anything for you. Because I will.”

“Showing vulnerability isn’t weakness, Jake. Telling you about my dad didn’t make me feel weak, it made me feel closer to you.”

“I’m not built that way.”

“So, what? You want me to understand all of this and forgive you? And then expect to never have you open up to me because it makes you feel weak? That’s bullshit. No,” I say, pulling away from the wall and walking away. But Jake pulls me back again.

“I’m not letting you walk away from me, darlin’.”

“You can’t stop me. I’m done, Jake.” I try and get out from his grasp, but I can’t.

“No, you’re not.”

“I’m not staying with someone who won’t talk to me about anything remotely emotional. You never tell me how you feel!” I yell in his face.

Breathing hard, he pins me with his stare, a battle of wills that I refuse to back down from.

“I spent the past five years alone and isolated because a woman took everything from me. But then you came crashing into my life in the middle of the night like a fucking meteor. The second you opened the door in those little silk pajamas, I was a goner. I’d never seen a more beautiful woman in my life. And when I looked into your eyes…baby, I found heaven. I had found my light. I couldn’t take my eyes off of you. I still can’t. Just being near you, holding you, kissing you…I’ve never felt more alive or at peace in my entire life.”

Reaching out, Jake brushes away the stray tear that rolls down my cheek, and I close my eyes at that simple touch, heat spreading across my skin.

"Seeing her last night brought back all of the anger and pain I used to live with every day. I didn't want you to see me like that. I couldn't let you see me like that."

"You didn't have to hide from me. I can handle shit, Jake. I'm not weak."

"I know you're not. And that's when something occurred to me today, and I was able to let go of it all." His thumb brushes my cheek. "She doesn't matter. The past doesn't matter. *You* matter. You make me smile, and laugh, and feel alive for the first time in a long time. You make me happy," he confesses, caressing my cheek. "I love you, darlin'. You're my everything."

Tears spill from my eyes and I pull him those last few inches that separate us, kissing him with everything inside of me.

He loves me.

Jake Taylor loves me.

I've never heard sweeter words spoken.

Gripping his hair, I pull him closer, needing him like my next breath. Jake lifts me up, and I wrap my legs around his hips. Arching against the wall, I push myself against him, needing to be closer still.

He pulls away, and I try and chase him with my lips, but he doesn't let me. I know he needs to hear me say the words.

Looking into his stormy blue eyes, I cup his cheek, rubbing his scruff along my palm. "Jake," I whisper, tears flooding my eyes again. "I've waited for you my whole life. You're something I never thought I'd have, or was worthy of. I love you, mountain man. With everything in me, I love you. You broke down my walls, and made the heart I had long ago gave up on, beat again. It beats for you. With you, I feel strong, beautiful, sexy, confident, and seen. You see me, Jake."

Tucking a strand of hair behind my ear, he smiles softly. "And you see me, baby. You know me. Even when I don't say everything I feel, I show you in every kiss and every touch."

Blinking away my tears, I lean in and kiss him softly. I place my hand over his heart and feel the strong, wild beat beneath my fingers.

Kissing me soft and slow, I savor his taste, my head feeling light and dizzy.

"I need you, darlin'," Jake breathes into me.

"Yes," I whisper against his lips.

Peeling me off the wall, he carries me around the corner of the building, hiding us in the shadows.

"Here?"

Jake smooths his fingers up my bare legs, leaving fire in their wake. "Yes, here," he says, pushing his hips into mine, letting me feel how much he needs me.

Groaning, I reach between us and undo his belt, popping the button of his jeans open and pulling down the zipper. Sliding my hand inside, I grip him in my hand and squeeze, my eyes burning into his. "This is mine, Jake. You're mine. Don't ever let me feel otherwise again. Got it?"

"Yes," he answers, flashing me a satisfied grin as he pushes my panties to the side. "And this is mine," he growls, sliding his fingers up and down my folds. "You tease me, and every man around, when you wear a dress like this. But I know that I'm the only one who gets to have you. I'm the only one who gets to see what's beneath," he says, shoving two fingers inside of me. "I'm the only one who can make you forget your name."

"Yes," I moan, and Jake slams his mouth on mine, his fingers following the same rhythm and dance as his tongue.

Wrapping my arms around his neck, I grip his hair and pull, telling him I need more. But he pulls out of me and I grunt, biting his lip.

"Don't worry, darlin'. I'm giving you more," he says smoothly, entering me in one swift motion.

My head falls back against the bricks, and my mouth opens in a silent cry, trying not to let the whole world know what we're doing in the shadows.

Kissing his way across my collar bone and up my neck, I grab his face and make him look at me. "I need it fast and hard, mountain man. I can't wait right now."

With a wicked gleam in his eyes, Jake pulls out and slowly pushes back into me.

"Jake, no, no, no. Please," I plead, but he just grips my hips and pins me against the bricks. I have no space to move, and I have no choice but to take what he gives me.

His slow, arduous pace gradually picks up until he's slamming into me with so much force, I know I'll have bruises on my hips from his grip.

Looking into his storming eyes, I see the love he has for me, and that's all it takes. Clamping down on him like a vise, I lean forward and bite his shoulder, my screams muffled by his shirt.

Jake grunts, pumping into me as I strangle him. And with one final stroke, he buries himself deep inside of me and groans into my neck, the vibrations humming through me.

Our ragged breaths fill the night air, and I tug on his hair, pulling his head up to look at me.

"I love you," I whisper, and he flashes me a sexy smile.

"I love you, too."

"Do we have to go back inside?" I ask, wishing I could leave with him right now.

"Yeah, darlin'. I have to meet your girls. I can't have them thinking I kidnapped you."

"I guess," I sigh, not wanting this moment to end.

Setting me back on the ground, I smooth my dress down as Jake fixes his jeans.

"They're definitely going to know we just had sex," I say nervously.

"Baby, everyone in there is going to know we just had sex. And I'm good with that."

I roll my eyes. "Of course you are."

"Your lipstick is a little messed up, though." He smirks, swiping his thumb across my chin.

"Great." Swatting his hand away, I rub it off myself. "Well if it's messed up on me, what do you think your face looks like?" I say smugly back, and his eyes go wide. "Let me." I smile, taking the hem of his black shirt and rubbing all around his lips. "All good. Back to your manly self."

Laughing, Jake opens the door for me, and we step back inside the bar, completely ignoring the looks we're getting from everyone as we walk up to my friends.

"Guys, this is Jake," I announce.

Releasing my hand, he holds it out to each of them to shake. "Ally talks about you all the time. It's good to finally meet you."

"You too, Jake," Mel says, smiling at us.

"Do you often have sex outside of bars, Jake?" Ellie asks, acting put off.

"Only if it's with Ally." He smirks, sliding his hand

around my waist.

"Good." She nods, biting back a smile.

"Do you have any brothers, Jake?" Ashley asks, leaning forward on the table and resting her chin on her fist.

Ellie rolls her eyes. "Jesus, Ash, really?"

"Well, excuse me for wanting to know if his gene pool was passed on to another. And you were right, Ally, he does look like Thor."

Laughing, Jake shakes his head and squeezes my side. "I have three brothers. You can meet them tomorrow at the BBQ."

"Oh, good lord, thank you," Ash says, smiling as she leans back in her chair.

"Keep it in your pants, Ash."

"Sorry, Ally-cat, no promises."

"Ally-cat?" Jake smiles at me. "That's cute."

"She's cute, but fierce."

"That I know," Jake says, laughing lightly. "I know not to cross her."

"Well, have a seat, Jake. We want to know all about the man who did the impossible and caught our girl here."

Rolling my eyes, we sit down and the three of them dive in, asking Jake question after question.

Every few minutes Jake would squeeze my hand under the table, and I would squeeze back, letting him know I loved him, too.

Chapter 24

Waking up, I stretch out in my bed, and then curl back into my covers, a smile playing at my lips.

Jake loves me.

My God, I'm so in love with him.

I can't believe I let myself doubt him. It was always right there. Every touch, every kiss, and every look told me he loved me. I just didn't recognize it for what it was.

It's hard to break habits that have been engrained in me, but I have to stop letting my past dictate my future. Jake isn't like my dad, and he isn't like any of the other guys I've been with.

Since that first night, Jake's shown me that a man can be a woman's savior and not the reason for her demise. We've saved each other, and we've inspired each other.

Alone, we were just pieces of ourselves, but together we're whole. We make each other stronger.

My phone buzzes on the nightstand and I smile, already knowing who it is.

Morning, darlin'. I can't wait to see you in a few hours so I can kiss your sweet lips. My bed was cold without you, but I know I'll get thousands of nights with my arms wrapped around you.

Swooning, I feel my cheeks heat as tears gather in my eyes from all of these new, overwhelming, emotions swirling through me.

Good morning, my sexy mountain man. I'm lying here, wishing I could kiss you senseless. I've never been happier in my entire life, and it's all because of you.

Making you happy is the only thing that matters to me now, baby. See you soon, I'll be waiting.

Smiling like a fool, I hold my phone to my chest and sigh.

If this is what my life is now, I can't think of anything better. I can't stop smiling.

Rolling out of bed, I grab my easel and a canvas and set them up on the back porch. Making coffee, I grab my other supplies and settle into a chair outside. It's another beautiful day in Pine Cove, and I honestly expected nothing less. With how I'm feeling, even if it was supposed to rain, I would have willed it away with the happiness bursting out of me.

That's why I have to paint. With every emotion inside of me heightened and swirling, I have to get them out of me. I have to solidify them.

Squeezing out a variety of colors on my palette, I dip my brush in the yellow first, and take a deep breath. With that first stroke, the world around me dissolves, and all I'm focused on is what I'm feeling.

I have no idea how much time passes, but when the back door opens and Mel pops her head out, I'm snapped back to the present.

"Hey, I don't mean to interrupt, but it's one o'clock. What time is the BBQ?"

"Oh, I didn't realize I've been out here for so long. It's at three."

"Can I see what you're working on?" she asks with hopeful eyes.

"Sure." I smile.

Stepping out onto the porch, she walks over and stands next to me. "Ally, that's beautiful."

"Thank you," I whisper, feeling a little shy at the praise.

"This is amazing. I'm so glad you started painting again. This place, and Jake, has breathed a new life into you. I've never seen you like this."

"I know, me either." I laugh lightly. "I feel different, too, in the best possible way."

"I'm so happy for you, Ally-cat. I hope to find it one day."

"You will. If I did, there's no doubt you will."

"I've been thinking a lot about life lately, and what I want. I love being a nurse and helping people, but the big, busy hospitals back home are starting to drain me. I'd love to just work at a small-town doctor's office where I know the patients on a personal level."

"Have you tried looking for one?"

"Yeah." She shrugs. "But I don't see myself living in Jersey forever."

"Do you want to move in here with me?" I smile.

"I would actually." She laughs. "It's so beautiful and peaceful."

"My door is always open, Mely."

"Thanks. I actually may take you up on that."

"Good. Now, we have to get ready. I don't want to be late."

Walking back inside, I find Ashley and Elizabeth sitting in the kitchen with coffees.

"Thanks for not asking Jake the questions you were really wanting to ask last night."

"We wanted to make a good first impression, too," Ellie says.

"So, what happened when you went outside? Other than having sex of course."

"We talked. Well, we yelled, and then talked. It was pretty hot to see him all riled up." I laugh. "He told me everything, though. Everything that was holding him back. Then he told me he loves me and nothing else mattered. *Then* we had sex." I smile.

"Well," Ash says, placing her hand over her heart. "I approve of him for you, Ally."

"I second that," Ellie adds.

"And I third that." Mel smiles.

"Wow, thank you all so much," I say, my voice dripping with sarcasm. "I may just cry."

"Oh, shut up, bitch." Ash laughs. "We just want you to know we support you."

"I know." I smile. "You guys are the best."

"We know."

"Well then, since you're the best, I'm going to need your help with an outfit. I need to make a good first impression with his family.”

“Let's go find some options.” Jumping up, Ellie heads to my room, and we all follow after her.

“I was thinking a sundress?” I pull out my favorite one from the closet.

“Oh, that's perfect!” Ash exclaims, clapping her hands together. “Only put on a little makeup, curl your hair in loose waves, and then wear your Keds. It'll look put together and cute, but not like you're trying too hard or look slutty.”

“Yeah, we don't want that,” I say, rolling my eyes. “Wearing my tight leather skirt and crop top was my second choice.”

“Alright, bitch. Just go get ready.”

“And nothing slutty for you guys either!” I yell behind me as I head into the bathroom.

“No promises!”

Pulling up to his parent's house a little after four, we're an hour late, I'm sweating, and I'm starting to freak out. I park next to a Jeep and pull out my phone.

I'm here, and I'm freaking out.

Be right there, darlin'. He sends back immediately.

“Okay, he's meeting us here.”

“Are you okay?” Ellie asks, her eyebrows furrowed.

“No, I'm nervous.”

“It'll be fine, Ally. They'll love you. How could they not?”

Her words don't even register with me. All I can focus on is my breathing as I wait for Jake. The second I see him come around the side of the house, I get out of the car and weave through the sea of vehicles to meet him halfway.

The second he sees me, a huge smile breaks out on his face and he grabs me around the waist. Lifting me up, I laugh as he spins me around, forgetting that I was even nervous just a second ago.

Setting me back down on my feet, he brushes a few curls from my face and leans down to kiss me. The second our lips touch, an electric current runs down my spine, and my heart skips a beat.

"You're beautiful, darlin'," he whispers against my lips.

Smiling, I pull back to look into his ocean eyes. "And you look handsome as always." I run my fingers across his jaw, loving the feeling of his scruff against my skin.

"Are you still nervous?"

"Not this second, no. But I will be in a minute when I have to meet your family."

"They're going to love you because I love you."

Hearing him say those three little words again, my heart swells, and I know it'll all be fine with him by my side.

"Okay," I whisper.

Nodding, he kisses my cheek and takes my hand. "Ready then?"

"Mhmm. Let me just get the girls." Walking back with Jake, I find the three of them leaning against the car, fixing their makeup. "Ready?"

"Yeah, are you done making out?" Ash asks, rolling her eyes.

"For now." I shrug, smiling.

Making our way through the cars, we walk along the side of his parent's house where the sound of music and laughter starts to get louder.

Squeezing Jake's hand for reassurance, we walk around into the backyard, and holy shit. It's probably half a football field in size with a breathtaking view of the ocean.

There's a huge patio area off the back of the house with couches and chairs around a fire pit, and speakers blasting country music. On the grass in front of the patio, is a full bar set-up where a crowd of people are gathered around, talking and laughing.

The right side of the yard is lined with tables of food and a man, who I'm assuming is one of Jake's brothers, manning the grill. He's tall, with broad shoulders, high cheekbones, a square jaw, short hair, and a smile that looks all too familiar.

In the middle of the yard, there are tables and chairs set up where maybe a hundred or so people are sitting and eating, and on the other side of them, near the tree line, I see a few people playing corn hole, horseshoes, and even beer pong.

Children run around screaming as they squirt each other with water guns, slide down a slip n' slide, and jump around in a bounce house.

This is the greatest BBQ I've ever seen.

I can see now why Courtney said the town looks forward to them every summer.

"Holy shit, this is amazing." Ellie laughs.

"Let's go get some drinks," Ash says, and the three of them walk off towards the bar.

"I guess they're going to meet my parents before you."

"What?"

"My dad is bartending, and my mom is next to him." Lifting his chin, he nods to a handsome older man laughing with a beautiful woman as he shakes a cocktail. "Come on, darlin', you need a drink."

"That's an understatement," I mumble.

Laughing, Jake squeezes my hand and walks us forward. "I don't know why you're nervous."

Pausing, I pull on his hand so he'll stop walking. "Jake, your family is really important to you. I want them to think I'm good enough for you."

Frowning, he gently lifts my chin with two fingers, searching my eyes. "Ally, you're too good for me. How have you not realized that yet? My family is important to me, but so are you. And there's no way in hell they'd ever see you as anything but amazing. Don't ever think you're not good enough."

His assurances melt away every doubt and insecurity I had. "I love you," I whisper, my eyes watering.

"What was that?" he asks, a slight smile on his lips, leaning closer to me. "I didn't catch that."

"I said I love you," I say a little louder, smiling.

"That's what I thought I heard," he says, capturing my lips with his. Throwing my arms around his neck, I kiss him back, feeling the electric current between us growing stronger every time we kiss.

Forgetting where we are, I pull away quickly, and my eyes dart around, taking in everyone staring. Shit. "Jake, everyone's staring. Now they probably think I'm some sex crazed woman who can't keep her hands off of you."

Throwing his head back, he laughs so freely, and I can't take my eyes off of him. His thick neck vibrates with laughter while his pouty lips frame a set of perfectly straight, white teeth, and his dimple is on full display.

The Jake in front of me now is so different from the one I met a month ago. He's happy, carefree, and doesn't look like he carries the world on his shoulders anymore.

"They wouldn't be wrong, though, would they, darlin'?" He smirks, making my face turn even redder than it already was.

"No, I guess not." I smile, realizing that what I said is exactly what I am.

Taking my hand again, Jake walks us over to the bar, his parents looking up and smiling at us when we get close. "Mom, dad, this is, Ally."

His mom immediately comes around the bar and hugs me. "It's so good to meet you."

"You too, Mrs. Taylor. Thank you for having me, and letting me bring my friends as well."

"Oh, call me Pam." She waves. "And of course your friends are welcome here. The more the merrier we say, right, Dave?" She smiles, turning to Jake's dad.

"Yes, dear." He smiles at his wife. "Hello, Ally, it's so nice to meet you," Dr. Taylor says, holding his hand out for me to shake.

"You too, Dr. Taylor."

"Oh, it's Dave, dear. No formalities with us."

"My son has been keeping you all to himself," Mrs. Taylor says, throwing Jake a look. "We'd love to get to know you, Ally."

"I'd like that, thank you."

"Now, what would you like to drink, dear?" Mr. Taylor asks,

"Gin and tonic?"

"I can do that." He nods, getting to work. "And Jake, your usual?"

Jake nods, and Dr. Taylor pours some kind of fancy

whisky into a cup and adds a couple ice cubes before making my drink.

"Thanks, dad. We're going to go grab some food."

"Of course, yes, please enjoy yourself, Ally. I'm so glad my son has found you," Mrs. Taylor says, her eyes glassy.

"Me, too," I say, smiling up at Jake.

"Okay, please stop." Jake laughs, uncomfortable with the attention. "See you guys later."

"Sorry about that," he says once we're out of earshot.

"No, I like them. They're really sweet."

Squeezing my hand, we approach the grill, and the man behind it looks up. "You must be, Ally." He smiles. "We've all been waiting to meet the girl who's made my brother less of an asshole. I'm Ryan, the older and better-looking brother."

"Well, that's debatable," I say, looking up at Jake.

Ryan is hot in his own way, but it's more in the polished, law enforcement, good boy kind of way. I prefer my rough mountain man.

"Huh, well, look at that, brother. A beautiful woman has finally found your woodsy, recluse look, appealing." Ryan laughs, turning the burgers over.

"Oh, she finds it way more than appealing." Jake winks down at me, making Ryan laugh.

"Oh my god," I groan, downing the rest of my drink. I can't believe he just said that.

"Sorry, darlin'." Jake smiles. "Alright, catch you later, Ry."

"It was good meeting you, Ally. Take care of my brother."

"I will. I promise," I assure him, and he nods.

Jake leads me over towards a group of guys eating at a table next, and as we get closer, I recognize Jack as one of them. Then, when I look closer, I see that all of them are wearing Pine Cove fire department t-shirts.

"Ty," Jake calls, and one of them turns around, and all I see is a younger version of Jake with shorter hair.

"This is Ally."

"Hey, Ally," he says, standing to shake my hand. "I'm Tyler. Good to finally meet the girl who's been keeping my brother busy all the time." He smirks.

"Ty," Jake warns.

"It's okay. It's true." I laugh. "Hi, Tyler, good to meet you."

"You're definitely too beautiful for my burly lug of a brother. Why don't you let me take you out?"

Laughing, I squeeze Jake's hand. "Thanks, but I love my burly man."

"Alright." He shrugs. "But let me know if that changes."

"It won't," Jake snaps, wrapping his arm around my shoulders.

"I tried." Tyler laughs, holding his hands up in defeat.

Pulling me away, Jake shakes his head. "Sorry about that."

"Why? He's funny. Both of your brothers are."

"They're assholes is what they are."

"You love them."

"I guess," he reluctantly admits. "Well, that's it for you, darlin'. You survived. You can meet Chris when he gets home on leave in the winter. Was it horrible?"

"No. It definitely went better than I thought it would. I need another drink, though."

"I'll get it for you. Your friends went over to the pong tables, so I'll meet you there."

"Oh, lord, of course they're there."

"Ally?" I hear a small voice say to my left.

Turning, I see Dottie standing there and I smile. "Hi, Dottie. How are you?" I ask, hugging her.

"I'm good, dearie. I see you're with Jake?" she whispers in my ear so only I can hear.

"Yes, I am."

"I knew you'd be perfect for him."

"What?" I ask, but she's already pulling away and turning towards Jake.

"My boy." She smiles, hugging him.

I watch as Jake's eyes widen in surprise and then dart over to mine. No doubt she's whispering something to him as well.

"You two enjoy yourselves." Dottie smiles at both of us. "Ally, call me sometime soon so we can have another baking lesson. I'll teach you how to make Jake's favorite cookies next."

"Sounds good." I smile, and she walks off towards the tables of food.

"What did she say to you?"

"What did she say to you?" he asks right back.

"I think she fancies herself a matchmaker."

"I'm not complaining," he says, wrapping his arms around my waist and kissing me softly. "I'll go get you another drink."

Staring after him for a second, I let my eyes feast on his fine as hell ass in those jeans, and his back muscles bulging through his t-shirt.

Trying to hide my smile, I head over to the pong tables and am not surprised by what I find.

"Hey!"

"No!"

"Chug that shit, bitch!" Ash yells at Mel across the table.

Her and Ellie have teamed up against Mel and Courtney,

and Ashley tends to get very intense when it comes to drinking games.

"Looks like Ash and Ellie are kicking your asses," I say to Mel and Courtney.

"Yeah, sorry, Courtney." Mel coughs, trying to breathe after chugging a cup of beer. "I haven't played since college. Ash, on the other hand, was a frat house junkie and her skills never went away."

"Excuse me for wanting to see if any of those boys would use their paddles on me."

"Ashley!"

"Oh, please Ellie, like you never wondered."

"Eh." She shrugs. "Not my thing."

"So, you did try it! I knew it! It was that kid Anthony, right?"

"You remember him? You should use your memory for something else."

"I don't need to. I have room to remember everything. Now, it's your turn, so go."

Watching them play out the game, Jake comes over to hand me another drink and then heads off to hang with Ryan.

"Meeting everyone went well?" Courtney asks.

"Yeah, they're all really nice. His brothers gave me a little bit of a hard time, but I just went with it. I feel like they were testing me."

"Boys," she sighs, rolling her eyes.

"I know. Well, I'm starving, can we get food now?"

"Yes!" Ash claps. "I could eat the whole buffet."

Walking over to the tables of food, we pile our plates with a little bit of everything, and then make our way to the grill.

"Holy shit, he's fucking gorgeous," Ash whispers behind

me.

"Hey, Ally." Ryan smiles.

"Hi, Ryan. These are my friends from back home – Ashley, Melanie, and Elizabeth. Guys, this is Jake's older brother."

"Ladies," he greets, bowing in a mock gentlemanly manor. "It's a pleasure to meet you."

"Oh, the pleasure is all mine," Ashley practically purrs, holding her hand out for him to take. "I'll have a wiener," she says, holding her plate out to him. "I like them extra juicy."

I don't know if I'm seeing things, but I think Ryan's eyes go a shade darker as he and Ash stare at each other.

Lord have mercy!

"Um, so I'll have a cheeseburger, thanks," I tell him, and he looks away from Ashley, serving up burgers and hot dogs to all of us.

"Thanks," I say, forcing a smile as I push Ashley towards a table.

"Ally! Stop pushing me, what's your problem?'"

"You! You're eye fucking Jake's brother a second after meeting him."

"So? He's the hottest man I've ever seen. He could man my grill anytime."

"What does that even mean? Your vagina is a grill? That's gross. He's also the sheriff of Pine Cove, so don't do anything that will get you arrested."

"He's the sheriff?" she asks, a hint of thrill in her voice.

"Yes, but don't get any ideas, Trash-ley."

"We'll see." She shrugs, a suspicious gleam in her eyes.

"Ash, keep it in your pants," Ellie chimes in.

"I say go for it." Courtney laughs. "He needs some fun in

his life."

"See, Ally, I'm fun."

Shaking my head, I find us an empty table and sit.

I've always envied Ashley's feminine prowess. If she wants a man, she goes after him without hesitation. But under all of her confidence, I know she's fragile. She hops from man to man to keep her distracted, but she's never satisfied. She always claims she's never going to fall in love because men can never seem to hold her attention for long, but I know she's going to fall hard and fast one day.

After we finish eating, we see one of the pong tables is free so we go back over and play another few games. This time, though, Mel decides to watch, and I teamed up with Courtney against Ash and Ellie.

"Yes! Ha Ha, suck it!" I yell, jumping up and down as Courtney and I soundly kick their asses. "I'm going to get another drink, be right back."

"Rematch!" Ash yells after me, and I turn to flip her the bird.

Looking around as I walk towards the bar, I take in how many more people have showed up since we got here. The yard is packed with probably half the town now, all laughing and having a good time. The Taylor's sure know how to throw a party.

Jake's dad isn't bartending anymore, so I walk behind the bar and grab a fresh cup of ice, searching for the gin on the table full of liquor.

"Let me," Tyler says, coming up next to me and taking my cup. "What's your poison?"

"Gin and tonic with extra limes. Thanks." I smile.

"No problem. So, you and Jake…"

"Yes?" I ask tentatively.

"You make him happy," Ryan states, coming to stand next to Tyler. "We haven't seen our brother happy like this in a long time."

"He makes me happy, too," I tell them.

"Did he tell you about Jen?" Tyler asks bluntly.

Jake didn't mention her name, but I'm assuming Jen is his ex. "Yes, and I'm nothing like her. I love Jake."

"They were in love, and she fucked him over."

"That wasn't real love. If it was, she never would have hurt him like that." They both look at each other, a silent conversation happening with just their eyes. "You're both really important to Jake, and I know that. I'm just hoping you'll give me a chance."

Smiling, they nod.

"You're good for him," Tyler says, making my drink.

"But don't think I won't do a background check on you," Ryan adds.

"Uh, what?"

"Standard procedure." He smirks.

"You won't find anything, so go ahead." I shrug, not knowing if he's kidding or not, when I feel a familiar arm snake around my waist.

"Hey, darlin'," Jake murmurs, kissing my cheek.

"Hey." I smile warmly up at him.

"Are they bothering you?"

"No, we're just discussing my upcoming background check."

"Ry, seriously?"

"No, it's fine," I reassure him before he gets worked up. "He's just doing his due diligence on a new Pine Cove citizen, right?"

"Right." He nods, smiling down at me, his eyes showing me his approval.

"I'm stealing you away, now. Don't gang up on my woman again," he tells his brothers.

Tyler hands me my drink and Jake steers me away. "Jake, they weren't being mean. They were just being protective brothers, which makes me like them even more."

"Really?" He seems surprised.

"Yes, and I can handle myself with them, so don't worry about that." I smile, leaning into him as we walk.

"They like you."

"I know, they told me," I say smugly, making him laugh.

We approach the pong tables, and Courtney rolls her eyes when she sees me with Jake. "I guess I'll have to take Mel back as my partner?"

"Hey!" Mel yells, making everyone laugh.

"Sorry, yeah," I tell her, leaning my head on Jake's arm.

"You owe me."

"Whatever you say." Blowing her a kiss, I keep on walking with Jake.

Nearing the edge of the yard by the water, Jake finds us a quiet spot to sit away from everyone. I settle between his legs and lean back against his chest.

Sipping my cocktail, I watch as the sun starts its descent into the water. "I painted something this morning," I confess.

"What's it of?" he asks, nuzzling my neck.

"I was feeling so much this morning that I just had to get it out of me. It's something special."

"Will you show me?"

Sighing, I lean into him further. "Mhmm. I made it for

you. But it's for your eyes only."

Stilling, he turns my chin so he can look into my eyes. "Darlin', please tell me you painted a nude of yourself for me." His eyes are a blazing blue, burning into mine.

"Not quite," I whisper.

I painted him and I in the throes of passion as the sun bursts to life around us. Finding each other meant we found the light again, and we no longer need to live in the shadows of our own making.

I've never painted something so intimate before, but it felt right. I wasn't even embarrassed to show Mel because I knew she'd see the art in it. It's more than just Jake and I having sex. It shows our souls coming together in a way that can't be broken.

"I could take you right here and now, darlin'. I'm so hard just thinking about you painting anything like that for me," he growls, his deep voice even sexier when he's turned on.

Staring into his darkening eyes, I shift my hips and feel him against me. Reaching back, I grip him through his jeans, holding what's mine as my eyes dart down to his lips, needing a taste.

Leaning in so he's just a breath away, Jake rests his forehead against mine.

"Jake," I whisper, closing the distance between us, melting into him the second our lips touch.

Gripping him harder, he groans into my mouth, and slides his other hand up my thigh. When my tongue meets his, the air around us electrifies, and my skin tingles with need.

Remembering where we are, though, I pull away, my breathing ragged. "You drive me crazy, mountain man. We have to stop before I let your hand go up any farther. It would be hard for me to stop you after that."

Flashing me a wicked grin, he grips my thigh and takes my earlobe between his teeth.

Stifling a moan, I bite my lip, trying not to draw attention to us.

"I want to hear you scream, darlin'," he growls.

"Jake, not here. Please," I beg.

"Soon." Kissing me hard and quick, I look into his eyes and see the dark promises I know he's going to keep.

I try and settle back against him like we were before, but I can't relax. My body is practically buzzing it's so wound up, and trying to focus on the sunset isn't helping in the least. Squirming against him to get comfortable, Jake grabs my hips, stopping me.

"Darlin', you're going to have to stop doing that if you want me to behave."

Opening my mouth to say something, I close it, trying to focus on not moving. But one of his hands drifts down to my leg again, tracing patterns on my bare thigh.

"Can you figure out what I'm writing?" he murmurs in my ear.

Focusing all of my efforts on his finger on my thigh, and not his sweet, hot breath on my neck, I smile when I figure it out.

"I love you, too."

Changing his pattern, he starts to write something else. It takes me a while to decipher it, but when I do, I look up at him.

"Please," I practically moan.

"When the fireworks start," he promises, his molten eyes glowing in the setting sun.

Nodding, I stare back out at the water, willing the sun to go down faster. But when I don't think my body can wait another second for what it's craving, the ocean finally sucks the sun under, and the sky begins to darken.

"Stand up," Jake commands, his voice strained.

Getting up, I smooth my dress down, and he grabs my hand, leading me over to the edge of the tree line. Looking around to see if anyone notices us, Jake takes me into the dark cover of the trees that extends back as far as I can see.

I have to make sure to watch where I'm stepping so I don't trip as I'm led deeper into the forest. And when we're far enough away for privacy, Jake suddenly turns and lifts me, throwing me up against the closest tree, his lips slamming down on mine.

Wrapping my legs around his waist, I grip his hair in my hands and pull, feeling his low groan vibrate through me. He runs his hands up my thighs and under my dress to grip my ass, squeezing hard enough to leave marks.

Moaning, I scratch his scalp, and he presses me harder against the tree. Jake quickly undoes his jeans and shoves my panties to the side, sliding into me in one, quick motion.

My back scrapes up the bark of the tree and I cry out, squeezing Jake inside of me with every muscle I have – the pain and pleasure mixing together in an intoxicating sensation.

Gripping my hips, Jake pulls out almost completely before slamming back into me, the explosions of the fireworks covering the screams being ripped from my throat.

Digging my heels into his ass, my back is dragged up and down the tree with every stroke, my skin feeling like it's on fire.

Looking into Jake's eyes, I see them light up with the colors bursting above us, and I know he can feel the pressure in me building, and it drives him to go harder and faster.

Digging my nails into the nape of his neck, Jake presses his thumb against my clit, and I throw my head back with a scream, dragging my nails across the back of his neck as he lets out a guttural groan.

Holding me tight against him, my body is racked with wave after wave of pleasure as my inner muscles squeeze him, taking everything he's giving me.

I try and suck in air, my chest tight with emotions so powerful that I don't even know how to put it all into words. The only word that could remotely cover it, is love. An all-consuming, life altering, stomach clenching kind of love.

Tears gather in my eyes as I'm struck with the intensity of how much I love this man. Slipping from my eyes, they roll down my cheeks, but Jake catches each of them with his lips.

"Don't cry, baby. Please," he pleads.

"I'm not sad, I promise. I just…" Pausing, I trace my fingers across his jaw. "I'm scared," I whisper, hoping he'll know what I mean.

"Don't be. This is real. We're real," he says, kissing me slow and deep. "I love you, darlin'."

Letting the tears fall freely now, my heart swells to the point where I think it might burst. "I love you, Jake."

Wiping my tears away, he smiles, his dimple on full display. "I'm really going to have to thank Dottie for arranging this."

Laughing, I lean my forehead against his and kiss him soft and sweet. But that's when the pain of the scrapes on my back comes to the forefront of my mind and I cringe, trying to move away from the tree.

"What's wrong?" he asks, his voice going into savior

mode.

"My back," I tell him, my voice strained.

"Shit, I'm sorry, baby." Pulling out of me, I groan at the sudden loss. I wasn't ready to let go of him yet.

Setting me on my feet, he turns me around and sweeps my hair over my shoulder.

"Fuck. You should have told me I was hurting you."

"You weren't hurting me, trust me. It's only starting to hurt now. I didn't mind it before," I say, feeling my cheeks heat. "I liked it."

Kissing the nape of my neck, his fingers gently move over the sensitive skin, removing any bark that was left behind.

"It doesn't look too bad, just red."

Kissing his way across my shoulder and up my neck, Jake sweeps my hair back over my shoulder so it falls down my back again, hiding the evidence of our tree shaking forest tryst.

"There, no one will know," he whispers, kissing me behind my ear.

Taking my hand, he starts to lead us back towards the party when I hear the moans of a woman, followed by manly grunts.

"Uh…" I giggle, covering my mouth. I don't think they're too far away, but it's too dark now to see anything.

"I guess I wasn't the only one who thought the fireworks were a good cover for sex." He laughs, stealing a quick kiss.

Navigating our way through the trees, we finally emerge near the water. "Just walk with me along the edge and no one will know I just fucked you into oblivion against a tree."

Laughing, I lean into his side and smile up at him. "I'm too happy to care if they all know."

Smiling, Jake leans down and kisses me, and I feel it all the way down to my toes. "You look so beautiful right now, darlin'. Your hair is wild and sexy, your skin flushed, your eyes bright, and your smile so carefree."

Feeling my cheeks heat further, I tuck my head against his chest and smile.

Chapter 25

3 months later...

Taking the pie out of the oven, I place it on the stove to cool. Jake has been holed up in his workshop for the past week, and I plan on using his favorite blueberry pie to lure him away from his boats to spend some extra time with me.

Over the past few months, I've spent almost every night at Jake's, and it's really starting to feel like home to me. Mostly because wherever Jake is, is my home. But it's also because he's made sure I have my own space here.

One day after work, he surprised me with my own painting room, and I've steadily filled it over the summer with too many paintings to count.

Jake and I have spent so many days driving along the coast

to find the perfect spots for me to paint, and if it was a secluded enough spot, those painting sessions may have ended up as a little roll around in the sand.

He's tried to tell me I should have a show, but I don't think I'm ready for that. I'm really just enjoying painting again because I love it, and not for any kind of profit. Jake inspires me every day, and every day I fall a little bit more in love with him.

Hearing my phone chime on the counter, I'm pulled from my thoughts.

Come to the workshop, darlin'. I have a surprise for you.

Smiling, I cover the pie and head outside. The bright summer sun shines in my eyes and I squint, seeing it reflect off of the calm lake.

Walking down the deck stairs, I make my way around to the open bay door to see Jake standing next to what looks like a boat covered with a sheet.

"Come stand over here, darlin'," he says, holding out his hand. When I place mine in his, he pulls me against him, stealing a quick kiss.

"What's my surprise?" I ask, a little breathless.

"You'll see." He smiles. "Cover your eyes. I'll tell you when to open them." Closing my eyes, I place my hand over them. "I promised you something a few months ago…" he says, and I hear the swoosh of the sheet being pulled away, a little breeze blowing my hair in my face. Coming back in front of me, he places his hand over mine on my eyes. "…and I always keep my promises."

Taking his hand away, I let mine fall to my side and open my eyes, blinking to adjust to the light.

Gasping, tears prick the back of my eyes immediately. "Jake," I whisper, covering my mouth with a shaky hand, taking a tentative step forward.

Reaching out, I run my fingers along the smooth wood.

He made me my boat.

This is what he's been working on? A couple months ago, I joked with him, telling him I wanted my own. But I didn't think he'd really make me one so soon.

My fingers gently glide along the side of the boat as I make my way towards the bow, feeling every carve he made just for me. Rounding the front, I turn to face the beautiful myth he's created, smiling through the tears pooling in my eyes.

He made me a mermaid.

Her torso extends up and off the bow of the boat as her wavy hair flows down from her head, running along the sides. Her soulful eyes draw me in, and a small smile plays on her lips.

She looks like me.

Tears spill down my cheeks as I keep circling around the boat, running my fingers over the intricate carvings of her tail that curls around from the back to rest along this side. I've never seen anything so beautiful in my life.

"Jake, it's so beautiful," I whisper.

Mesmerized, I look inside, and see that he even took the time to carve shells and starfish across the benches and down along the oars.

"This is amazing."

Jake stands a little distance away, watching me, his body rigid. Holding his gaze, I never let it waiver as I make my way to him and grab his shirt, pulling him down to me to kiss him hard.

"This is the most special thing you could ever give me," I tell him, blinking away my tears. "I love it, and I love you. I didn't know this is what you've been working on."

Snaking his arms around me, Jake smooths his hands down and over my round ass. "Well, if you remember, I did tell you how you'd be paying for my services if I made you one." He smiles, squeezing his favorite part of me.

Laughing, I rest my head on his chest and wrap my arms around him. "Yeah, I remember. And I think you've received overpayment."

"Nope, not possible."

Turning in his arms, I stare at my boat again, not wanting to look away. "It's perfect."

"It was hard to wrap everything you are into a simple design. I went through a whole notebook of sketches before it suddenly came to me. The mermaid is the legendary myth of the sea. She lures men in with her siren song, and casts a spell over all who come close and look upon her. She's a creature so beautiful that it hurts to look at her."

Sighing, I lean back into him. "Just when I think I can't love you any more, you prove me wrong."

"I love you, darlin'," he whispers in my ear. I'll never get tired of hearing that. My heart skips a beat every time. "Check inside the boat, there's something else for you."

"Jake, I don't need anything else."

"Just look, darlin'," he urges.

Walking back over, I peek over the side and see an envelope about the size of a postcard sitting on one of the benches that I hadn't seen there a minute ago. Picking it up, I turn it over and slip my finger under the seal to open it, pulling out a thick piece of stock card and reading the gold script.

Wait.

No.

Oh my god.

It's an invitation to an art show. *My* art show.

I spin around, the card shaking in my hand. "Jake, what is this?" I ask nervously.

"It's an invitation. Did you read it?"

"I did. I just don't understand."

"I put together an art show for you."

"But…" I start to say, but can't find any other words.

Stepping towards me, Jake takes my shaking hands in his. "You deserve this. You've been working hard for months, and loving every second of it. Your paintings are amazing, darlin'. People should see how talented you are."

"But…"

"It's tonight at seven. Courtney helped me organize it, and everything is already set up."

"But…"

"You just have to show up, baby. Go back to the cottage and pick out one of those sexy dresses you have, and I'll pick you up at 6:30."

"But…"

Searching my eyes, he asks, "Do you want me to cancel it? I will if you really don't want this, but I think you do."

"I do," I say quietly, studying the invitation again.

He organized an art show for me and sent out invitations. I can't wrap my mind around this.

Looking back up at him, I see his love for me shining out from his eyes.

I fucking love him so much.

A smile breaks out on my face and I throw myself at him,

jumping into his arms. I catch him off guard, but he quickly recovers and wraps his arms around me as I kiss him with all the love I have inside of me.

"Thank you," I whisper against his lips.

"Anything for you," he whispers back.

"No," I say back, shaking my head. "Thank you for knowing what I want even when I don't."

I trace his dimple with my finger, then lean in and kiss it softly, swirling my tongue around the little indent.

"Is this why you shaved this morning?"

"Yes." He laughs lightly.

"I was wondering why you did. I know you only do it when there's a reason." I smile, feeling his smooth skin beneath my palm.

Setting me back down on my feet, I push my hair out of my face and look at my boat again.

It's amazing. He had to have been working on it for months.

"What time is it?" I ask.

"Two."

"Oh, I have to go then if I'm going to be ready in time. I'll see you at 6:30?"

"Yes." He nods, his arms tightening around me.

"See you then, handsome," I say, giving him a kiss goodbye.

With my hair swept up into a low bun, I curl the pieces that don't reach all the way back so they hang softly around my face. My blue eyes shine back at me in the mirror, framed by thick eyelashes that I made sure to add an extra layer of mascara to. I even went a little bolder and added winged eyeliner over my gold shimmery eyeshadow to make my eyes seem more exotic and enticing.

Walking into my room, I take my robe off and slip my dress over my head, making sure to avoid ruining my hair. The red silk floats down and around my body, highlighting my curves.

A conservative rounded neckline is held up by thin spaghetti straps, while the back of the dress is the showstopper. A deep scoop cuts down almost the entirety of my back, and is held together with a crisscrossing of thin, red satin strings.

The dress has a looser fit to it, but with every step I take, the silk clings to my body and showcases every curve I have.

Jake is going to love it.

I'll be surprised if he even lets me leave the house before tearing it off of me.

Smiling at that thought, I do a little twirl in the mirror, and make sure I have smooth lines everywhere. It's hard to wear a bra with this, so the stickies I have on better hold up. I don't need the girls in full headlight mode when everyone is going to be there for me and there's nowhere to hide.

Swiping a bold red lipstick across my lips that matches my dress perfectly, I slip into my heels just in time to hear a knock at the door. I throw the lipstick into my gold clutch, and take one last look in the mirror, smiling through my nerves.

Taking a few deep breaths before opening the door, I almost faint when I see the Jake that's standing in front of me.

Damn.

I rake my eyes up and down every inch of the man I barely

recognize in a sleek black suit that looks to have been perfectly tailored to his Viking size. His normally wild hair that I love is combed back and tamed to show off his freshly shaved face.

I barely notice the bouquet of lavender roses he's holding because he looks so damn good.

Smiling, I meet his heated eyes.

"Darlin'," he rasps, slowly taking me in. "You're beautiful. More than beautiful."

Reaching up, I smooth my hand up his chest, feeling the soft fabric of the suit beneath my fingers. "You're so handsome, Jake. You know I love your rugged mountain man look. But damn, baby, you're smoking hot in a suit."

Smiling wickedly, he wraps his arm around my waist and kisses my cheek, not daring to ruin my lipstick.

"There's no back to your dress, darlin'," he states, his voice strained as his hand caresses my bare skin.

Smiling seductively, I reach for the roses. "They're beautiful. I love the color." Holding them close, I inhale their sweet scent. "What do these mean?" I ask, knowing he loves picking flowers for me based on their meaning.

"Enchantment and love at first sight."

Smiling wide, I lean up on my toes and kiss his cheek, leaving behind a perfect set of red lips. Good. Now every woman will know he's mine.

"Let me put these in water and then we can go."

I turn to walk to the kitchen, but I only make it a few steps before I hear Jake growl behind me. "Darlin', you're killing me in that dress. I'm waiting outside. Otherwise, I'm going to rip it off of you and we're never leaving."

I smile over my shoulder. "I knew you'd like it."

"I fucking love it," he groans. "Tonight's going to be

torture."

"Yes, it will be. Especially when all I'll be thinking about is peeling that suit off and kissing every inch of you, leaving my red lip prints all over your body."

"I'll be outside," he says, his voice hard as he abruptly turns and walks back out to his truck to wait for me.

Laughing lightly, I go into the kitchen and put my roses in a vase. I love torturing him with my outfits. It's always fun to see how long he'll last before giving up and just taking me wherever we are.

There have been many nights when he's had to pull over on the shoulder of some back road because my dress was too much for him and he couldn't concentrate with so much of my legs showing. He always said that wherever we were going could wait, even if we were on our way to meet his family.

Smiling, I leave my roses on the kitchen table and lock up the house. When I join Jake outside, he's already behind the wheel, so I decide to saunter my way over to the passenger side to torture him some more.

It's a silent ride into town as Jake grips the steering wheel tight, keeping his eyes trained on the road and not once straying over towards me.

When we park in front of the café, he gets out and opens my door, holding his hand out for me to take. I have to maneuver my way out of his truck in a way that doesn't rip my dress or flash anyone the goods, but it's not easy.

As soon as my feet are safely on the pavement, I look up at Jake and smile, seeing my lipstick still on his cheek. Licking my thumb, I reach up and rub it off. "Sorry. I may have left a mark."

"You did it on purpose."

"I know." I smirk, and he loops my arm through his.

"Are you ready?"

"As I'll ever be." I nod. "Thank you, Jake. This means so much to me."

"Making you happy is all I care about, darlin'," he says, kissing me by my ear. "And for the next two hours," he whispers, sending chills down my spine, "I want you to think about all the ways I'm going to make you pay for not being able to touch you when you're dressed like this."

Squeezing his arm, my core clenches, and my skin tingles.

But the second I walk inside, tears pool in my eyes, and I take in what Jake and Courtney have done for me. I'm speechless.

The tables and chairs have been moved out and replaced with easels that are displaying my paintings, while the larger pieces hang along the walls.

This is surreal.

"Ally!" Courtney exclaims from behind the counter as she pours glasses of wine with Dara.

Smiling, I leave Jake for a second to go and hug them. "Thank you so much, Courtney."

"It was all Jake. Don't let him try and say I did more than offer the café and help set up."

"I can't believe this," I say, looking around again.

"You're so talented, Ally. People should have the opportunity to see that."

"Thank you." I smile, feeling my cheeks heat.

"And you look hot as hell. Damn, girl. I'm surprised Jake hasn't dragged you into a corner yet."

"He wanted to." I laugh. "But he decided to show some self-control for once."

"Oh, how nice," she says sarcastically, laughing with me. "Well here, have a glass of wine and try to relax."

"Thanks, I need it. I've never had people look at my work like this, let alone buy it."

"Don't worry about it. It's going to be great."

"If you say so."

"I do." She smiles.

Coming up next to me, Jake wraps his arm around my waist. "I have one more surprise for you," he says, turning me to face the window.

"Jake!" I exclaim when I see my family walking towards the door. "You invited them?"

"Of course."

"Thank you!" I say, kissing his cheek, not caring that I left another mark.

When the door opens, and my mom and sisters walk through, their eyes light up when they see me.

"Ally!" Kelly greets with a huge smile, coming in for a hug.

"Don't mess up my hair or dress." I laugh.

"Oh, right." She smiles, going a little gentler. "You look freaking amazing."

"Thanks, sis."

"Ally! How are you?" Marissa cuts in, grabbing me for a hug.

"I'm really good."

"I can see that," she says, looking around at my art. "You did all of these?"

"Yes."

"They're amazing, baby sis."

"They really are," Kelly agrees.

"Thank you," I say softly, feeling shy.

"Hi, sweetie," my mom says from behind Marissa and Kelly.

"Mom." I smile, hugging her. "I've missed you."

"Me too, sweetie. I'm so proud of you," she says, a catch in her voice as she looks around the room. "This is all so beautiful. My baby is so talented." I feel the blush creeping up my cheeks, not used to so much praise. "Now, are you going to introduce me to your young man?"

"Oh, right. Of course." I smile. "Mom, this is Jake Taylor. Jake, this is my mom."

"Hello, ma'am, it's nice to finally meet you," Jake says, shaking her hand.

"It's nice to finally meet the man who's in love with my daughter."

"Mom," I groan, embarrassed.

"No, it's the truth, darlin'." He smiles, and this time I know my cheeks are red.

"And I'm Kelly," my sister interjects, shaking his hand.

"Good to meet you. You must be Marissa then," he says, shaking her hand next.

"Yes," she sighs, a dreamy look in her eyes.

"Okay guys, thanks for that. Why don't you go and get a glass of wine and stop embarrassing me?"

"We'll never stop." Kelly laughs as the three of them go over to Courtney and Dara.

"Why don't you go with them, darlin'. I'll be around if you need me, but I want you to spend time with them."

Squeezing his arm, I lean against him for a moment. "Thanks, handsome."

Joining my sisters and mom, I introduce them to Courtney and Dara, and then we walk over to one of the high-top tables.

"Ally, holy lord, Jake is hot!" Kelly says, eyeing him across the room.

"Yeah, for a second there I forgot I was married and I wanted to throw myself at him."

"Marissa!"

"What?" she asks innocently, and then smiles. "But seriously, Ally. Damn."

"I know," I sigh, raking my eyes up and down my sexy mountain man. I know he can sense my eyes on him because he turns his head and meets my heated stare – my skin breaking out in goosebumps with just one look.

"Okay, please save that for later."

"What?" I ask absentmindedly, still staring at Jake.

"Hello? Earth to Ally." Kelly waves her hand in front of my face, and I shake my head, breaking the spell.

"Ah, she's back." Mar jokes.

"Sorry." I blush.

"It's okay, sweetie. I'm happy to see you happy. You two are obviously very much in love."

"We are," I say shyly. My family is definitely not used to seeing me like this.

"Come and show us your work, sweetie. I want to hear about each one." Taking my arm, my mom guides me over to a painting I did from one of the Adirondack chairs at the cottage. There were so many sailboats in the water that day that I just *had* to paint them. It was too pretty not to.

"It's beautiful, sweetie. This is where you've been living?"

"Yes. I can take you tomorrow to see it if you'd like."

"Please." She nods, and we continue on to the next painting.

As I take my family around, the people of Pine Cove filter in and out of the café over the next hour, and they all make a point to come over and say hello, telling my family how much they love having me here.

Being the girl who brought Jake Taylor out of hiding had made me the hot topic of gossip for quite some time around town. But then everyone started coming to the café to investigate me, and those visits soon turned into genuine conversations, that then evolved into friendships. I really love this town and everyone in it.

I can definitely see myself living here for the rest of my life.

"Hi, Ally," Mrs. Taylor says next to me, pulling me from my thoughts.

"Hi, Mrs. Taylor." I smile. "This is my mom, Linda, and my sisters, Kelly and Marissa."

"Hello, it's nice to meet you all. I'm Jake's mom, Pam. Ally, honey, this is all so amazing. You're so talented."

"Thank you. Jake organized this whole thing for me, but only told me about it this afternoon." I laugh. "He probably knew I'd freak out if I had time to think about it and say no."

"Why would you say no? You should showcase yourself. I saw sold tags on more than half of the paintings already."

"What?" I choke out. "Really?"

"Yes." She smiles. "We love hometown art, and you've really captured the essence of coastal Maine in every piece."

"Ally, dear, how are you?" Mr. Taylor walks up and interjects before I can thank his wife.

"Hi, Mr. Taylor. I'm good, thank you. Overwhelmed, but good. I still can't believe Jake did this for me."

"That's my boy," he says, the pride evident in his voice.

My eyes automatically find Jake's through the crowd again, and I smile sweetly at him. "Yes, he sure is something." He's stayed away as I mingled and spent time with my family, but I always felt his eyes on me – watching me, and making sure I'm okay.

It isn't until the evening starts to wind down that Jake comes to my side, slipping his arm around my waist. "Hey, darlin'. You ready to head out?"

"Is that allowed?" I ask, looking up at his handsome face.

"Why not?"

"Well, don't we have to pack everything up or something?"

"No, I got that covered. You don't have to worry about a thing."

"Okay, then. If you're sure."

"I am." He nods, squeezing my waist gently.

Turning to my mom and sisters, I hug them goodbye. "Thanks for coming. I've really missed you."

"We're staying at the Inn in town for a few more days, so we have more time together. Maybe we can do something tomorrow?"

"Yes, that's not even a question."

"I hope to see you as well, Jake," my mom says.

"Yes, ma'am." He smiles wide, showing off his dimple, and giving my sisters another reason to swoon over my man.

"Have a good night, sweetie," she says, her eyes flashing to Jake's.

"'Night." I wave as we make our way outside.

The ride back is peaceful as I hum along to the radio and steal glances over at my man. I have to get in all the looks of him in a suit before I slowly peel each piece from his body –

unwrapping him like the gift he is.

When we get to his house, Jake helps me out of his truck, but I stumble on the rocks in my heels. Luckily, he's right there to wrap his arm around my waist to steady me.

"Thanks," I say breathlessly, thankful I didn't just break my ankle.

"Take a walk with me, darlin'." With the way he's looking at me, I'd go just about anywhere with him.

"Okay. I just have to take my heels off."

"Not yet," he says, and lifts me up into his arms. "I want those sexy things on you when you have your legs wrapped around me later."

Smiling, I kiss his jaw as he walks us around the house and into the backyard, only setting me down when we reach the dock. Taking his hand, we walk to the end, listening to the water lap gently against the dock as the crickets talk to one another.

I look up to the sky, but the full moon is shining so bright, it's drowning out the stars.

"Darlin'?"

"Yes?" I answer, my eyes looking out over the dark water of the lake. But Jake squeezes my hand, and tugs gently, making me look at him.

He reaches out, sweeping a curl away from my eyes. Cupping the side of my neck, his thumb caresses me softly. "You're my light, Ally. I was in the dark for so long, but your light broke through and freed me. You took the darkness away. You're the best thing that's ever happened to me, and every day I'm with you is the best day of my life. I'm the luckiest man in the world because I have you, and I love you more than you'll ever know."

"Jake," I whisper, "I–" And the words die on my tongue the second I see Jake fall to one knee.

Pulling out a square box from inside of his jacket, he opens it, revealing a beautiful pear-shaped diamond that's sparkling in the moonlight.

I have no words.

His ocean eyes swirl with so much hope and love as he looks up at me. "You're my everything, darlin'. Will you marry me?"

Words fail me.

Jake is asking me to marry him.

He's asking me to spend the rest of my life with him.

Reaching out with a shaky hand, I brush my fingers over his forehead and down across his jaw, his eyes closing briefly at my touch.

He really does love me.

My legs give out and I fall to my knees in front of him, my tears blurring my vision.

"Yes," I whisper, and Jake's lips crash against mine. The fire in my heart spreads through my veins as I give him every ounce of love I have.

He's my forever.

ACKNOWLEDGMENTS

A very special thank you to my mom and Rachel. Your support, encouragement, and belief in me kept me going even when I doubted myself.

ABOUT THE AUTHOR

Rebecca is a dreamer through and through with permanent wanderlust. She has an endless list of places to go and see, hoping to one day experience the world and all it has to offer.

She's a Jersey girl who dreams of living in a place with freezing cold winters and lots of snow! When she's not writing, you can find her planning her next road trip and drinking copious amounts of coffee (preferably iced!).

Website, blog, shop, and links to all social media:
www.rebeccagannon.com

Follow me on Instagram to stay up-to-date on new releases, sales, teasers, giveaways, and so much more!
@rebeccagannon_author

9 798986 705934